The Last to Fall

"Authors Jim Rada and Richard Fulton have done an outstanding job of researching and chronicling this little-known story of those Marines in 1922, marking it as a significant moment in Marine Corps history."

- *GySgt. Thomas Williams*
Executive Director
U.S. Marine Corps Historical Company

"Original, unique, profusely illustrated throughout, exceptionally well researched, informed, informative, and a bit iconoclastic, 'The Last to Fall: The 1922 March, Battles, & Deaths of U.S. Marines at Gettysburg' will prove to be of enormous interest to military buffs and historians."

- *Small Press Bookwatch*

Saving Shallmar

"But Saving Shallmar's Christmas story is a tale of compassion and charity, and the will to help fellow human beings not only survive, but also be ready to spring into action when a new opportunity presents itself. Bittersweet yet heartwarming, Saving Shallmar is a wonderful Christmas season story for readers of all ages and backgrounds, highly recommended."

- *Small Press Bookwatch*

Battlefield Angels

"Rada describes women religious who selflessly performed life-saving work in often miserable conditions and thereby gained the admiration and respect of countless contemporaries. In so doing, Rada offers an appealing narrative and an entry point into the wealth of sources kept by the sisters."

- *Catholic News Service*

Between Rail and River

"The book is an enjoyable, clean family read, with characters young and old for a broad-based appeal to both teens and adults. Between Rail and River also provides a unique, regional appeal, as it teaches about a particular group of people, ordinary working 'canawlers' in a story that goes beyond the usual coverage of life during the Civil War."

- *Historical Fiction Review*

Canawlers

"A powerful, thoughtful and fascinating historical novel, Canawlers documents author James Rada, Jr. as a writer of considerable and deftly expressed storytelling talent."

- *Midwest Book Review*

"James Rada, of Cumberland, has written a historical novel for high-schoolers and adults, which relates the adventures, hardships and ultimate tragedy of a family of boaters on the C&O Canal. ... The tale moves quickly and should hold the attention of readers looking for an imaginative adventure set on the canal at a critical time in history."

- *Along the Towpath*

October Mourning

"This is a very good, and very easy to read, novel about a famous, yet unknown, bit of 20th Century American history. While reading this book, in your mind, replace all mentions of 'Spanish Flu' with 'bird flu.' Hmmm."

- *Reviewer's Bookwatch*

BLACK FIRE, BOOK 1

SMOLDERING

BETRAYAL

Other books by James Rada, Jr.

Non-Fiction

- Battlefield Angels: The Daughters of Charity Work as Civil War Nurses
- Beyond the Battlefield: Stories from Gettysburg's Rich History
- Clay Soldiers: One Marine's Story of War, Art, & Atomic Energy
- Echoes of War Drums: The Civil War in Mountain Maryland
- The Last to Fall: The 1922 March, Battles & Deaths of U.S. Marines at Gettysburg
- Looking Back: True Stories of Mountain Maryland
- Looking Back II: More True Stories of Mountain Maryland
- No North, No South: The Grand Reunion at the 50th Anniversary of the Battle of Gettysburg
- Saving Shallmar: Christmas Spirit in a Coal Town

Secrets Series

- Secrets of Catoctin Mountain: Little-Known Stories & Hidden History Along Catoctin Mountain
- Secrets of Garrett County: Little-Known Stories & Hidden History of Maryland's Westernmost County
- Secrets of the C&O Canal: Little-Known Stories & Hidden History Along the Potomac River

Fiction

- Between Rail and River
- Canawlers
- Lock Ready
- October Mourning
- The Rain Man

BLACK FIRE, BOOK 1

SMOLDERING

BETRAYAL

by
James Rada, Jr.

LEGACY
PUBLISHING

A division of AIM Publishing Group

SMOLDERING BETRAYAL

Published by Legacy Publishing, a division of AIM Publishing Group.
Gettysburg, Pennsylvania.
Printed in the United States of America.
First printing: August 2018.

ISBN 978-0999811474

Cover design by Grace Eyler.

315 Oak Lane • Gettysburg, Pennsylvania 17325

For Elena Bittinger,
a fine writer and a better friend

Chapter 1

February 8, 1922

The black iron steam engine slowed gradually as it approached Cumberland, Maryland, from the east. When the wheels finally stopped turning, metal screeched and groaned as the trucks slid along the iron rails, pushed by the weight of four Pullman cars and two baggage cars. Everyone aboard felt one last gentle jolt as the train shuddered and stopped in front of the Queen City Station.

Matt Ansaro opened his dark eyes and lifted his chin off his chest where it rested while he napped. He looked out the window to his right and stared at the train station. The sun was bright, but he believed he could see a grayish haze in the sky. He might be imagining seeing the coal dust in the air. After all, it had been five years since he'd been here. Things could have changed.

Cumberland was a transportation city. Nestled in the Allegheny Mountains, it was where the National Road started, and the Chesapeake and Ohio Canal stopped. It also had two railroads running through it—the Baltimore and Ohio Railroad on the east end of the city and the Western Maryland Railroad on the western end. From Cumberland, a person could buy a ticket to anywhere in the country.

Yet, Matt's ticket had brought him back to Cumberland. He

had left here a coal miner and returned a veteran of the Great War. The coal miner had sworn he would never return to Eckhart Mines, and yet the veteran was in Cumberland and on his way home. Did that make him a liar or just a poor fortuneteller?

As an eighteen-year-old man leaving Allegany County for the first time, Matt thought the Queen City Station resembled a palace, with its two-story center section and flanked by its two four-story wings. It was the largest building he had ever seen. On his occasional visits to Cumberland as a child, he wondered what the city looked like from the cupola atop the center section. Now he could appreciate the Italianate style and the decorative ironwork on the eaves. He even knew what those things were. Although most of the building was made of hotel rooms and offices, the ground floor had a ballroom, waiting rooms, and a restaurant.

The building no longer fascinated him, though. Since he'd last been in Cumberland, Matt had walked inside real palaces in Europe that dwarfed the Queen City Station in comparison. This train station was just a large building to him now; beautiful but far from a palace.

He stood and stretched, easing the kinks from his back. The trip from Baltimore lasted five hours. He tried sleeping, but every time the train slowed and pulled into a station, it had shaken him awake.

Matt stepped off the Pullman car and onto the platform. The air smelled of smoke, coal, and burnt metal. People crowded the platform, either waiting to climb aboard or looking for someone. Matt turned and offered his hand to the elderly woman behind him.

"Allow me, ma'am," he said.

As Matt helped the white-haired woman wearing a blue dress slightly out of style step down the platform, she smiled and thanked him.

That's when she noticed the scar on Matt's neck. She reached up and ran her fingers across the pink and white scar tissue contrasting against his dark skin. Matt leaned away. This never happened to him before. People stared. Some commented on it, but no one ever touched it, especially a stranger.

"The war?" she asked, lowering her hand.

Matt nodded.

"Bad business, war. My husband–may he rest in peace–fought in Cuba. He had a similar scar. He used to tell people he rode with Teddy Roosevelt up San Juan Hill, but really, he was just a navy ensign. He didn't even see much fighting, except when his ship sank. During the confusion, a hot steam pipe burst and fell against his neck. It left him with a burn mark, just there. Like yours." Her gray eyes took on a misty look as if she was someplace else.

Matt wondered if that story was true or if her husband hadn't wanted to talk about something worse that had happened to him. Matt could count on one hand the number of people who knew the story of his scar.

He took the woman's hand between his hands, in part, so she wouldn't touch his scar again. "I'm sorry for your loss, ma'am."

The old woman blinked and focused on Matt. "The burn made him look like he had escaped the gallows, like some desperado in a western novel. It quite upset him. Here he was the kindest, gentlest soul you'd ever meet, and people would see that scar and think something totally different about him. He took to wearing high-collar shirts to hide it."

Matt had tried that for a time, but his head felt too constrained in high collars.

"Yes, ma'am," he said.

He couldn't imagine a woman from Baltimore saying these things to him. People saw lots of unusual sights in a big city, but in Cumberland, it just seemed natural. People treated each other as friends.

The woman grinned and then laughed. She patted his hand. "You think I'm just an old lady telling tales, don't you?"

Matt hesitated, and then admitted, "The thought did cross my mind."

"And why wouldn't it? I am an old woman telling tales, but like most tales, there's a point to what I'm saying. Don't let that scar define you. I saw you on the train, young man. You act like a man alone in the world, but someday you won't want to be. When that time comes, don't let what that scar tells people be who you really are."

Matt smiled. "I'm trying my best not to. May I walk you into the station?"

"No, no. I may have some trouble with up and down, but I still handle forward and back pretty well."

She waved to him and headed into the building. Matt watched her leave. He shook his head slowly. That was certainly not how he had expected to be greeted, no matter how friendly people could be here.

He found a porter who looked barely old enough to shave. Surprisingly, his white shirt managed to look clean although he worked on the platform all day with its cinders and coal dust.

"Welcome to Cumberland, sir," the young man said.

Matt nodded. "I've been here before."

"Then you know why they call her the Queen City." The porter grinned as if he had a secret to share, proud that he lived in Maryland's second-largest city.

"My guess is that no one here has seen a queen or a real city," Matt said.

Taken aback, the porter managed to keep the smile on his face. "What can I do for you, sir?"

Matt flipped the man a quarter. "I need the suitcases for Matt Ansaro as quickly as you can find them."

The porter glanced at the generous tip. "Yes, sir!" He hurried away.

Matt turned in a slow circle. It felt like a dream … or a nightmare … to be standing here. He looked down and brushed at the shoulder of his brown suit jacket. Coal dust from the train was already accumulating on him.

The porter returned carrying two large suitcases. Matt thanked him, took the luggage, and walked down the sidewalk that ran alongside the tracks. He crossed at Baltimore Street and headed downtown past Rosenbaum's and McMullen Brothers department stores, the *Cumberland News* newspaper offices, a dance hall, and two theaters. He felt cinders crunch beneath his shoes with every step he took. The people on the street consisted of well-to-do businessmen and professionals, wives, miners, and railroaders. They moved along the sidewalk, either hurrying past or weaving around him, avoiding his slow pace from lugging his suitcases.

Matt found the Liberty Trust Bank at the intersection of Centre and Baltimore streets. At six stories, it was taller than the Queen City Station, but not as impressive. It was a simple brick design with slightly rounded corners. Before Europe, Matt had never been inside a bank. His family had been poor, only ever needing a Mason jar kept in the back of a cabinet for their minimal funds.

He bypassed the tellers behind their frosted half windows and headed for the desks at the far end of the floor, stopping at the first person he found.

The portly man wearing a crisp white shirt and wide blue tie looked up from his work.

"May I help you, sir?" he asked in an unusually deep voice.

"I'd like to open an account, and I will also need to rent a box," Matt told him.

"Please take a seat." The man waved at the wooden chair in front of the desk. "I can help you with both of those things."

Matt gave the man his personal information and passed him $200 to deposit into his new account. The bank employee looked surprised at the amount of money.

"May I ask what your profession is, Mr. Ansaro?"

"I am a consultant for businesses that need information."

The man pursed his lips as if to say something. His eyes drifted to Matt's neck, lingering too long on his scar. Matt smirked and wondered if he should tell the clerk he'd ridden with Teddy Roosevelt and the Rough Riders.

The clerk decided against pressing for more details, and instead said, "It sounds like interesting work."

"It can be. It depends on the business and the information needed."

"Is your business located in Cumberland?"

Matt wasn't going to admit he was a Pinkerton detective hired by Consolidation Coal Company. It would start rumors that would make their way up the mountain to Eckhart Mines. He shook his head. "My business is in Baltimore, but I'll be in Cumberland long enough to need a local account through which I can handle my business transactions."

"Well, we're happy that you chose Liberty Trust Bank. Let me get you a receipt for your deposit, and then we'll get you a bank box."

The clerk walked over to a teller and handed her the money. Matt watched, and when he was satisfied no one was paying attention, he surveyed the bank. Six teller windows, although not all of them were open, and four clerks seated at their desks between Matt and the vault. The door was open, but a gate blocked the access. The lobby held two entrances, while a third, he assumed, was at the back located near the staircase. When he first entered the bank, he had passed a different staircase. These were the types of details he learned and noted since starting his work for the Pinkertons.

The clerk returned and handed Matt the receipt for his deposit. Then he passed Matt a key.

"If you'll follow me, I'll show you your box."

Matt grabbed one of his suitcases and followed. The man opened it with a key on a length of thin chain attached to his belt, then searched the numbered plates for Matt's box. He found it and tapped on it.

"Here you go, sir. Number 407."

Matt nodded. "Thank you. Is there a place where I can go and add some items in private?"

"Of course, sir. If you will take your box and follow me."

Matt unlocked the bank box, slid the steel container out, tucked it under his arm, and went to a nearby room outside the vault. When left alone, he set one of his suitcases on the table.

He opened it and lifted out a small cardboard box. Inside was a diamond ring. He had spent most of his savings on it two months ago. It was a beautiful ring for which he now had absolutely no use. He wasn't sure why he was still carrying it, except that it was valuable. Matt set the ring in the bank box.

He added a stack of papers and letters, most of which identi-

6

fied him as a Pinkerton agent. They would only be useful if he got in trouble with the law or the mining company. Some of the letters were personal ones he hadn't wanted to leave in Baltimore. He lifted his revolver from his suitcase, stared at it for a few moments, and set it back amongst his clothes. He might need a weapon at the mines.

He took out a wrinkled photograph of Priscilla standing under a maple tree last summer. The black and white photo couldn't capture the glow of her skin or the light brown of her eyes, but somehow, though, when Matt stared at it, he saw every feature in color. Her blonde curls draped over her shoulders as she stared back at him and smiled. He crumpled the picture, and for the twentieth time since Priscilla had broken his heart, he smoothed it back out. He could tell himself to get over her. She undoubtedly was over him, but he couldn't do it, not yet. He dropped the picture into the bank box. He might not be able to throw it away, but he could keep it out of sight. It was the best he could do for now.

Next, Matt removed his father's pocket watch. Geno Ansaro gave it to him before Matt had enlisted in the Marines. It looked different now than it had five years ago. What had been a brand new watch then, now had a bullet protruding from its near center. The same attack that had left Matt's neck scarred had also destroyed the timepiece. Matt believed he had used his lifetime of luck that day.

Finally, he took out his Pinkerton badge and dropped it into the box. He might need it at some point, but he certainly didn't want to be caught with it where he was going.

Matt closed the bank box and his suitcase. He walked back to the vault door and waited for the clerk to let him inside. He locked the box away and hoped he wouldn't need to revisit it before returning to Baltimore.

He headed back up Baltimore Street to the Queen City Station. Rather than boarding a train, he went into the station and found a washroom. He opened one of his suitcases and changed into a long-sleeved green shirt and a pair of denim jeans. He traded his brown wingtips for leather work boots and topped off his ensemble

7

with a cap. Now, he looked like any other worker in town, except he wasn't filthy. That would come later.

He walked to Centre Street where Cumberland and Westernport Electric Railway had an express office and waiting room in the same building as the Liberty Trust Bank. Matt could have changed before visiting the bank, but a worker with $200 in cash would have raised suspicion. For that reason, he didn't want to arrive in Frostburg looking like a businessman. He didn't want to draw the wrong sort of attention to himself.

For the twenty-six-mile journey to Frostburg, trolleys stopped every hour at the Cumberland and Westernport station. According to the clock on the wall, Matt had fifteen minutes to wait. Four other people sat on benches in the office; five if you counted the toddler with his mother. Not that he was doing much sitting. Matt found a seat that gave him a view of the door.

The pudgy-faced toddler moved away from his mother and wobbled over to him. Matt watched him walk over, guessing the little guy was three or four.

"Hello," Matt said, smiling.

The child made a noise, but Matt could only guess as to what he was trying to say.

"Matthew, come back here," the young mother said. "I'm sorry, sir. He's very curious nowadays."

"That's quite all right," Matt said. He leaned over and said to the child, "So, Matthew is your name. Do they call you Matt? That's my name."

Matthew reached out and grabbed the bill of Matt's cap. Matt took it off and placed it on the boy's head. Matthew laughed and started bouncing up and down.

"You've made yourself a friend now, sir. Do you have children of your own?" the mother asked. She looked like she might still be a teenager.

"I'm not even married yet, ma'am." Not for lack of trying, but the result was still the same. He wasn't sure how a family fit in with the work that he did.

"Well, it looks like you will make a good father when you do."

That made one of them.

"I hope so."

Matt played with Matthew for a little longer to pass the time while waiting for the trolley. When it arrived, Matthew's mother scooped him up and boarded the streetcar.

The trolley headed north out of Cumberland through the Narrows, a gap between Haystack and Wills mountains. The reason the National Road began in Cumberland in 1811 was to go through the gap rather than over the mountains. The space between the two mountains was so narrow that Wills Creek, the Western Maryland Railroad, and the National Road all ran side by side.

Once through the Narrows, the trolley headed west to LaVale. Matthew and his mother got off at the LaVale stop, and Matt waved goodbye to his little friend.

He took a deep breath of mountain air, filled with less coal dust, and settled back against his seat for the twelve-mile trip to Frostburg. The change in elevation from Baltimore to Cumberland was 800 feet, whereas the much shorter trip between Cumberland and Frostburg had nearly twice the difference in elevation.

The trolley stopped at Kelly's Pump in Eckhart. Matt could have hopped off there, but the town had no hotels. It was a coal town, not a tourist destination. He'd get a room in Frostburg for the night.

Besides, the longer he could delay going home, the better.

Chapter 2

February 8, 1922

Two Allegany County Deputy Sheriffs arrived in Eckhart Mines at noon. They were stout men with the bearing of ex-soldiers. They came in one black car without the siren blaring, but their presence was noted by everyone above ground in the small coal-mining town. The lawmen had been expected.

The car stopped in front of the Eckhart Mines General Store, and the two large men climbed out of the car. They were armed with both shotguns and pistols, although they kept the guns holstered, and the shotguns pointed down.

The store had a wide front porch and double doors, but they went around to the left and entered a side door where the Consolidation Coal Company office was located.

Joseph McCord saw the men walk in and stood up from his desk. He pulled his vest down because it had slid up over his slight belly bulge while he was sitting.

"I assume you know why you are here, deputies?" he asked.

The men nodded. It wasn't their first time doing this duty. They didn't like it much. Joseph could see that in the stoic expressions on their faces. It wasn't Joseph's favorite part of his job either, but it was something that needed to be done from time to time.

Joseph put on his herringbone jacket and homburg. He didn't often wear a full suit to the office, but on days like today, he needed to look the part of the man in charge.

"Okay then, let's be on our way. I'll lead you to the house," Joseph said.

The deputies filed back outside while Joseph locked the office door. The paymaster was still at lunch. He had his own key so he could let himself in when he returned.

Joseph had driven his Renault GS to work this morning. Usually, it stayed in the garage at his house, and he walked to work. Truth be told, he felt a little guilty driving the car through Eckhart. Gasoline and oil were supplanting coal, and automobiles used both. It wasn't like he could drive a coal-powered car around town, but as the mine superintendent, he had to think about appearances. Besides, the office was close enough, and it gave him a chance to walk through town so people could see him and realize that he was part of the community. He was one of them. He was responsible for them and would take care of them.

He drove the short distance down the mountain to Parkersburg Road and stopped in front of one of the company-owned houses that miners rented. They were small but constructed from stone so that they were sturdy. Most importantly, miners could afford the rent.

Ralph Scarpelli stood inside the white picket fence that ran around the house's small yard. His shoulders sagged, and his black hair was unkempt as were his worn clothes. He had been fired yesterday and told that he would need to leave the company house by noon today, which had already passed ten minutes ago.

Joseph and the deputies climbed out of their cars. The deputies held their shotguns with the barrels pointed at the ground and stood next to their vehicle. Joseph walked up to Ralph.

His wife and two children stood inside the house. Joseph could see them through the open door.

"Mr. McCord, please don't do this," Ralph said when Joseph stopped in front of him.

Joseph tried to look sad and a bit contrite because it was ex-

11

pected of him. "You left me with no options, Ralph. You knew this could happen when you joined the union."

Members of the United Mine Workers were not welcome in any coal mining operation. The union had forced its way into some mines, much to the chagrin of the owners, but since the violence in Blair County, West Virginia, last year, the mining companies had started taking back control of their mines once again. Being a union member was grounds for firing.

"I'm just trying to make a better life for my family," Ralph pleaded.

"You should have thought of that before you joined. Now, I have agreed not to blacklist you since you were a good worker, but you won't be able to work for a Consolidation Coal Company mine."

Ralph raised his hands in frustration. "But that means I won't be able to work just about anywhere hereabouts. Consolidation owns nearly all the mines."

That wasn't far from the truth. The Consolidation Coal Company had started in the Georges Creek Region of Allegany County during the Civil War, and the No. 4 mine in Eckhart Mines was one of its first mines. The company continued buying mines throughout the late 1800s and early 1900s. It now operated eighty coal mines and was the largest supplier of coal on the East Coast. The company's general offices were in New York, but it had a regional office in Cumberland.

"At least you still have some options," Joseph said. "You can try Garrett County or one of the smaller mines along the Creek."

Joseph knew that he was being generous. He should have blacklisted Ralph to keep him from being able to work in a coal mine anywhere using his own name. Joseph also knew his generosity was far less than it appeared. Word would get out that Ralph had been fired for being a union member. Everyone in Eckhart Mines probably knew of it by this morning. It would spread through Frostburg today, and by the end of next week, most miners and mine superintendents from Mount Savage to Westernport would know Ralph Scarpelli was a member of the United Mine Workers.

Joseph needed his miners to fear the consequences of union membership and to fear those consequences more than any benefit they would get from joining the union. He didn't want to impoverish union miners. That would just make matters worse because such heavy-handed action would drive miners to the union. Joseph walked a narrow line as superintendent. The miners needed to fear what he could do to them, but not be able to say that he wasn't fair. Sometimes, he went too far one way or the other, but not today. Today, he was hitting just the right look as superintendent.

He heard a sob and looked to the left. Ralph's wife cried as she hugged her children to her breast. She was bedraggled, but then she probably hadn't slept last night, knowing that this would happen today.

He saw a group of four miners approaching from the National Road. The deputies tensed, fearing that it was the beginnings of a mob. The deputies started to raise their rifles, but Joseph waved them down.

"I brought them here," he said.

He had hired the men to carry out all of the Scarpellis' goods from the house and place them outside of the picket fence and off company property. The miners hadn't wanted to do it, but Joseph had insisted. He reminded them that it would be better if friends emptied the house because they would show care. If Joseph had to hire men from Frostburg, they wouldn't be so careful. Joseph hadn't told the miners that he wanted them to do the moving because it would put them close to the situation and remind them that it could just as easily be them and their families being evicted.

Joseph pointed to the house. "Everything needs to come out, and be careful to not break anything," he said loud enough for the gathering crowd to hear

He could care less whether they were careful or not, but it sounded good.

The four miners couldn't look at Ralph as they passed by him to walk into the house. They set about doing their work in silence.

"Please, Mr. McCord, I have a family," Ralph said.

"You already said that Ralph, and I have been as kind as I can given the circumstances."

As the men began carrying items out of the house, a crowd formed. It was made up of women since most of the men were at work in the mines.

Antonietta Starner pushed through the crowd carrying a large basket with a red napkin covering it. She was a middle-aged miner's widow with a narrow face and strong features, which would have made her a beautiful woman to be courted when she was younger. She had black hair pulled into a bun on the back of her head with just a few wisps of gray in it. She wore a white dress with blue polka dots. Since her husband had died in the mines three years ago, she had become very anti-mining.

She paused in front of Ralph and laid a hand on his shoulder. "I'm so sorry."

Ralph hung his head in shame.

Antonietta walked into the house and hugged Eliza Scarpelli with one arm. "This should help for a day or two," she said as she passed the basket over.

"What am I going to do, Toni?"

"You'll find a way. We're survivors. At least Ralph is still alive."

Eliza nodded and started crying again. Toni hugged her and glared over the woman's shoulder at Joseph. He didn't flinch or turn away. He had no reason to be ashamed or turn away from her stare. He had been fair with his miners, and they knew it.

The deputies continued their post next to their car, watching for any sign of an armed mob gathering. Ever since the Matewan uprisings in Blair County that had started with evictions, coal companies had been nervous about evicting miners. This was only the third time since the West Virginia riots that Joseph had evicted a family. He knew that Ralph wasn't the only union member in Eckhart Mines. He needed to find a way to root them out.

Joseph had to show that he could run an efficient operation and a productive coal mine that was non-union. He needed to run the ideal mine for Consolidation Coal to prove that he deserved more.

The pile of furniture and bags of clothing grew quickly. It

wouldn't take long to empty the small house. The miners worked fast, but they were careful not to damage anything. One or two of them seemed on the verge of tears.

Joseph stood with a severe expression. He puffed on a cigar and watched the work progress.

Antonietta walked back to Ralph and said, "What will you do now?"

Ralph's shoulders sagged, and his head drooped. "I don't know. We need to leave, but I don't know where to go."

"What about your belongings?"

"I've been trying to find someone with a truck, but I haven't so far."

Most people in Eckhart Mines didn't need a vehicle. If the stores in town didn't have what they needed, they could walk or ride the trolley to Frostburg.

"I'll ask around. Maybe I'll have some luck," Antonietta said.

She passed through the gate, glaring at Joseph. She walked back through the crowd heading toward The National Road.

Joseph stood with his back straight, and his chin lifted. The miners needed to see that the superintendent wouldn't bend; that he was strong, that he was a leader, and if they did not follow his rules, there would be consequences.

"Please, Mr. McCord, you can't do this to my family," Ralph said.

Ralph suddenly grabbed the lapels of Joseph's suit coat and pulled him closer. Ralph had an inch or two on Joseph and was lean muscle. The deputies started to raise their rifles, but Joseph waved a hand for them to stand down. Ralph wasn't threatening; he was pleading.

"I have not blacklisted you, Ralph … so far," Joseph said quietly. "You still have a chance to make a new life."

"Until the next mine finds out that I'm in the union."

Joseph nodded slowly. "Yes, unless you quit the union. This company gave you work and a place to live. We kept you working even as demand dropped for coal, and this is how you repay us? It is unacceptable."

Ralph let go of Joseph and dropped his hands to his sides, defeated. He waited for his family to come out of the house and they stood on the dirt road next to their pile of household items. The children looked dazed, and Eliza Scarpelli was still crying.

When everything was out of the house, Joseph took the key from Ralph and locked the door. He dismissed the miners and thanked the deputies. The miners joined the crowd, but the deputies got back in their car and drove off.

Joseph got into his car and drove back to the office. He still had work to finish today.

Chapter 3

February 8, 1922

The Cumberland and Westernport trolley car rolled up the National Road and turned west into Frostburg. Matt recognized St. Michael's Catholic Church with its tall spire on the right and prepared to hop off. He grabbed his suitcases and stepped off when the trolley halted in front of the electric railway office at the corner of North Water Street and West Main Street. It was less than a block from the triple arch entry for Failinger's Gladstone Hotel. This was Frostburg's Main Street, and unlike Cumberland, which had cross streets full of businesses, most of Frostburg's business district sat on the busiest street in town. This was understandable since Frostburg was one-fifth the size of Cumberland and at a higher elevation. Being built on a mountain ridge, the wind blew through downtown bringing colder temperatures than were typical further down the mountain in Cumberland.

Although the town was named after the founding family, it also seemed an appropriate name because, on some winter days, an inch or two of snow covered the ground in Frostburg while Cumberland's streets were bare.

Matt hurried through the front door and into the lobby of the hotel. It was a large room with a grand staircase that rose up half a flight before turning left and right to continue to the second floor. The fireplace to the right of the entry door was set with a large fire burning. A few people sat in armchairs talking to the left of the door. Halls on either side of the staircase led back to the restaurant, ballroom, and barbershop. The basement held other things that one would not expect in a hotel.

It wasn't the typical hotel where a miner would stay, but Matt thought it might be the last time that he got to enjoy himself for a while. The Gladstone Hotel might be twenty-five years old, but it still looked new and beautiful. It didn't appear large from the outside or even the lobby, but it had 100 guest rooms on three floors, so Matt shouldn't draw too much attention among the guests. He could pass for a traveler on the National Road.

He paid for a room at the front desk, and a bell boy came over to help him with his suitcases. Matt waved him away.

"I've only got the two bags," he said. "I can manage on my own."

The bell boy walked away, and Matt picked up his bags and headed up the grand staircase. Once in his room, he fell back on the bed and ran through in his mind what he still needed to accomplish. He hoped that it could all be done today or tomorrow. The mining company wouldn't start anyone working on a Friday because it was considered bad luck. Matt put his clothes away in the armoire and headed back out to the National Road.

He was walking past the five-story Frostburg Opera House, keeping his chin tucked into his chest and his coat pulled tight as the wind whipped around him. He noticed a young woman walking south on the other side of the street. For a moment, he thought she was Priscilla. She had shoulder-length blonde hair and stood a little over five feet tall. She struggled to carry four, thick books, shifting them from under her arms to holding them in front of her. Matt wondered if she'd make it to wherever she was going before those books tumbled to the ground.

From her age and the fact that she was carrying books, Matt guessed that she was a student, and any student her age would be attending the Maryland State Normal School. Matt slowed down to watch her walk as quickly as she could while trying to balance the books. She was unbalanced and was either going to go sprawling or lose the books that she was carrying. He wondered if she was late getting to a class. Once she passed, Matt noticed two miners hurrying to keep up with her. They spoke loudly and wobbled a bit as they rushed after her. They appeared drunk, though it was not yet five o'clock in the afternoon. Had they been enjoying moonshine or drinking in a speakeasy in town.

Frostburg was quickly gaining a reputation as a place where it was easy to get liquor, even though it was illegal. One story said that six out of ten families in Frostburg made their own wine. Matt had heard stories about Frostburg's flaunting of Prohibition and lawlessness in Baltimore.

"Hey, pretty teacher lady, why don't you teach my friend and me something?" one of the men called, slurring slightly.

The woman glanced over her shoulder at the men and quickened her pace. The men kept up with her.

"Don't leave us ignorant, ma'am," the other man said. "If you teach us, we'll teach you about love."

When she glanced over her shoulder, Matt saw her eyes wide open, and her mouth parted as if she wanted to scream. Though Matt was reasonably sure that the miners wouldn't have done more than taunt her, she obviously didn't believe that. He ran across the street and stepped between the young woman and the men.

"Enough!" Matt said in the same tone of voice he had used when he commanded Marines in Europe.

The miners halted, swaying a little as if they might topple over. They stared at Matt.

"We're just having a little fun with the school teacher," one of the miners said. Matt noticed that he had one blue eye and one green one. Both of them were bloodshot.

"She doesn't think it's funny. You'd know that if you weren't drunk," Matt said.

"Well, she didn't say anything. Did she Frankie? Get out of our way," the second miner said. He was the larger of the two and smelled of sweat. He tried to push past Matt, but Matt put his arm out to stop the man.

"She might not have said anything, but she was trying to get away from you."

"You're the one who best get away from us," the miner said. "There's two of us and only one of you."

Maybe Matt should have told the men that both the Marines and Pinkerton Agency had trained him to fight. He should have, but he didn't like bullies. Matt swung hard with a right uppercut that hit the man in the jaw. His head snapped back, and he dropped to the ground. He rolled around in pain, but he didn't get up.

"Now there's just one of you. Get out of here before you get the same thing," Matt told Frankie.

Matt's arms hung at his sides, inviting the remaining miner to try his luck. Matt kept his fists clenched. Frankie stared at Matt. Matt thought Frankie might actually take a swing at him, but then the miner glanced at his companion on the ground. The man rolled back and forth holding his jaw.

A bit of sobriety came back into Frankie's mismatched eyes. He stepped back from Matt, leaned down, and grabbed his friend by the arm. He pulled the fallen miner to his feet. They hurried off down the street.

Matt flexed his fist easing the pain from his knuckles. That had felt good!

"You ruffian! How dare you attack that man!"

Matt turned and saw the student yelling at him, her cheeks flushed red from the anger or exertion. Matt would have bet the former. She probably would have shaken a finger at him, but she was still trying to balance her books in front of her.

"Miss, that man and his friend were chasing you up the street," Matt said.

"I could have protected myself."

Matt's eyes widened. "Really? Against two men and you with an arm full of books? Besides, you didn't seem to be protecting yourself. You were nearly running."

She moved up close to Matt. She was a head shorter than him but made up for it with righteous indignation. Her blue eyes nearly bulged. Her nostrils flared, and each breath gave off a bit of water vapor that gave her the appearance of a tiny demon.

"They wouldn't have touched me!"

Matt sighed. A thank you would have been nice. He would never understand women. That much was becoming evident to him.

"You don't know what they would have done," he said calmly. "Maybe they wouldn't have bothered you if they were sober, but they weren't. Liquor can make a man do stupid things."

"I am a modern woman, and a modern woman can take care of herself without resorting to violence!" She wasn't the one who had resorted to it, and Matt hadn't minded. After all, he was a modern man.

"Why are you yelling at me? Maybe you should have yelled at them. Let them see the kitten turn into an alley cat, and they would have left you alone." His voice rose as he spoke, but he was losing his patience with this woman.

That gave her pause as she considered what he had said. When she realized it was an insult, her face reddened only emphasizing Matt's earlier impression that she looked like a demon.

He sighed. So much for this woman's resemblance to Priscilla. Priscilla had always kept her emotions in check as she thought a proper lady should. Anger for her was raising her voice, not yelling, mind you, just speaking loudly.

Matt tipped his cap to the woman and started to walk away.

"Men are barbarians!" she called from behind him. "The world would be better off without them!"

Matt stopped and turned back. He'd had just about enough of this ungrateful woman. He took a couple steps toward her as he rubbed his chin. "Miss, I may not have had all of the education that you do, but if there were no men, the world would run out of people right soon. I may not go to college like you, but I did learn in the little school where I went that you need both men and women to keep having people in the world."

He grinned as he said it and watched the color rise in her cheeks. Then he turned and resumed walking.

Despite the ungrateful woman, Matt found himself in good

spirits. It had been a while since he had been in a fight if you could call it that. He had boxed some in Baltimore to stay in shape, but he had given it up more than a year ago because Priscilla hadn't liked seeing him bruised. It felt good to be back at it. It had released much of the stress that had been building in him all week as he had gotten ready for the trip out here. Now he nearly bounced as he walked down the street. He wondered if anyone in Eckhart Mines did any boxing.

He headed east and walked through Frostburg, surprised at how well he remembered the different stores and businesses. He saw the Hitchins Brothers store, Betz Brothers Grocery, Betz Brother Jewelry Store, and Stanton's Hardware. The buildings weren't as tall as those in Cumberland, but he wondered if taller buildings wouldn't blow over in Frostburg's strong winds.

His family had rarely come to town because they never had a lot of money to spend. His mother would save what cash she could and pay with company scrip to buy food at one of the stores in Eckhart. If she had the money, she would spend it at one of the other stores in town where prices were reasonable. For more expensive items, she scrimped and saved pennies and nickels. When she had enough money, they would walk into Frostburg to buy clothing and other non-perishable items. It was always tiring to walk home with their arms full, but the hassle was worth it because the prices in Frostburg were much lower than those at the company store.

Once he had passed through town, Matt headed down the mountain to Eckhart Mines. It had never been a city, but it laid claim to being the location of the first Maryland coal mine. Sure, there were other mines before then, especially in Western Maryland, but they had been for iron. Coal was found in Eckhart Mines in 1814 while the National Road was being built. It had been hauled in wagons along the road to Cumberland and then onto Baltimore.

That initial discovery had grown into four coal mines and a town of nearly 2,000 people. Eckhart had seven saloons, three barber shops, two halls, two churches, a meat market, a reading room, a library, and a school. Consol No. 4, Consol No. 10, Sullivan

Brothers, and Ocean No. 3½ were the four mines, of which, the Consolidation Coal Consol mines were the largest.

Although Consolidation Coal was a massive company, it did not control all of the mines in Western Maryland. Small operations and towns dotted the Georges Creek region and the North Branch Potomac River. They had names like Vindex, Dodson, Pekin, and Shaft. Some of these towns lived only a few short years, dying when the coal in the mine played out. Other coal camps found reasons besides coal mining to exist and so they continued on even after the coal was gone. Although Eckhart Mines still had coal mines, its nearness to Frostburg kept it from being as isolated as other coal towns. This meant that Consolidation Coal couldn't maintain a stranglehold on Eckhart like those towns where the company owned every business, every home, every school, and every church.

Coal was big business, and the mine owners used their power to keep the unions out if they could. The more money that the unions forced the mine owners to spend, the more their profits were reduced. Having grown up in a family that just barely got by, Matt sympathized with the miners. What he didn't sympathize with were the miners who resorted to violence to get their way. To Matt's way of thinking, they were just another type of bully that needed to be dealt with.

That business last year in West Virginia had been a nasty affair. Around 13,000 miners, law enforcement officers, and soldiers had fought in Logan County in southern West Virginia after miners had gunned down Baldwin-Felts detectives working for the Stone Mountain Coal Company. They had been evicting union members from their company homes. The security agents had retaliated, and the fighting had grown until President Warren Harding had sent the military in to quell the fighting. In the end, fifty people had been killed. It hadn't looked good for either the mining companies or the union. Right now, the companies were enjoying their victory over the union, but if they weren't careful, such problems would spread and strengthen the United Mine Workers.

Although the Pinkertons had sent Matt to Eckhart, he had been willing to return to help keep Allegany County from turning into another Blair County. It would help protect his family. As a miner's life went, things weren't too bad in Maryland, but the UMW kept trying to get a foothold in Western Maryland by stoking anger against the companies while ignoring the positive things about Maryland's coal mines. Maryland mines had a reputation for being better than coal camps in many other states. They paid more, the houses were larger and better kept, and the mines safer. While all this was true, Matt knew from having worked in the mines that safety could be improved, wages needed to be increased, and coal companies should stop taking excessive payroll deductions.

The mine owners didn't see it that way, though. They provided above average working conditions and expected loyalty for that. They got it for the most part. Some miners did join the union, but they did so in secret. Consolidation Coal Company executives worried that another Matewan Massacre was coming, and the owners wanted to head it off by getting rid of the union organizers before they built a following. Those were the men Matt had been sent to find.

Shutdowns were bad news for the mine companies and miners, neither of which earned money when the mine wasn't operating. The UMW would call for a strike and support the miners until the coal companies gave in to the UMW's demands. Successful strikes improved the union's reputation, and miners joined seeking improved pay and benefits. Failed strikes meant lots of miners lost their jobs, and the remaining ones had to settle for whatever the coal companies were willing to provide. So far, most Western Maryland strikes had ended with the coal companies winning, and because the coal companies hadn't taken advantage of their wins, miners were relatively happy.

Since the Great War had ended, coal prices and demand had settled back down to their pre-war prices. That meant lower profits, which held down miner's wages. Dissatisfied miners offered an opportunity for the UMW. Matt was in Eckhart to blunt that opportunity if he could.

He walked into the Consolidation Coal office. It was attached to what was, in all but name, the Eckhart Mines company store. This portion of the store served as the mine office, and miners lined up here on Fridays to collect their pay for the week. The hope in having the office attached to the store was that the company would get some of the wages paid out returned as miners with pockets full of money bought goods on their way out. The office walls were covered with charts and notices. A large blackboard also took up most of one wall. It was filled with notes and figures concerning the mine's production.

Matt stepped up to the front of the counter and waited. Two desks dominated the room; one of them was for the paymaster, and the other was the superintendent's. He wondered if Winston McCord was still the superintendent. He had been when Matt worked in the mines before the war. Only one of the desks occupied at the moment. A large man with carefully combed blond hair looked over papers spread out before him at the superintendent's desk.

He noticed Matt waiting and said, "What do you want?"

"I've come to see if you have any jobs for a miner."

Matt had heard that the local mines had become increasingly suspicious of union activities. The fact that he was here was proof of that. The mine owners were firing anyone they caught supporting the union. At the same time, the mine owners suspected a strike was on the way and were trying to maximize production while they still had workers to get the ore out of the ground.

Some of the owners realized that such outright animosity toward the union wouldn't make them any friends, especially in the wake of the riots and killings at Matewan and Blair Mountain. The Baldwin-Felts Security Agents there had been heavy-handed and cruel. Consolidation Coal Company had hired the Pinkerton Agency to spy on the miners and find union supporters before they caused trouble.

The man stood up from his desk while smoking a cigar. He stared at Matt. Finally, he said, "Do I know you?"

"My name is Matt Ansaro. I used to live here."

The man plucked his cigar from his mouth. "Ahh, yes, I do

25

know you. Matteo Ansaro, the boy who left and became a war hero. Your parents talked about you often. I'm Joseph McCord."

Matt thought for a moment trying to match the name with a face. Joey McCord had been a scrawny teenager the last time Matt had seen him. Now he was a thick man, somewhat muscular, but also a bit given to fat, something rarely seen in a coal miner. He also had a hard expression, nothing like the whiny teen Matt remembered.

"Joey McCord?"

Joey had grown up in Eckhart Mines with Matt, but he had never really had a group of friends. The town was made up mainly of Poles and Italians, who tended to socialize amongst their own except in the mines and town events. Not only was Joey Scottish, but he was also the son of the mine supervisor.

"It's Joseph, and if I hire you, it will be Mr. McCord because I am the superintendent of this mine now," Joey said.

"I thought your dad was the supervisor."

"He was promoted to the Cumberland office to oversee the Consolidation Mines in Western Maryland, and I was promoted to his job."

Promoted? That would have meant that Joey had actually worked for the Consolidation Coal Company, and the last Matt had heard, Joey had been attending college in Baltimore. He had apparently risen through the ranks quickly.

Joey walked up to the counter and stood close to Matt. The man must have hit a growth spurt after Matt left home. Not only was he now heavier than Matt, but he was also an inch or two taller than Matt's five foot eight inches.

"Congratulations, Mr. McCord. That's quite a responsibility."

Joey leaned his beefy arms on the counter and leaned in, so he was face to face with Matt. "I'm in charge of keeping this mine profitable for the company, which means that 300 miners have work."

"Well, I'm hoping that I can be the 301st."

"It's been a while since you've been back here, Matteo." He blew a cloud of smoke in Matt's face. Matt closed his eyes and held his breath. He wasn't sure what was worse; the smell of the tobacco or Joey's breath.

"I was in the war." Matt never said that he had fought in the war. It hadn't been a choice to make like he had with the miners in Frostburg. In Europe, he'd fought because he'd been in a situation where he had to if he wanted to live. He had been no more than a bullet fired from a rifle. The officers had been the rifles. Even when Matt had become an officer, he had discovered that he was a rifle being held by someone else to aim and shoot. He had survived, and that only barely.

"The war ended four years ago," Joey said, staring Matt in the eyes. "Most everyone came home three years ago. Most everyone. Sam Marino did not. He died when his ship was sunk. My older brother never even got out of the country. He died in a truck crash. The Barry Brothers were both killed. They were the heroes. You are just a survivor."

"I wouldn't argue that," Matt said.

He had known all of the men Joey had named. He and Sam Marino had been good friends. His generation seemed to be growing smaller all of the time.

"Your father and uncles used to come in here bragging about how Matteo was an officer in the Marine Corps. They would save all the newspapers articles of Marines in your division and come into the store and read the stories of Belleau Woods, Champagne-Marne, and Meuse-Argonne, giving you credit for any heroic act mentioned."

Matt couldn't help but smirk. He could imagine his father and uncles doing just that. "My family does like to tell stories."

Joey blew smoke in his face again. "Well, to hear them tell it, you won the war single-handedly, but lots of Eckhart boys went to war. We've got veterans working in the mines now, and some of them were officers as well. They came home after the war."

"I've been in Baltimore."

"Why didn't you come home? You've still got family here. Were you worried that the town wouldn't throw you a parade? What were you doing in Baltimore?"

Matt shrugged. "Mostly just manual labor. When I could find better-paying jobs, I did them. It wasn't easy, though. When I came back from the war, so did a lot of other men who were all trying for the same jobs," Matt said.

Joey stepped back from the counter and glanced at some of the charts on the wall.

"Well, I do have some openings, but I need to be careful about who I hire nowadays," Joey said.

"Why's that?"

"Union talk's been flaring up again. Not only here, but nationwide, but unlike a lot of other places, we've been able to keep the union out of Eckhart Mines. It's not only what's best for us, but it's also what's best for the miners. If you don't believe that, you don't need to be working here."

"None of my family are union nor have they ever been."

"That doesn't mean they don't want to be, and it's my job to make sure those types are kept out of my mine."

His mine as if Joey owned it. Maybe Matt should put that in his report.

Matt shrugged. "I'm just looking for work, and I can work hard."

"Can you take orders?"

"I was in the Marines. We had to take a lot of orders. Some of them, well, some of them were ones that you wished you didn't have to follow." They were the ones that gave Matt nightmares even now, four years after the war had ended.

"I didn't serve in the armed forces myself," Joseph said. "I was kept here to run this mine to make sure there was enough coal for the ships to get you boys to Europe and back."

Matt doubted that Joey had been "kept" here. Even his brother had gone off to fight. Either Joey's father had kept him out of the service, or Joseph had taken his chances against getting drafted.

"Everyone did what they could, sir," Matt said.

Joey smirked at the "sir" reference, which is partially why Matt had used it. He needed to ingratiate himself with this man because he needed to be hired. If he wasn't, he might find a job at one of the other mines, but this was the one where he had worked before the war. He was familiar with it. His family was here. He needed a job in Eckhart Mines to help them.

It would have been easier to get a job if Joey knew that Matt was a Pinkerton detective working for Consolidation Coal, but that had been one of the conditions that Matt had insisted on. Neither the miners nor the superintendent could know that he was a Pinkerton. Matt needed to be accepted by the miners. He couldn't risk the superintendent giving him special treatment or too harsh treatment. Matt was alone on this assignment. He had no company officials to back him up.

Right now, he was glad of that. Joey would have found a way to make Matt's life miserable by holding that secret over his head. Joey could have exposed him as a private detective to the miners and blamed it on Matt's incompetence. Worse, Joey might have mentioned to the wrong person in Cumberland that Matt used to live in Eckhart Mines.

Joey tapped a finger on the counter. "That's right, and this was where I could be best used. My skills as a manager helped keep you boys alive. How long did you work in the mines before you left?"

"Three years."

"Had you started mining or were you doing other jobs?"

"I started off as a breaker for about a year. Then I was a mule driver for a little while. My last year and a half I worked as a miner."

Joey nodded. "So you know how things work in the mine. Do you have your own equipment?"

"No, sir, I haven't needed them for a while. I sold them when I left."

Joey pointed to the door leading to the company store. "Fine. You can go next door to the store and get what you need. It will go on your account, and a portion of your wages will be deducted each week to pay it back."

Matt nodded that he understood. He also assumed that he would wind up paying dearly for that equipment. The attached store might not be a company store in the sense that the coal company owned and operated it, but the company pushed business toward stores that accepted scrip. If those stores didn't support the mining company, the company might blacklist them, which could harm their businesses. That didn't mean those businesses were the preferred places for miners to buy goods. Frostburg stores offered lower prices, but his new employer might not like it too much if he bought too many things there.

"You can start tomorrow. I'll let the shift foreman know that you're coming. His name is Tom Gianconne. Be prepared to work."

Matt left the office. He'd been in a fight, yet not a punch had been thrown. He'd let Joey intimidate him, or rather, pretend to let Joey intimidate him. It had taken all the control Matt could muster not to lash out at Joey.

Matt walked into the store. It wasn't massive because of the competition from other stores in Eckhart Mines and Frostburg, but it carried the necessities, clothing, food, household goods, mining equipment, and more. What wasn't stocked could be ordered.

The clerk behind the u-shaped counter helped one of the women buy food. Matt browsed the aisles, waiting patiently. He checked the prices on some of the items and shook his head. Better prices could definitely be had in Frostburg, and these prices were probably better than a lot of other company stores in out-of-the-way places that had no competition.

Matt glanced over at Harry Portnoy. He had run the store when Matt had been a kid. Portnoy was older, with more wrinkles and less hair. The man had taken a switch to Matt's backside after Matt had stolen some penny candy when he was ten. What an ass! It was one thing for his dad to do it, but not this man. Harry was always sharp-tongued with his customers, and he always seemed to be saying something more than what he actually said and none of it good.

Portnoy finished with his customer, and she left. Rather than smile as most clerks did, Portnoy frowned.

"Can I get you something?" he asked.

He didn't even try to hide the fact that he was staring at the scar on Matt's neck.

"I'm starting at the mine tomorrow and need a shovel, pick,

drill, lunch bucket and hard hat."

"You'll be going on the books for it then." Matt nodded. "What's your name?"

"Matt Ansaro."

Portnoy's stare moved up to Matt's eyes. "You have the Ansaro look about you, but not as crazy-looking as your uncles."

Portnoy went to one of the shelves behind the counter and pulled down a round, metal lunch bucket and a hard hat. Matt had brought coveralls and other mining clothes with him so he wouldn't be gouged entirely.

Portnoy set the items on the counter. Then he opened a ledger and wrote down what Matt was buying and the cost. When he finished, he turned the ledger around said, "Sign there or make your mark if you can't write."

Matt said nothing. He just signed his name to be invoice agreeing to pay back the amount of the hat and lunch bucket in weekly payments.

"We take it out of your pay before you even get it," Portnoy said.

"I remember how it works."

"You need anything else?"

Matt shook his head. "Not from here, I don't."

He put the hat on his head. Then he looped the pail over the handle of the drill and laid the tools over his shoulder. When he walked out of the store, he was a coal miner once again.

Chapter 4

February 8, 1922

Matt walked down Federal Hill toward the Consol No. 10 mine. The mine tapped into the Tyson Coal Seam and was above the Consol No. 4 mine, which drew its coal from the Big Vein Coal Seam. Their closeness often caused drainage problems in the lower mine.

Matt felt like he was walkng backward in time. He was erasing all of the progress that he had made the past five years since he had left Eckhart Mines. Each step was another month regressing in his life. Going into the mine tomorrow would feel like a surrender to fate. He would be fifteen years old again and walking underground for the first time. Only this time, he knew what was to come, and he was still going.

As he reached the larger houses further away from the mine, he started looking for the Starner house. These houses were better kept than the ones closer to the mine. Those homes weren't neglected, but their owners couldn't afford repairs and paint. Those homes were smaller. The coal company owned them and rented them to mining families. Although the rent was overpriced for the size of the house, it was all the miners could usually afford. The further the homes got away from the noise of the mines, the larger they became.

The houses that were right on the edge between mining houses and larger houses closer to Frostburg were where the boarding houses were. They were larger than a mining house but close enough to the mines for single miners to easily walk to work. The trolley also ran miner special cars to take miners to the mines in the morning and home in the evening.

Matt saw the two-story house that he was looking for. It had a sharply peaked roof that hid the third floor, although the dormers gave it away. The wide front porch had a porch swing on it. He was relieved to see that it was well kept. Boarding houses owned by coal companies sometimes weren't.

Matt walked up the three steps to the front door. He set his tools down next to the door and knocked. A middle-aged woman answered. Matt recognized the woman immediately, although she now had gray in her hair. It was his aunt.

Seeing her so unexpectedly stunned him into silence.

The woman's eyes narrowed as she took him in. Matt saw the sparkle in her tired green eyes return, and he knew that she recognized him. Then those eyes filled with tears.

"Oh, Matt."

"Aunt Toni," he said.

She opened her arms and took him in a fierce hug. He was surprised at how strong her grip was.

"Oh, my boy, you are a sight. I never thought that I'd see you again. What are you doing back here?"

"I've got a job at the mine," Matt replied.

She pushed him back. "The mine! I thought you'd gotten away from all that."

He suddenly felt ashamed at disappointing this woman whom he hadn't seen in five years. Aunt Toni had been the woman who had slipped him home-baked cookies when his mother chased him from the kitchen. She was the one who had sat and talked with him after he had messed things up with Laura Henshaw.

"I thought I had gotten away, too, but I guess mining's in my blood."

Antonietta shook her head. "No, it's not in your blood, but it will take your blood if you let it." Matt couldn't understand her anger. His family had been miners for generations. Then she added, "It took my man last year. He was alone, and the black damp got him. He fell, and no one found him in time. Not an injury on him. He just stopped breathing."

Mine fans kept air circulating through the mine, but occasionally methane released from mining found places to gather. A man walking through one of these dead areas would pass out unable to breathe, and if no one was nearby to pull him away, he would suffocate. It was one reason no one was supposed to be alone in the mine.

"I'm so sorry, Aunt. I didn't even know that you had gotten married. Did I know him?"

"His name was Michael Starner."

Matt thought for a moment. "I knew a Peter Starner."

Antonietta nodded. "That's right. Michael was his brother. When Michael died, the coal company kicked me out of our house down the street. You know how it is, but Samuel and Enos put together their money with what little I had, and we put a down payment on this house. I was lucky to have your uncles to help me."

"I saw your ad in the newspaper, although I didn't know it was you at the time."

His aunt laughed. "Yes, I'm a businesswoman now." She grabbed Matt by the arm. "Come inside, boy, and let me look at you."

She pulled him into the sitting room. It had a couch and two wooden armchairs in it. It also had a large radio against one wall. The walls were whitewashed, but she had hung a few framed pictures from magazines and books to give the walls some color. Antonietta positioned him on the braided rug in the center of the room and then circled him like a vulture.

"You seem healthy enough. You've put on some muscle since I last saw you and maybe an inch or two."

"Yes, ma'am, I'm doing fine in that regard." He unconsciously drew himself up straighter. Her scrutiny made him more nervous than being yelled at by a drill instructor at Parris Island. She ran a finger along the four-inch scar along his neck. "I don't remember you having this before."

Matt unconsciously flinched away from the touch. "It's from the war."

Antonietta stared at him for a moment and nodded. "I didn't think it was from falling out of bed, Matt. It looks like it came might close to taking your head off your shoulders."

It wasn't the closest he had come to death during the war, and he didn't want to remember any of them.

"They took care of me in the hospital, and I'm fine now."

Antonietta snorted. "If you were fine, you wouldn't be back here."

"I need work, and I know this place, Aunt." It was a half lie.

Matt and his aunt sat down on the couch.

"Do your uncles know you're back?" she asked him. She ran her fingers through his hair, combing it back. She could not stop touching him. He wondered if she thought he was a ghost.

"No, ma'am, I haven't seen them. I just got in today on the morning train in Cumberland."

"Well, won't that be a surprise for them when they come home? Though the way news spreads around here, they probably already know it. Geno Ansaro's boy has returned to Eckhart Mines."

"Do they live here, Aunt?"

She nodded. "They do. We combine our money to afford this place. It not only saves us rent, but we pay the mortgage and gro- cery bill with what the boarders pay us. Your uncles live in the rooms on the third floor. Samuel and Myrna have one room, and Enos lives in the other." Myrna was Matt's Uncle Samuel's wife. Enos was apparently still single.

"Do you have another room to rent like the ad said? I'm in need of one," Matt asked.

"You can stay here, Matt. You don't need to pay rent."

"Yes, I do. I won't be a burden on you by depriving you of a boarder. I'll pay rent just like anyone else, and I'll be glad to do it."

Antonietta crossed her arms over her chest and stared at him. "If you want it that way, I won't tell you that the money won't help, but I'm going to give you a better room than the one I have to let. Where's your bag?"

"I took a room at Failinger's for tonight until I could figure things out. My tools are on the porch outside."

"Well, you must be rolling in the money if you can afford a hotel." He only wished that was true. If so, he might still have Priscilla.

"I'll come down tomorrow morning for breakfast, drop off my suitcases, and then head into the mine," Matt told her.

"Descend into hell, you mean." She sighed. "Well, you can leave your tools and lunch bucket here. Pick them up when you drop off your bags in the morning, and I'll make sure that you have something to eat for lunch."

She pulled at his arm. "Come with me, Matt. Let me show you your room. There are two rooms on the third floor, the ones your uncles have. Then I've got four rooms on the second floor. Those are the ones I rent. I've got three boarders right now. All miners. On this floor, there's the kitchen, the common sitting room, my bedroom, and sitting room that we have just for family." She led him down a short hallway and opened a door on the left. "This is the private sitting room, but it's your room now."

Bookcases lined two walls. A sofa and two chairs also filled the room. It looked much like the living room without the radio. A small painting of Jesus Christ hung on one wall.

"Are you sure you want to give it up?"

"You're family, Matt, it ain't no trouble. I'll have your uncles move out the furniture tonight, and put a bed and bureau in here. I may have some other pieces in the shed that might suit, too."

Matt looked around. The room had two windows covered by light blue curtains. One looked at the side of the house next door, and the other looked toward the mine. It was about twelve feet square which would suit him.

"It looks like just what I need," Matt said.

Antonietta hugged him. "I'm happy to see you, Matt, really I am, but I'm sad that you saw such that it would make this place look like a haven."

They sat in the room and talked for a half an hour about what had been happening with the family. Matt steered as much of the conversation away from his life in Baltimore as he could. Finally, he stood up, kissed his aunt on the cheek, and started back to Frostburg.

Walking back to the hotel was all uphill, and Matt was somewhat winded by the time he got back to his room. He sat down in the chair next to the window and stared out onto the National Road.

He found himself shivering. He wasn't sure whether he was cold or worried. He was beginning to think that he shouldn't have come back here, but he didn't have much say in his assignments. Of course, if he had told his boss the truth, he might still be in Western Maryland just not in Eckhart Mines.

Matt decided that he didn't want to sit around in his room for his final evening as a regular person and not a coal miner. He had one last evening of freedom, and he wanted to make the most of it. He walked down to the front desk in the lobby.

"I need a place to get a good meal and a drink," Matt told the man behind the front desk. He was about Matt's age but better dressed.

"Our restaurant serves excellent food, but you won't find alcohol hereabouts. You can thank the Volstead Act for that."

The federal government had passed the Eighteenth Amendment to the U.S. Constitution in 1918, outlawing the production, transportation, and sale of alcohol. It was ratified the following year, but then the Volstead Act had been in effect for two years now. It defined what an alcoholic beverage was and created an enforcement agency for the new law.

"I saw two drunk miners on Main Street just a few hours ago," Matt said.

"I couldn't say where they found their drinks."

Matt leaned in closer to the man. "Listen, I used to live around here. I know the hotel used to have a bar that is supposedly shut down."

The clerk stared at him and then grinned. "Not supposedly."

"I also know that a place like this gets a lot of travelers with a heavy thirst. Count me among them. I'm not a police or government agent. I'm someone who just wants a drink and a meal and is willing to pay."

Matt slid a silver dollar across the countertop. The man stared at the money and then at him. He picked up the money, and said, "Follow me."

They walked across the lobby to the restaurant entrance. Plenty of people filled the tables, but these people were drinking lemonade or coffee with their meals or at least appeared to be. The dim electric lights helped hide what people might be drinking.

"You can order food and drink here. They will bring the drinks up from downstairs. You can also go down if you want to drink and watch a cockfight."

Matt shook his head. He had no desire to see two roosters rip each other to shreds. He'd seen enough brutality to last a lifetime and then some. "That's all right."

"Then take a seat. I'll let the head waiter know that it's all right to serve you. Don't be loud about it, though. Not everyone here is drinking."

Matt patted the desk clerk on the shoulder. "I understand."

The desk clerk walked over and said something to the head-waiter – a thin man dressed in a black suit – who glanced at Matt and nodded.

The restaurant was long with the tables and dining area near the front of the hotel. The middle of the room was a dance floor with a band set up on a platform next to the wall. What had been the bar before Prohibition was at the back of the room. The shelves were now empty of bottles, though, and more tables had been added to the space.

The band played, "A Pretty Girl is Like a Melody." Some couples danced while others contented themselves to eat and drink. Matt wanted to be part of the latter group.

"Can I get a table away from the music and dancing?" he asked the headwaiter who had walked over with the desk clerk.

"Certainly, follow me."

They walked to the far side of the room where the wall seemed to be made of new brick. At the rear of the room, Matt thought that he saw a staircase leading down to the basement. If the hotel kept its booze down there, it would be easier to hide if the police ever raided the restaurant.

Matt sat down at a small table large enough for two people. A small candle burned in the center of the table, but it didn't give off much light. The headwaiter handed him a menu.

"I don't need it," Matt said. "I want your best steak. Cook it medium well, a potato with butter, green beans, and carrots. To drink, I would like bourbon."

"Yes, sir."

The headwaiter moved away, and Matt relaxed and listened to the music. The waiter brought his bourbon, and Matt took a sip. If he got any liquor to drink in Eckhart Mines, it would probably just be moonshine unless someone had hidden away some bottles of the good stuff before stores stopped selling it.

He watched the dancers moving quickly to "Ja Te Digo." Matt had never learned to dance, but it certainly looked like fun.

One of the dancing women laughed loudly, and he realized that it was the student he had met on the street earlier. Only now, she wore a loose-fitting cream-colored dress that barely reached her knees. It was covered in fringe and rhinestones that swung wildly with her movements.

It appeared that she could have a good time if she chose to. She even seemed willing to dance with the hated male of the species. Matt wondered if he should tell her that if she got rid of men, she would be dancing by herself.

The song ended, and the woman walked back to her table. Matt noticed her dancing companion moved off to another table. So their joining on the dance floor had been a temporary truce between the woman and all men.

She didn't sit when she reached her table. She just took a drink from her glass and began scanning the room, probably hunting her next dance partner. It shouldn't be too hard. She was an attractive woman and dancing didn't require conversation.

When she looked in Matt's direction, he turned away. He didn't feel like getting into another argument. He just wanted to drink his bourbon and enjoy a good meal.

The woman walked over to him and stood next to his table. He almost stood up, but then he figured that she wouldn't appreciate it.

"Hello," she said. Her tone was pleasant, unlike the way it had sounded this afternoon.

Matt looked up at her. He couldn't get past how much she looked like Priscilla, but the resemblance ended at looks.

"I was very rude to you this afternoon," she said. Matt didn't say anything. He wasn't sure what would light her fuse. "I have to admit that I was a bit ... unnerved by those men, and I took it out on you. I'm sorry."

Matt couldn't believe what he was hearing. This woman was the total opposite of the one he had met earlier. Then he realized that she had been drinking. It had apparently mellowed her.

"Would you like to sit down?" He motioned to the chair opposite him.

"Thank you, no. I'm here to dance. Would you like to dance with me?"

Matt shook his head. "I'm afraid that I never learned how."

"That's too bad. It's quite fun."

"I have to say, and please don't take any offense, but you are leaving me somewhat confused."

She put her hands on her hips and laughed. "Why is that?"

"This you..." He waved a hand at her. "...is a wonderfully charming person, but the you that I met earlier today was bitter and angry. At first, I thought it was that you were drinking this evening, but then I realized that both of these women are inside the same person. It seems sad that this one only reveals herself when you are drinking."

"Do you prefer your women demure, Mr. ...?"

"No, I prefer my women kind, friendly, intelligent, and my name is Matt Ansaro."

"I am Samantha Havencroft." She held out her hand. Matt

shook it.

"I am pleased to meet you. May I ask why you are so angry with men?"

Her cheeks flushed, and Matt thought that she might erupt again. "Since you seem sincere, I will answer in a kind, friendly, and intelligent manner. Men hold women back."

"That answer was certainly to the point." Matt stood up and pulled out the other chair. "Please, do sit down, Miss Havencroft. I think I might wind up with a sore neck if I keep having to look up to you."

She reluctantly sat down across from him, although she kept herself turned out from the table as if she wanted to be able to bolt away.

"I understand what you said, and to a certain degree, I can see how that might be true," Matt sat and said, "However, times are changing, women won the right to vote."

Samantha nodded. "Yes, but there is still so much more that needs to be done."

"So you say that men hold women back. How are they holding *you* back?"

"I have to live in a society where I can't be what I want to be."

"What do you want to be?"

"If I wanted to be president ... if I wanted to be a corporate owner, I could not."

"I agree with the part about the president, but you could certainly own a company," Matt replied.

"Can I? Can you name one corporation owned by a woman?"

Matt shook his head. "No, but I can't name many male corporate owners either. I do know that some women do own companies."

"They are few and far between."

"Yes, but as a percentage of women who have tried, it might not look as bad. The percentage of men who have tried and created successful corporations is rare as well. The difference is a lot more men try."

"I'm surprised you know math like that," Samantha said.

Matt frowned. "I'm a miner, Miss Havencroft, not an idiot. You might be surprised at the types of things miners know, not from being taught them at school but from practical experience learned in the mine."

"You seem to have a bit of anger yourself, Mr. Ansaro, although yours seems to be about social classes."

Matt thought for a moment. He had left Eckhart because he wanted to get out of the poverty of the area. Then he had begun to earn some money as a Pinkerton detective, but it hadn't been enough for Priscilla. And yes, that had angered him. Her family money hadn't meant anything to him, but it was more important to her than Matt's love.

Matt raised his glass toward Samantha. "You may be right about that. I apologize for any offense. I guess we are both trying to move mountains and realizing the futility."

Samantha stood up. "I came here to dance and be happy, Mr. Ansaro. This is not my time to be serious."

Matt nodded. "I know, and it's a joy to watch you succeed at both."

She walked away, and Matt admired her shapely legs. Very soon was back on the dance floor spinning and bouncing with a new dance partner. The waiter brought Matt his meal. He hoped food in his stomach would sop up some of the alcohol.

He cut into the thick steak and popped the piece in his mouth. Juicy and easy to chew. *Perfect.* Honestly, the rest of the meal could be lousy, and he would think it was still the best meal he had ever eaten because of this steak.

A man plopped down in the chair on the other side of the table. "Matt Ansaro, right?" the man asked.

Matt put down his knife and fork. "Do I know you?" "I'm Paul Nowak from Eckhart."

Matt recognized the name and then saw his childhood friend in this man's face. He was older and cleaner. He now wore a trimmed brown beard and mustache, but it was his friend.

Matt smiled. He reached across the table and slapped Paul on the shoulder.

"Paul, yes, of course, I remember you, but you look respectable now."

Paul laughed. "Not too respectable. I am here." He swung his arms in a circle to indicate he was talking about the room.

"Then you aren't alone in your pursuit of debauchery. Join me for dinner. This is the best steak that I have ever eaten."

Paul held up his hands in surrender. "Sorry, I can't. I have food coming to my table. I'm here with a date. I don't want to leave her alone for too long, or she might realize that she can do better than me."

"What are you doing these days?" Matt asked.

"I'm a bank clerk."

"How did you avoid the mines?"

"The army saved me. I was assigned to the quartermaster corps, which taught me a lot about managing goods as well as some other useful stuff. After the war, I came back to Eckhart to work in the mine with my father. Joey McCord was superintendent by then, and I couldn't bring myself to work under him, so I came to Frostburg. There were a lot of jobs available with all of the soldiers returning, but the bank manager was a veteran himself. He said that he could use a man who was skilled and organized enough to be in the quartermaster corps."

"Do you like the work?"

Paul nodded vigorously. "I do. I can see the daylight. It pays well, and I don't have to worry about the roof falling in on me."

"I'm glad for you."

"What about you? I haven't seen you for years."

Matt considered what was safe to say. "I was in the war and then Baltimore. I just came back today."

"Are you back here to stay?"

Matt shook his head. "Probably not, but I'll be here for a couple months at least."

"What are you going to be doing?"

"I'll be in the mines."

Paul's mouth fell open. "Really? In Eckhart?" When Matt nodded, Paul said, "Why the hell would you want to work there?"

"Not really my choice. I needed to go there."

"How so?"

Matt lied. "Personal reasons. I can't explain it."

Paul shook his head slowly. "So have you met Joey?"

"You mean, *Mr.* McCord? Yes, he certainly has changed."

"Yes, and not for the better. I don't envy you."

"I don't envy me either, but it will not last forever," Matt said.

"Well, good luck to you, Matt. If you want to get together some-time, stop by Citizens National Bank, and we'll set something up."

Paul stood up and shook Matt's hand. He walked back to his table, and Matt sat down to eat his meal.

It had felt good to see Paul. They had run in the same group of friends before the boys had started going to work as coal breakers in the mines.

Matt felt ashamed that he had to pretend to be a coal miner. He had gotten out of the mines just as Paul had, but Matt had to hide the fact. He wanted people to know that he had beaten the system. He wasn't a coal miner any longer. He was a private detective and security agent, but for the next few months at least, he would also have to be a coal miner.

He was about halfway through his steak when he felt a hand on his shoulder. He looked up and saw an attractive woman about ten to fifteen years older than him. She was doing her best to look younger with a healthy application of make-up, although Matt didn't think she needed it. Her dark hair was cut short so that it curled around her ears in a style was starting to gain in popularity among women. Her sleeveless loose-fitting dress shifted gently with her movements, suggesting more than revealing.

"I see that you are alone. May I join you?" she asked.

Matt nodded and wiped his mouth on his napkin. Then he stood up and pulled the other chair out for the woman.

"How do you do," he said. "My name is Matt."

"My name is Calista."

Matt cocked an eyebrow. "Really?"

Calista propped her elbows on the table and rested her chin on top of her hands. "You don't believe me?"

Matt shrugged. "I suppose that it could be your name, alt-hough, in all my time growing up here, I never heard of anyone named Calista. I also don't know of any French families hereabouts. However, a lot of veterans from here returned from France who would have heard the name. I'm sure that the name and you remind them of the beautiful ... and grateful ... women they met over there."

Calista smiled. "You make quick deductions, Matt."

Matt tilted his glass in her direction. "Don't get me wrong, the name suits you. I believe it means, 'Woman of most beauty,' doesn't it?" He had picked up some French during his time in the country.

She leaned forward and admitted, "I don't know, but I liked the way it sounded. It almost makes you lift your voice at the end so that it sounds full of anticipation and longing."

Now it was Matt's turn to smile. "You almost sound like a poet. May I buy you a drink?"

"I was hoping you would ask."

Matt waved the waiter over, and Calista ordered a French 75. Matt wasn't familiar with the drink, but he was sure that it cost more than bourbon.

"So Calista, why am I the envy of all the men in this room because I am graced with your company?" Matt asked.

Her eyelashes fluttered. "You think them envious?"

"Certainly the ones who have less-attractive companions."

Calista smiled. "You were alone and not wooed to the dance floor by the beautiful suffragette."

"Oh, you know Samantha?"

"Most people in Frostburg do. She does a lot of street preaching trying to encourage women to stand up for their rights. Vote. Get a job. Don't feel forced to marry."

"And I take it that doesn't interest you?"

"My rights won't quiet a rumbling stomach or quench my thirst for a drink."

"Would you care for something to eat?"

She shook her head. "You don't need to. Most men just want to go to their room or the alley."

Matt plucked a piece of steak from his plate with his fork and held it out to her. "Taste that steak."

Calista hesitated and then leaned forward to pull the meat off

45

the fork with her mouth. She chewed slowly, and he saw her eyes widen slightly. "It is delicious, and I haven't eaten all day."

Matt nodded. "So you can understand that as lovely as you are, I'm not leaving until I finish my meal. Now wouldn't it be rude of you to sit here watching me eat?"

"I suppose it might," she said hesitantly.

Matt reached out and laid his hand over hers. "Don't worry, Calista. It will be worth your time. However, just so you know, I will need to get up early and be on my way."

She nodded. "You are not what I expected."

That gave Matt pause. He needed to be just what people expected from a coal miner. If he stood out too much, they might begin to suspect him.

When Calista had ordered her meal, Matt said, "I was in France during the war, and I knew many ... Calistas over there. Some were as lovely as you. Others not so much, though they may have been at one time. Some were surprisingly young and others, well, let's say, they weren't so young."

"But you enjoyed evenings with all of them."

Matt shrugged. "Some. It is hard to enjoy yourself if the woman is crying. Don't get me wrong, some of the ladies enjoyed their work. They all had suffered loss and tragedy, whether they admitted or not. Who in their country had not? It was war. I was there to help liberate France."

She smiled demurely.

"Do you see yourself as my liberator?"

"No, but I do not have to be your conqueror either. We will spend this evening together, and I fully expect to enjoy myself. You have already done much to make that happen. I, in return, will try to make sure that you don't hate yourself and maybe enjoy yourself, too."

She looked down at her hands on the table.

"Jenny." She looked up. "My name is Jenny."

"Oh, is that the American translation of 'Woman of most beauty'?"

Jenny laughed. It was a short laugh, but genuine.

"Pleased to meet you, Jenny. My name is still Matt."

Chapter 5

February 8, 1922

Samantha stopped in front of the door to her father's house on College Avenue. It was a three-story brick Georgian home with six bedrooms. It was far larger than what she and her father needed, but he thought the president of the college should live in a house befitting his position.

She took a deep breath to clear away the cobwebs from the gin she had been drinking. She hoped that she didn't reek of alcohol and tobacco, though she doubted that. She could still smell the scent of cigarette smoke on her dress. The restaurant had been full of smoke tonight.

She opened her coat and ran her hands down her dress, trying unsuccessfully to push the hemline past her knees. Giving up, she straightened up with her shoulders back, and her head held high.

She opened the door and stepped into the foyer. She took her coat off and hung it on the rack then started down the hallway, trying to keep her heels from clicking on the oak floor.

As she passed by the living room, she saw her father sitting in his leather armchair next to the fireplace. It was his favorite spot on a winter's evening. He would get a fire going and settle down to read until he decided to go to bed. Samantha had hoped that he would have already gone to bed.

"Good night, Father," she said as she headed for the stairs.

John Havencroft glanced at the grandfather clock, then snapped his book shut. He removed his wire-rimmed glasses and wiped them with his handkerchief.

"Samantha, how many times have I asked you not to stay out so late?" he said.

"I'm a grown woman, Father. I can stay out as long as I want."

Her father snorted. "You're a grown woman who is still living in her father's house, which means that you're not a grown woman at all, despite what you might like to think. And look at how you're dressed! Why must you dress like that?"

"It's fashionable."

"It is low and common." He sighed and rubbed his eyes. "Samantha, I have a reputation and appearance to uphold in this community. I'm the president of the college and a leader in the community. People look to me and those in my household to set the example. When they see you dress like you do, they believe that is how the young women of the college are being told to dress."

Samantha bent a bit at the knees, so her dress hung a couple inches lower.

"It is not my fault they make such assumptions."

Her father stood up. He was nearly six feet tall with broad shoulders. He looked more like a military general than a college president.

"You don't mind it when they think such things about your soapbox sermons trying to convince women to overthrow mankind."

Samantha put her hands on her hips, which only pulled the hemline of her dress higher. "That's not what I'm doing."

"You can't have it both ways. And what kind of example of young womanhood do they see when they see you?"

Samantha lifted her chin a bit. "They see a modern woman who is confident, intelligent and able to take care of herself."

Her father harrumphed. "Well, we've already established that you are not taking care of yourself. A modern woman? Perhaps. Confident? Again, perhaps, but maybe unfounded."

"Why is that?"

"I was told of an incident today. You ran into a little trouble in town."

Samantha shook her head. "No trouble."

Her father walked over and put his hands on her shoulders.

"Really? I heard that two men nearly accosted you."

How had he heard that? "I had things under control," she said.

"Did you now? I also heard that a third man had to come and end their pursuit."

Samantha stepped back from her father. "I had things under control," she said sharply. "A third man did not *have* to help me. How are you finding out these things? Do you have someone following me?"

Her father gave a short laugh. "Hardly. As I said, we are a leading family in town, Samantha. We are watched by others and remarked upon."

She hadn't considered that. She wondered how much her father knew about her evening excursions to Failinger's restaurant. He certainly wouldn't approve. He had removed all the liquor from the house when the Volstead Act passed.

Her father walked back to her chair. "And this gentleman who helped you. I heard that you were quite rude to him."

"I didn't ask for his help," Samantha snapped. "I didn't need it. I was not attacked or even touched."

"But you were pursued, and from what I heard, you were quite upset at that pursuit. This man stepped in and helped you, and you treated him poorly."

"I did not ask for his help," Samantha repeated. "He insulted me."

"Insulted you? How did he do that?"

"He assumed that I could not take care of myself, and he was very violent to those men."

Her father rolled his eyes. "Those men who scared you?"

"Yes."

She could still picture how quickly Matt Ansaro had struck. Those miners hadn't been the only people surprised. How could such a gentleman as the man she had spoken with tonight be so violent?

"Samantha, you are intelligent, and someday I have no doubt that you will be quite a capable woman. You need to know that capable women–as do capable men–need associates who are willing to cooperate with them. The best way to accomplish that is to make friends. You, my dear, do not make friends well."

She was tempted to tell him that she had had a civil conversation with Matt Ansaro this evening and that it hadn't been unpleasant. Of course, to say so, might lead to her father asking where she had been. Besides, she didn't want to give him the satisfaction of feeling like he had won the argument.

"I don't make friends with men who overstep their boundaries," Samantha said.

"Yet, it is precisely those men whose help you may need in the future."

"I will not cater to the whims of men."

"I'm not asking you to cater to them. I'm asking you to be civil. I do not like living in this town any more than you do, but we are here, Samantha, for the time being. Some of these people I would prefer not to associate with, but I do so as I try to improve the college. If the college is improved, I will have that as evidence that I can do more elsewhere. Then we can move to a place that is not so backwoods as Frostburg. Don't be a snob, my dear."

She pointed a finger at her father. "And why not? You are."

"You can pursue your goal to be a modern woman. It does not mean that you have to be an unfriendly woman. I'm not saying that you have to date the man who helped you, but far be it from me to say that he deserved a tongue lashing. He deserved a thank you."

Which he had received, and it hadn't been as painful to do as she had thought that it might.

"So, you would have me be kind, friendly, and intelligent?" she asked, recalling Matt's words.

Her father rubbed his chin. "I might not have phrased it that way, but those traits are certainly praiseworthy."

She wondered what he would say if she told him that a coal miner had come up with them.

Her father continued, "Vernon called on you again this evening. I had to tell him that you were out who knows where."

Vernon Mitchell was a student at the college who had been pursuing Samantha for weeks. She had been quite blunt telling him "no," but he hadn't given up. He was a good-looking man, but he was arrogant and definitely overconfident. Despite his intentions, Samantha wasn't sure if his interest was in her or getting on her father's good side. Vernon acted exactly as her father urged her to do. Make friends and stay on people's good side.

"You should have told him that I was in a speakeasy getting drunk. I'm sure he would have rushed over to take advantage of me," Samantha said.

"Samantha!"

She wanted to see her father's reaction to determine if she might be able to tell if that is where she really was or not. She hadn't minded getting a rise out of him, though.

"Good night, father. I will see you for breakfast in the morning."

She walked upstairs to her room. She pushed the button to turn on the overhead light in her bedroom. It was dominated by a four-poster bed that was covered with a quilt that Samantha's grandmother had made. On one side of the room was an armoire and high bureau. On the other side of the room were her desk and chair.

Her Victrola sat in the corner of the room. She opened the cabinet and took out the record on top. It was the Happy Six playing "Na-Jo" and "Jabberwocky", two foxtrots. She put the record on the turntable and cranked the handle on the side to get the turntable spinning. Then she set the needle on the record and swayed to the music.

Samantha danced over and sat down at the desk. Mrs. Hopkins, their housekeeper, had left a copy of the *Cumberland Evening Times* on her desk. Samantha opened it up and began scanning headlines to see if there was anything of interest, mainly if there were any stories about women making progress in this world.

She had been excited when they first came to Frostburg because she had learned that Frostburg Miner's Hospital had had a female doctor when it first opened in 1913. Dr. Helen Binnie ran

Maryland's first state-supported hospital for a few months. Then she had left to join her father's practice in Wisconsin.

The woman had been a pioneer and then given it up! And for what? To help her father!

Samantha didn't find anything in the newspaper, which was usually the case. Western Maryland didn't care for progressive women. Cumberland might be Maryland's Queen City, but it was still dwarfed by Baltimore where half of the state's population lived.

She opened one of her desk drawers and pulled out a scrapbook. It was filled with clippings from newspapers and magazines about women who were inspiring Samantha to reach her full potential. Annie Arniel was a suffragette who had been part of the Silent Sentinels and was arrested in front of the White House in 1917. In fact, she had been jailed eight times for supporting women's rights. Sophonisba Preston Breckinridge was the first woman to earn a Ph.D. in political science and economics and the first woman to pass the Kentucky bar. Tennessee Celeste Claflin and her sister Victoria Woodhull were the first women to open a Wall Street Brokerage firm.

When the record stopped playing, Samantha got up and turned it over. She paused and flipped it over again and then again.

Matt Ansaro had said she was two different people like two sides of a record. The suffragette and the dancer. Were they really different, though? Could they be? They were both her.

Well, Matt Ansaro was two different people, too. He was the uncouth street fighter she had met in the afternoon and the sincere gentleman in the restaurant.

So why did it bother her that he thought she was two different people and he didn't like one of them? He was just a foolish man who wanted her to act demure. That wasn't her, no matter what side he was looking at.

Still, she hadn't known what those drunk miners were going to do. She heard stories from other students at the college about miners getting too aggressive. Matt Ansaro had faced down two men just to help her.

She didn't want to admire that, but she couldn't help herself.

She changed out of her dress, which she admitted to herself was not the wisest thing to wear in the winter, and into a flannel nightgown. Then she climbed under the heavy comforter on her bed. She fell asleep dreaming of a world where women ran the government, and oddly, Matt Ansaro.

Chapter 6

February 9, 1922

Matt woke at 5 a.m. His internal clock was reasonably accurate, so he knew that he would be within a minute or two of that time without even looking at the clock on the wall. It was still dark out. The National Road was quiet for now. By the time he left the mine this evening, the sun would have gone down. He probably wouldn't see daylight until Saturday afternoon. The thought caused him to shudder.

He slid out of bed, careful not to wake Calista. He had paid her last evening, so he had no debt to settle with her this morning.

He dressed as quietly as he could and repacked the suitcase he had used. No use washing off. He was only going to get filthy in the mine.

When he was ready to leave, Matt sat down on the bed and shook Calista's shoulder. She stirred and mumbled something that he didn't quite catch.

"What did you say?" he asked.

Calista blinked open her eyes. They were light blue, so light that she seemed to have a perpetual dreamy look about her.

"I said that you mumble in your sleep," she said.

Matt froze. He knew he had bad dreams sometimes, but what

if he said something about his assignment? "Did I say anything interesting?" He tried to sound casual and not concerned.

"I could only make out a word here and there. I was listening for my name, but I didn't hear it." She grinned mischievously. "You also thrash around a good bit."

Matt shrugged. "Sorry about that." He stood up. "I need to leave now. The room is paid for. I'll leave the key at the front desk and tell them that someone is still in the room. You can leave whenever you wake up and feel like going."

Calista rolled onto her back and stretched her hands over her head. The sheet slid down below her breasts, and Matt smiled. "Will I see you again?" she asked.

"I imagine that I'll come to town, so you may see me, but in bed again...I doubt it."

"I thought we had fun last night," she said with a smile.

Matt grinned back. "We did, but it's been a while since I've been with a *Calista*. In truth, I thought that I would be married by now. That plan didn't work out."

"I'm sorry."

Matt believed that she meant it. He shrugged. Priscilla was his past. Nothing could be done about it, even if he hadn't been in Western Maryland.

"I wish I had met you years ago," he said.

"Do you think you could have saved me from this wicked life?"

"I was thinking that you might have saved me from mine. I might not have gone to Europe."

"I was already married by then, and it didn't stop my husband from going to Europe," Calista said. "He never came back."

Sadly, she wasn't the only woman with that story.

Matt brushed a loose strand of hair off her face. "Now, I'm the one who's sorry." He stood up. "I go into the coal mines this morning, and you've given me something to smile about in the darkness. If you do see me again, I'll understand if you want to ignore me."

Calista laughed. "Why would I do that? Usually, it's the other way around."

"I'm sure that I'll be looking a lot grubbier the next time we meet, and what 'woman of most beauty' would want to be seen with a filthy coal miner?"

"It depends on the miner." She got a faraway look in those beautiful blue eyes. "My husband was a coal miner." She hesitated, and then added, "You be careful in those mines. I know women who have lost someone in the mines."

She didn't have to say that some of them would have wound up like her, needing to sell themselves to make ends meet. Matt, at least, had no one depending on him whom he might leave destitute if he died.

Matt leaned over and kissed Calista on the forehead, then he headed out of the room.

A layer of frost covered the ground outside the hotel, but at least it hadn't snowed. He put on his work gloves to keep his hands warm. The electric streetlights glowed, casting enough light to see by, although most people were still moving shadows.

Life on the street slowly stirred as he headed south. Drivers in their trucks and a few wagons made early-morning deliveries. Bakers fired up their ovens. Various workers, like Matt, headed toward work.

As he moved out of town, Matt noticed that the other people dressed as miners walking on the road. Eckhart Mines was close enough to Frostburg that miners could live in Frostburg and walk to the mines. It might be a miserable walk in the snow or rain, but it got them out of a small coal town where they had to live under the thumb of the mining company. They could also find cheaper rents and prices in Frostburg.

Coal camps were first and foremost towns built for the convenience of the mining companies because towns were rarely located where coal was found. Eckhart was an exception. It had been in existence for more than sixty years before coal was discovered in Maryland.

Matt had been born in Eckhart Mines and lived there for his first eighteen years of life. He thought he had gotten out of the coal town, but here he was walking back into it to live and work.

As coal towns went, Eckhart Mines was actually not bad. The miners' homes were small, but they were made of stone, and most of them were in good condition. They even had small yards bounded with picket fences. The town had a theater, stores, a school, churches, and even an ice cream parlor.

But it was a coal town. Those businesses depended on coal miners, and the miners depended on the coal mines. Even if the coal company didn't own Eckhart like they did other coal towns, the mine owners had a lot of say over how things ran. If they blacklisted a business, it would fail.

Eckhart Mine's lifeblood since coal had first been discovered there in 1852 had become increasingly dependent on the ore. Although coal towns had done well during the Great War supplying coal to power the ships, now that the conflict was ended, coal prices and demand had fallen below pre-war levels. The lessening demand was affecting towns like Eckhart Mines reducing the number of hours and money to be had. Consolidation Coal had already cut back to two shifts in its Eckhart coal mines and reduced the per ton rate. Miners were angry over decreasing wages and nervous about their jobs.

The National Road ran right through the center of town. Matt could see lights on in some of the houses. Chimneys puffed smoke as coal was thrown into furnaces. He turned off on his aunt's street and walked up onto the porch. He considered knocking, but he lived here now.

Matt opened the door to the boarding house and stepped inside. He was swept into a bear hug that pinned his arms to his sides. His feet dangled off the floor.

"What do we have here?" someone said. Matt felt whiskers giving his face brush burn and tried to pull back.

"It's an intruder," another man said.

Matt stopped struggling and let his legs become entangled with his captor's. The man tripped, and they fell with a great thud. The man's grip broke, and Matt rolled to the side, grabbing for his boot knife.

"Enough horsing around," Aunt Antonietta snapped. "Someone's going to get hurt, and from the looks of it, it will be you, Enos."

Matt tried to catch his breath as he looked around the room from his squatting position. His hand still rested on the top of his boot, ready to pull the knife.

"Enos? Uncle Enos?" Matt said.

The bearded man on the floor laughed and rolled onto his side.

"Who else did you think it would be?" He paused. "Well, I guess it might have been Samuel, but he's too serious about things nowadays."

Samuel Ansaro walked out of the kitchen and offered his younger brother a hand up.

"One of us needs to think about the future," Samuel said.

"I think about it, and then I ignore it since one day is pretty much like the next," Enos Ansaro.

Matt slowly stood up and tried to relax. He had nearly stabbed his uncle.

"I could have hurt you, Uncle Enos," he said.

"You may have gotten away from me, but I wasn't trying to hurt you only hug you. It's good to see you, Matt. The Marines treated you well."

Enos was the youngest of the Ansaro brothers. He was also the one who looked most like Matt's father with his dark hair and eyes, broad face and welcoming smile. He was ten years older than Matt, and although they could have passed for brothers when Matt had last seen him, his years in the mines were catching up with him. He looked older than his age now.

"The Marines kept me alive," Matt said.

"That's the best we can do–live to see another day," Enos said.

"It's good to see you, too. Both of you," Matt said.

"I'm surprised that you came back here," Samuel said.

He was the oldest brother nearing fifty years old. He still stood tall at six feet. The mine hadn't taken that from him. He actually appeared to be bearing up to the stresses of working in the mine better than his youngest brother.

"Toni says you're going back into the mines with us," Samuel said.

Matt nodded. "Yes, sir."

"You're a man now, Matt. Don't sir me. I'm not Mr. McCord."

Enos added, "He's too high and mighty now to allow himself to be called Joey. It's always Joseph."

"It could be worse, Enos," Samuel chided. "He's not heavy handed on the miners, just high minded."

"Your aunt packed your lunch pail," Enos said.

"I need to put my bags in my room, and then I'll be ready to go," Matt told him.

"We can all walk down together."

Matt carried his suitcases back to his room and set them on his bed. He would unpack them later this evening. He picked up his hard hat off the bed and walked back out to the sitting room.

Antonietta was there holding his lunch pail. He took it from her, and she kissed him on the cheek. He felt like a schoolboy preparing to head off for his classes for the day.

"The other boarders already left," Enos said. "You will meet them this evening when we get home."

"I'm looking forward to it," Matt said.

Samuel led him back to the mudroom where their tools were lined up against one wall. Matt put his pick, auger, and shovel on his shoulder and headed out the back door.

The three men headed out of the house to join the growing stream of men and boys walking to the mines. The men mined the coal while the boys worked as breakers, going through all of the mined rock and separating the coal from it. The lights from the headlamps on the men's hard hats were a mix of battery powered or carbide, and it made the men look like a line of fireflies. While Frostburg had streetlights, the innovation hadn't come to Eckhart Mines yet.

The men were all dressed similarly in overalls or jeans with flannel shirts or even sweaters. They also wore leather gloves, hard hats, and heavy boots that could offer some protection for their toes in a rock fall. The sweaters and flannel shirts were worn even in the summer because the mine temperature was around fifty degrees even at the height of summer.

"So what's Baltimore like?" Enos asked. "Are the girls pretty?"

"Some are," Matt told him. "Just like here. Now the French girls, though, the French seem to have more than their fair share of pretty girls."

"So why didn't you marry one? I heard a lot of doughboys came back with a French wife."

Matt chuckled. "I couldn't pick between them."

Enos started laughing. It sounded loud in the early morning with so few of the miners saying anything as they walked to the mine.

"What do you think about this Prohibition?" Enos asked.

"I think it doesn't seem to be taking in Frostburg."

"Uh huh, uh huh. It's not taking around here either if you know what I mean."

"I'm glad to hear it. I hate to drink alone," Matt said.

Matt didn't mind the chit-chat. It kept his mind off of where he was going. He was also glad that it was dark out, or his uncles might have seen that he was growing paler the closer they came to the mine.

"What do you think of our investment?" Enos asked. "We're landlords now."

They had achieved something that a lot of miners wouldn't or couldn't, and they had done it by sticking together as a family and pooling all of their resources.

"It seems like Aunt Antonietta does most of the work," Matt said.

"We all have our jobs. Samuel and me, we do the big chores. We also help find most of the renters because we know the miners."

"So what are you going to do with your fortunes?"

"Good question. Samuel is saving his. He opened an account at a bank in Frostburg. I keep mine hidden in my room. Maybe we'll buy another boarding house, but I've been thinking about buying a car."

"What would you need a car for? You live a quarter mile from your work," Matt asked.

"I could be a taxi man, driving people up the hill to Frostburg or Cumberland, so they don't have to wait for the trolley."

"That's an interesting idea," Matt said.

"You think so? I just thought it up right now. That's what it means to be a man of means. You're always thinking of ways to make more money."

Matt laughed.

The Ansaros stopped at the equipment room first. Matt checked in with Tom Gianconne who assigned him to work with his uncles. The foreman also assigned him a number that he would use to register his daily tonnage. The miners grabbed their shovels and then went to the powder room to fill a bag with the black powder they might need during the day. They put their shovels, lunch pails and powder bags into a coal car that would carry the equipment to the layoff where the miners would pick their items up before they headed to the face.

They walked back to the maintenance shed and hung their miners' check—brass medallions about the size of a quarter and stamped with their miner number—on a board outside the shop. If the check was on the board, it meant that miner was underground. It was a safety precaution to make sure no one was left behind in the mine if there was an accident like a cave in. A quick glance at the board would tell the mine foreman whether everyone was out of the mine and if not, who was still inside. If there were problems in the mine, you wanted to see a miner's check on the board.

"So why did you come back?" Samuel asked as they headed toward the mine entrance. It was the first thing he had said on the walk from the boarding house. "The last I heard you were happy in Baltimore."

Matt shrugged, knowing he needed to be careful about what he said. "Things change. I needed to get away from there and start over."

Samuel shook his head and threw the butt of his cigarette on the ground, snuffing it out with his toe. "Hell of a way to start over. Why not just go back into the Marines?"

"The war's over, Uncle. They don't need all those soldiers, sailors, and Marines. Even after they let loose all the ones they drafted, they have still been reducing the numbers."

"Sounds like the mines. Now that the government's not buying so much coal, the mines have been cutting back on their miners or at the very least their hours."

"How's it been here?"

"We're down to two shifts, but a lot of men are giving up mining for factory work at the Kelly-Springfield plant in Cumberland."

"Oh, they got that open?"

Samuel nodded.

The Kelly-Springfield Tire Company had manufactured tires in Ohio, but the company had started work on a new plant in Cumberland in 1916. The city had offered a lot of incentives to get the new factory, including eighty-one acres of land, $750,000 toward construction, and infrastructure improvements. In return, the company provided around 3,000 jobs to area residents, and many of them paid better than mining. Tires had been manufactured at the new plant since last April.

"So is Eckhart down to two shifts because there's not enough miners or not enough contracts?" Matt asked.

"One thing about Consolidation Coal is that they're big enough to get the big contracts," Samuel said.

As the largest coal company in the eastern United States, Consolidation Coal had its headquarters in New York City where many national contracts were negotiated. The company did have a division office in Cumberland. The staff there coordinated the efforts of the Maryland mines, railroads, and C&O Canal to get coal out of the region.

The Ansaros and other miners climbed into a line of coal cars that would take them under the earth. Matt looked at the dark hole in front of him that was even darker than the night sky. This was the last place he wanted to go. He wanted to scream, but all he could do was smile and laugh at a joke Enos had cracked.

Chapter 7

February 9, 1922

Antonietta finished the morning dishes and dried her hands on a dish towel. The sun was up, although it still felt like it would be a cold day. Myrna was in the chicken coop in the backyard. She had milked their cow already and was now gathering eggs. The backyard was more of a small farm than a yard. An awning was attached to the coop that allowed the cow to get out of the rain. Antonietta also planted vegetables in a large garden. Last summer, Samuel had built an outdoor oven so Antonietta and her sister-in-law could do their baking without increasing the heat inside the house.

For the most part, having her brothers living in the same house with her was a good thing. It reduced the expenses any of them had to pay, and Myrna was a big help around the house, although Antonietta could do without some of her sermons.

Myrna and Samuel went to church every Sunday and read the Bible in the evening. Antonietta did as well. She was fine with religion, but she had developed her own opinions about God, Jesus, and the Holy Ghost. She didn't need Myrna getting worked up trying to make her believe something different.

Antonietta opened the door to the mudroom. She pulled one of the two steel tubs off the wall hooks and laid it on the kitchen floor.

She stuck a smaller bucket under the kitchen faucet and filled it, then emptied it into the tub, repeating the process until the tub was half full. Then she tossed some of the dirty clothes into the water and let them soak to loosen up some of the caked filth from the coal mine.

Instead of dusting the sitting room, she decided to help out Matt. Her nephew would be exhausted after his first day in the mines, whether he admitted it or not. Better he should come home and have one less thing to worry about.

She walked into his room where he had left his suitcases laying on the feather mattress on the bed. She flipped the latches on the case and lifted the top. Then she pulled open the bureau drawer.

Antonietta lifted out the brown suit that was on top. Below it was a pinstripe suit. They were very pricey outfits, certainly better quality than anything most miners would ever wear. She wondered what her nephew had done in Baltimore to be able to afford and need two suits. It wouldn't do to keep them folded in a drawer. She would have to get a hanger from the armoire in her room and hang the suits on the back of the door to Matt's room.

She set the jacket on the bed and tried to smooth out the wrinkles. Then she did the same thing for the pants.

A couple of shirts went into the drawer. When Antionetta lifted a pair of jeans out, she froze. A pistol was laying amid the clothing. What would Matt be doing with a weapon? It wasn't uncommon for men around here to have guns, but those were rifles and shotguns that they used for hunting. Antonietta couldn't remember the last time she saw someone with a pistol. Maybe it was something that he had kept with him from the war. That could be it.

Should she put it away in the bureau? What if he hadn't wanted anyone to know that he had the pistol? She hadn't told him that she would put his things away. If she had said something, he might have told her not to.

She stared at the weapon for a few moments longer, and then she began carefully repacking everything just as it had been. She closed the suitcase and clasps.

If Matt wanted to tell her about the pistol, let him do it in his own time.

Chapter 8

February 9, 1922

Joseph woke at 7 a.m. when his alarm clock rang. He reached over and flipped the button to disengage the bell. Then he stretched out and lay with his hands behind his head. The room was warm, and he was toasty and relaxed under the comforter.

He could see daylight beginning to shine around the edges of his heavy curtains, and he heard Maizy preparing breakfast in the kitchen.

His miners would already be at work for the day forcing coal from the ground. Joseph had walked through the mines with his foreman a month ago, looking at the low-ceiling tunnels and damp walls. The thing he remembered most was the sulfur smell as if the men were digging their way to hell. Even though he hadn't dug any coal, he had come out of the mine feeling dirty and in need of a bath.

It was not a place where he had enjoyed being, and he made sure to spend as little time as possible there. His job forced him to visit on occasion, but luckily, those occasions were few and far between.

He finally sat up and turned on a lamp next to his bed. Then he opened the curtains and let the morning light into the room. It hadn't snowed during the night, which was always a good thing, but there was frost on the window. Winter was here.

It was on mornings like this that Joseph was glad that he had indoor plumbing. Some of the larger homes in town also had installed plumbing and built bathrooms, but most people still used outhouses. He walked out of his room to the end of the hallway where the bathroom was located. He washed up and then walked back to his room.

This was the house that he had grown up in. Back then, his room had been on the other side of the hall. This room had been his parents. He had taken it over since it was the largest bedroom in the house. His old bedroom now served as his dressing room. His parents moved to Cumberland when his father had been promoted, and they owned an even larger house on Washington Street.

Joseph dressed in a shirt and tie. He only wore a full suit if an inspector from the company or the state was coming. Otherwise, he felt that a shirt and tie allowed him to look like a mine superintendent without flaunting his wealth.

He walked out of the room and headed downstairs to the kitchen. Maizy flitted back and forth between the stove and oven. She was a middle-aged widow of a miner who died in a rock fall three years ago. Although she had been evicted from company housing, Joseph had decided to hire her to cook and clean for him. He also gave her a downstairs room to live in.

"Good morning, Mr. McCord," she said when she saw him.

"Good morning, Maizy. What's for breakfast today?"

"Pancakes and bacon."

Joseph sat down at the table so that he could look out the large window. The house was built on the mountainside above Eckhart. At times, he liked to believe that he was actually closer to Frostburg than Eckhart, but he knew that wasn't true. He looked out the window at the clustered buildings with smoke trailing out of their chimneys.

Everyone in that town depended on the coal mines in some way, and that meant they depended on him since he was superintendent. Should the mines close, not only would the miners be out of work, but the businesses that depended on their trade would most likely close.

Maizy came in with a cup of coffee, sweetened with sugar. She set it on the table and went back into the kitchen.

Joseph took a sip of the coffee and then picked up the copy of the *Cumberland Evening Times* sitting on the table. He went through the newspaper once scanning the headlines to see if anything caught his attention. Those would be the first stories that he read. He would gradually read most of the newspaper throughout the day.

He kept himself informed, even if he didn't have someone to speak with about what he read. Sometimes he would talk to Old Man Portnoy, but that was only in times of desperation.

Joseph ate his breakfast by himself as he read the newspaper. When he had finished, he put on his overcoat and headed down toward the mountain.

He arrived at the office by 9 a.m. That gave Sidney Bloom, the paymaster, time to make sure the furnace was going and the building was warm. Portnoy usually showed up at 9 a.m. to open the store.

"Good morning, Mr. McCord," Sidney said when Joseph walked in. He was a mousy little man, the younger son of one of the shopkeepers in town. His older brother had inherited the store, leaving Sidney to find his own way in the world.

Joseph knew how that went. He had been the younger son. Frederick had been groomed by their father to take over the mine, but then the war had come, and Frederick had gone off to fight. He had never even made it out of the states. He had been killed when a truck he had been riding in slid off an icy road. Yet, their father had insisted that Frederick was a war hero.

That accident had changed Joseph's future. He had been in school, figuring that he would be drafted at some point, but his father had made arrangements so that it never happened. Not only that, but the old man had pulled Joseph out of school and set him to working for Consolidation Mines.

"Do you have good news for me today, Sidney?" Joseph asked.

"The tallies are on your desk. We are meeting our goals for the contracts, but the goals are getting lower. We'll be producing an excess before too long."

Demand for coal was down since the end of the war. Joseph had no say in getting the contracts that Consolidation Mines filled, but if the largest coal company in the region couldn't win a coal contract, what did that say for the industry?

That wasn't good. Once that started, Consolidation Coal would want him to cut back on the number of miners he employed.

His biggest worry was that the order would come down from Cumberland to cut back on production. If that happened, it would be the coal miners who suffered the most. That was something that Joseph wanted to avoid. Keeping the miners fully employed helped keep them busy and out of mischief, and if they were fully employed, they would be making a decent living, which would keep them happy. It was all connected.

Joseph hung up his coat and sat down at his desk. He flipped through the papers on his desk to get the general idea of what was happening in the mine. Then he went back to the beginning and looked at them in greater detail.

The miners were producing. Sidney was right. Companies just weren't buying as much coal.

He saw another set of papers and flipped through them. These were Tom Gianconne's safety reports. Joseph knew what they said. They always said the same thing. Equipment needed to be serviced. Supports needed to be replaced. The problem was that Joseph didn't have the money.

His job was to keep the mine profitable. With smaller orders being filled, it meant that his mine was being allocated less to run. It was either keep the miners working or make the repairs. He wouldn't get more money for maintenance unless something drastic happened, and with mining, something drastic usually meant that miners got killed.

He set the reports aside. He would need to have Gianconne

prioritize his list by cost and need. If Joseph could manage to hold back some operational money, he might make a few repairs.

Joseph heard movement next door in the store. He grabbed his cup and stood up. He opened the door to the store and saw that Portnoy had started the coffee. He had told the dour man to make that his first order of business each morning.

He didn't see Portnoy. He must be upstairs gathering some stock to fill in empty spots on the shelves.

Joseph walked over to the pot-belly stove in the middle of the room that helped heat the store in the winter. He saw the coffee pot on top and lifted the lid. It smelled delicious. Portnoy might be an unpleasant person, but he made a delicious cup of coffee.

Portnoy walked down the stairs with his arms full of items from the second-floor storeroom. He set them on the counter.

He frowned as he always did when he saw Joseph drinking his coffee without paying. It was one of the perks of being mine superintendent that Joseph often enjoyed.

"Good morning, Joseph," Portnoy said through clenched teeth.

Joseph held up his coffee cup toward the older man. Then he walked over to the counter and picked a peppermint stick out of a jar and began swirling it around in his coffee to sweeten it.

Although Maryland law required company stores to be operated as separate entities from the coal mine, most mining companies still owned a stake in at least one of the stores in their towns. Such was the case with Consolidation Coal Company and this store, which allowed Joseph to get away without paying for just about anything, but it also allowed Portnoy to feel that he didn't need to call Joseph Mr. McCord.

"How was business yesterday?" Joseph asked.

"We did well. Customers who usually walk to Frostburg for the best prices aren't so willing to do that in the cold."

"You know, you would probably have more customers if you weren't always so glum." It was a point that Joseph made at least once a month, not that it did any good. Portnoy had run this store for fifteen years, and Joseph didn't think that he had ever seen the man smile.

Portnoy's eyes narrowed. "I'd make more money if people would pay for their goods."

"Are you talking about me?"

"I'm talking about all of the people I have to carry on the books."

Joseph shrugged. "If you are going to charge high prices, then you need a reason to keep people coming in here. Easy credit makes them indebted to the company."

The front door opened, and a woman walked in with three young children trailing behind her. She nodded to Joseph and stepped up to the counter.

"I'm here to pay on my account, Mr. Portnoy," the woman said.

She opened her small purse and took out some coins that Joseph recognized as company scrip. Portnoy took it and counted it up.

"This is just the minimum, Mrs. Jablon."

"That's all I need to pay, isn't it?"

"Yes."

"Well then, until next payday."

She turned and walked out of the store.

"Her husband hasn't even gotten paid yet," Portnoy said. "She's probably had that money all along."

"As long as she's paying, what's the problem?" Joseph asked.

"The problem is I don't get paid for something until three months after I sold it."

"But when you do get paid, it's more than the item's worth."

Portnoy snorted and made a shooing motion. "You're too soft on them, Joseph."

"Have you been to the mines, Portnoy? These people don't lead soft lives. I'm trying to keep the union out of this town. The happier I can keep my miners, the less likely they are going to be to want the UMW in here."

"Then pay them more money so they can pay for their goods," Portnoy said. "That would make them very happy."

Two women entered the store talking. Joseph nodded in their direction, and said, "Good morning, ladies."

"Good morning, Mr. McCord."

The women stepped up to the counter. Portnoy kept stocking the shelves. They waited patiently for him to stop and look at them.

"Mr. Portnoy," Joseph said politely. "You have customers."

One of the women smiled appreciatively at Joseph.

"I can see them," Portnoy said. "I can also hear them. What do you want?"

"I need a pound of cornmeal and a pound of navy beans," one of the women said.

"Fine, and how about you?" Portnoy said, staring at the second woman.

"We're sharing those things," the nervous woman said.

Portnoy rolled his eyes. He grabbed two small bags and stepped around from behind the counter. He walked over to a line of barrels along one wall and scooped beans into one of the bags. He moved down a few barrels and scooped cornmeal into the second bag. Then he weighed them on the counter scale, added a few more beans and removed some of the cornmeal until he was satisfied with the weight.

"That will be seventeen cents," he said at the folded down tops of the bags.

"Seventeen?" the first woman said. "I thought the price of cornmeal had been coming down. This would cost fifteen cents in Frostburg."

Portnoy snorted. "I'm sure it would, but this is Eckhart, and here it costs seventeen cents."

Joseph just shook his head. Was it any wonder people didn't want to shop here? Portnoy's attitude and insistence on maintaining high prices were the reasons that his store stocked little in the way of fresh goods. At his prices, he couldn't sell them fast enough before they spoiled. Canned goods, dry goods, clothing, and supplies, he could let sit on the shelf as long as he wanted to. Joseph would have fired Portnoy years ago, but he was a part owner in the store. It was a large enough share that he didn't have to smile at his customers if he didn't want to.

The woman counted out some coins on the counter and then looked at her companion who added some more to the small pile. Portnoy swept them into his hand and deposited them into his cash register.

The women took the two small bags and left the store.

Joseph topped off his coffee cup and headed back to his office. If he had to watch much more of Portnoy, he might wind up throttling the man. He was preparing to shut the door between the two rooms when the front door opened again, and Laura Spiker walked in.

Joseph stopped, frozen in place. She was a beauty, but then she had always been since they were youngsters, although back then it had been the beauty of a happy, carefree girl. Now it was something more. Her shoulder length light brown hair was pulled back behind her head. Her high cheekbones were red from the wind outside, and she wore only a light coat to fight the cold. Her son, who toddled along behind her, was better dressed in a worn winter coat.

She saw Joseph and waved. "Good morning, Joey."

He couldn't help but smile. Only a few people could get away with calling him Joey, and she didn't even realize she was among such a small group.

"Good morning, Laura." He bent over. "And a good morning to you, Jacob," Joseph said to the younger boy.

Jacob moved to hide behind his mother's legs. Joseph didn't mind. He had actually bent over to look at Laura's dainty ankles and the gentle sweep of her calf.

"Say, good morning to Mr. McCord, Jacob."

"Morning," the boy said.

Joseph smiled. "He'll be half your height before too long."

Too bad. Joseph wouldn't have a reason to get so close to her legs then.

"He's growing faster than we can keep up with. How have you been?"

"Just doing what I can to keep the mine going. Demand for coal is not so high right now, and it's a struggle to keep all of the miners fully employed."

72

"We're grateful for that. It's hard enough to get by now."

"You could always pay more per ton," Portnoy interjected.

Joseph glared at him. "You know I have no say over the per-ton rate unlike you and your prices, Mr. Portnoy." That shut the man up.

Laura walked up to the counter and said, "Mr. Portnoy, I need a pound of bacon, a pound of cheese, three pounds of macaroni, a pound of sugar, and a pound of prunes."

Portnoy grumbled about not being able to get any work done, but he started collecting the order. They were necessary food items that he needed to gather mostly from the barrels. The bacon and cheese sat in a glass display cases at one end of the counter. It took him a few minutes to collect everything on the counter. He tallied the costs with a pencil and pad.

"That will be $1.36."

Laura's eyes widened. "Oh! So much, I'm not sure if I have enough money."

She dumped the coins from her coin purse and counted them out. "I've only got a $1.25. Can I put the difference on the books?"

Portnoy looked at his ledger. "You're already carrying a balance. In fact, since this is payday, you owe another quarter on that amount."

"Peter will pay that when he gets his paycheck."

"As long as it gets paid by tomorrow. This still comes to $1.36."

"I guess I'll have to put something back. I just don't have any more money right now." Laura turned red with embarrassment.

"What's it going to be? You need to cut eleven cents."

"Well, the prunes were a bit of a splurge, but I need the rest of the items."

Portnoy rolled his eyes. "The prunes are only three cents. I said you needed to reduce the bill by eleven cents."

She turned red with embarrassment.

"I heard you, Mr. Portnoy, but I have to think about what I was going to use these items for to know what I can do without."

Joseph stepped forward. "Don't worry, Laura. I'd be happy to make up the difference."

Laura shook her head. "I couldn't let you do that, Joey. I should have priced everything out before I ordered it. I just didn't think it would be quite so much."

"You're not the first person who has said that about Mr. Portnoy's prices. You go ahead and take the order. I'm more than happy to take care of the difference. After all, we're friends."

Laura smiled at him, and Joseph felt a slight shiver go through his body. Then she laid a hand on his arm and said, "That is so wonderful of you, Joey. You are a good friend."

She put all of the smaller bags that Portnoy had packaged up into a large cloth bag that she had brought with her. Joseph walked her to the door and held it open for her.

"Take care of yourself, Laura, and you, too, Jacob," Joseph called.

"Thank you again, Joseph. You were my knight in shining armor this morning," Laura told him.

He chuckled.

She walked out onto the porch and then down to the street, holding her bag in one hand and Jacob's hand in the other. Joseph stood in the doorway and watched the sway of her hips as she walked away.

"Close the door!" Portnoy snapped. "You're letting the cold air in."

Joseph stepped back inside and closed the door. Then he walked to the office door.

"Hey, you owe me eleven cents," Portnoy said.

"Put it on the same account as the coffee," Joseph said. Then he walked into the office and closed the door behind himself.

Chapter 9

February 9, 1922

One of the problems some detectives going undercover in coal mines faced was that they had never mined coal, much less been in a coal mine. They didn't understand a coal miner's life or the culture of a coal town. That meant they usually took a job other than that mining in a coal camp. Because of this, they were never part of the group they had been sent to investigate. That was why Matt's boss had wanted him on this assignment. Matt could fit in with the miners even more than his boss realized.

Of course, Matt's mining skills were rusty. He hadn't been inside a mine or held a pick for five years. Matt had expected as much, but he knew that his skills would return and that his uncles would help him if need be.

What he hadn't planned on was the sense of the mountain closing in on him. He hadn't been claustrophobic when he worked in the mines before, but now being underground made him nervous. Water occasionally dripped on his face, and he would jump in the darkness.

He needed to get used to being underground before the spring came, if he was even still here, which he hoped wasn't the case.

When spring arrived with its melting snow and spring showers, coal mines could become wet places as the rainwater and snowmelt soaked through the ground to fall on the miners and form puddles.

Besides the rain and thaw, seeds also started sprouting. It was a nervous time in the mine or at least a cautious one. If you were on top of the ground, well, things were fine, but when you were underground, all it took was a little shift to cause problems like mudslides and roof collapses. The diggers were also responsible for pumping any standing water out of the rooms where they worked, and it had to be done for no pay.

The coal cars had carried the miners about a mile underground to the face where they were working. It had been a rough, uncomfortable ride. With no cushions or springs, Matt felt every little bump up his spine. Ponies pulled single cars along temporary tracks further into the mine. The miners would fill those cars with coal and have the mine ponies pull them to the main track where the electric engine would take them to the surface.

"So how's it feel to be back, Matt?" Enos asked him.

Matt turned to his uncle so that his face was illuminated in the light on his hard hat. "It feels like I woke up in a strange house in the middle of the night and can't find my way to the outhouse."

Enos laughed. "Give it a week, and it will feel like you can't find your way out of that outhouse."

Matt wasn't sure whether he hoped that was true or not. He didn't want to feel comfortable here, but he needed to. He could tell himself the Maryland mines were considered among the safest coal mines to work. It didn't matter when he heard one of the black powder charges explode, or he felt the ground tremble. Every coal miner knew someone–usually more than one person–who had died in the mines.

The ceiling on the tunnel lowered until the men couldn't walk standing upright.

"You're going to have to bear walk the rest of the way, but at least we've cleared out enough now that we can work sitting down.

The coal mine was dug in a room and pillar system. A lot of coal was lost digging this way, but it was inexpensive, and with demand for coal starting to fall off, the mining companies were grateful for ways to keep their expenses low.

Unfortunately for miners, it was also a dangerous way to dig. Coal was mined in "rooms" that were about 100-feet wide so that a wall of coal and rock was left intact between rooms. These walls or "pillars" served as supports for the tunnel roof.

Once the edge of the coal company property was reached, the mining operation would essentially back itself out of the tunnels, mining the walls as they went. This would eventually cause cave-ins in the rooms as the weight from the mountain pushed down.

Matt sat down with his headlamp shining on the coal seam. He swung his pick at the coal, knocking chunks lose. He wasn't sure how long he kept at this. He didn't want to pull out his pocket watch and get it filthy with coal dust and dirt. He also didn't want to be reminded of how slow that time was passing.

His mind kept drifting to the hours he had spent in foxholes during the war. At night, the sides of the foxhole had made the trench darker, much like the mine tunnels. However, he could always look at the stars and see a way out. He had no such luxury in a coal mine.

When Matt had filled his section of the tunnel with chunks of coal and earth, he stopped working and called for a coal car. When the driver brought the coal car into the low tunnel, Matt squatted down and started to shovel the chunks of coal into the car. It was designed to hold about four tons of coal when it was filled. Once full, he hung his medallion on the car so that he would get credit for the tonnage when the driver took it to the surface.

Matt didn't need his earnings from this job since he was still being paid by the Pinkerton Agency, but he couldn't spend that money. He needed to live on his wages as a coal miner to maintain the pretense that he was a miner.

Soon after he sent the coal car up to the surface, he heard the call for lunch.

"Grab your pail and let's get out of here for a little while," Enos called from further along the tunnel.

Matt bear walked to the main tunnel and then stood up and

stretched for the first time in hours. He thought that he could hear the bones in his back clicking into their proper place. His muscles were cramped and aching. He couldn't do much about that now. His body would have to get used to the work.

When he reached the surface, Matt flopped onto the ground and stretched out and relaxed in the sun. He felt the warmth on his face. Although it was still cold outside, it was no colder than in the tunnels.

"Better not take a nap," Samuel said. "You need to eat, so you have the energy to work this afternoon."

"Besides, Toni packs a great lunch," Enos added.

Matt pushed himself into a seated position. He set his lunch pail in front of him and removed the lid. He pulled off his gloves and lifted the ham sandwich out of the top section. The ham was salty, but it had a rich flavor. The best part, however, was Aunt Antonietta's homemade bread. It was soft without being doughy and had a hint of sweetness that hid the yeast flavor.

The bottom section of the pail had two large pieces of apple pie that he savored. He washed it all down with a cup of water from a barrel next to the maintenance shed.

"It doesn't seem like much has changed here in five years," Matt said.

"Except that Joey is now the superintendent," Enos said.

"You mean Mr. McCord."

Enos laughed. "Well, Mr. McCord forgets that a lot of us re-member him walking around town in shorts showing off his knock knees."

Matt doubted that Joey would appreciate the fact that his name was a joke, but it was his own fault. Joey had been a snobbish child, and he was an even worse adult.

"Is he a good superintendent?" Matt asked.

"Are any of them?"

"His father was."

Samuel nodded. "Winston McCord was a good superintendent, but those were easy days for the coal industry. Demand has dropped since the war ended, and I don't see it coming back. I think young McCord is in over his head."

"Can't tell it by looking at him," Enos said. "He struts around Eckhart like he's king. You should slug him, Matt. I remember that you two used to like to fight and wrestle from time to time."

"What did you two fight about?" Samuel asked.

Matt shrugged. "Who can remember? A shove, a girl, an odd look. All I remember is that I won."

Enos asked, "Could you beat him now?"

Matt slowly repacked his lunch pail. "He was a might smaller back then. He looks like he'd be a challenge now. He's taller and heavier than me. He hit some growth spurt."

"That's what happens when you can eat properly," Samuel said. "Mining kids, they're all scrawny and wiry because they're always hungry."

The whistle blew signaling the lunch hour was soon to end, and they should return to their work areas. The miners grumbled as they stood up and headed back into the mine.

As they rode the coal car back into the dark earth, Matt asked, "Where does a fellow go for a drink around here? I'm going to want something to wash this coal dust out of me after work."

"Beer Alley is respectable now that Prohibition hit," Samuel said. Beer Alley was the street in Eckhart where most of the bars were located.

"Where there's a will there's a way," Enos said cryptically.

"I figured there might be. I found such a place last night."

"They aren't in short supply around here. I can show you a few places. They might not be as fancy as where you went last night, but they're good for what ails you."

They returned to the same tunnel to resume their digging for five more hours of backbreaking work. By the time Matt emerged from the mines at the end of his first day of work, he was as black as coal tar. The coal dust had also worked its way under his clothing and mixed with his sweat so that it had formed an irritating grit that he was sure had rubbed parts of his skin raw. His clothes were caked in coal dust and dirt. He was tempted to lay down where he had eaten lunch and just go to sleep. He trudged up the road with his uncles pulling him by the arms.

"You had a good first day, Matt," Samuel said. "Things will get easier."

Matt just grunted. He pulled off his gloves and flexed his hands. They were stiff, and he had blisters.

"You'll need to soak your hands and wrap them tonight," Samuel said when he saw Matt's red skin. "You'll toughen up soon enough."

"I had forgotten about this part," Matt said. "It reminds me of my first day in basic training. When I laid down that first night, I hadn't thought that I would get up for a week."

Samuel laughed and clapped him on the shoulder. Matt winced, which only made Samuel laugh harder.

"You'll be fine, Matt."

Samuel's wife, Myrna, stood behind the house, pumping water into metal buckets of water. She passed the buckets to Antonietta who would set them on one of the burners on the stove. They were heating up three buckets of water at once. They needed to use multiple buckets to fill the tubs as fast as they could. Some families could get by with using just one bucket, but six miners were living in the house now. Each of them would need to be clean before he would be allowed in the main house.

"Off with the clothes," Antonietta said when she saw the men filing into the mudroom.

"It's only Thursday," Matt said. Saturday afternoon was the usual bath day, and it still was, but Antonietta also had half the miners bathe on Wednesday and the other half on Thursday. They all bathed on Saturday. Even if it wasn't a full bath day, Antonietta expected all of the miners to wash their hands and faces before going into the house.

Enos and Samuel immediately began to strip down to their longjohns.

"Who's first?" his aunt asked.

"Let it be Matt since it was his first day. Strip down to your longjohns, boy," Samuel said.

Matt did as he was told and tossed his dirty clothes into a basket. Then he walked into the kitchen where his aunts had a placed a wooden tub that was steaming with warm water.

"Climb in and show us your back."

Matt peeled out of the top half of his longjohns and squatted in the water. Antonietta dunked the bar of Lava soap into the warm water. Then she poured water across his back. She began scrubbing at the dirt there. It didn't take too long. The parts of his body that were covered by clothing weren't as dirty as his face and hands.

"Don't think you're going to get pampered, Matt. I just do backs. Then I'll leave you to it to strip down and do the rest of you, and don't forget your hair. I don't want you making my sheets and blankets all filthy tonight."

"Yes, ma'am."

Antonietta started to leave the kitchen, but then she stopped. "Oh, since you didn't lay out clean longjohns to use tonight, I brought a towel. You can wrap it around yourself and go to your room to get dressed. Bring the towel back. The others will need it to dry off."

She walked out, and Matt began scrubbing at his hands and face. He wasn't sure whether the grit he was feeling was the coal dust or the Lava soap, but it was the best thing for getting rid of coal grime. Every miner used it. The secret to the soap's success for coal miners was that it contained pumice. The pumice made the soap rough, but that was what made it effective.

When he finished washing, Matt created what lather he could and rubbed it into his hair. Then he climbed out of the tub and dunked his head into the water to rinse it. He pulled his dripping head out of the water and saw that it was black.

Matt grabbed the towel off the counter and toweled himself dry. He wrapped the towel around his waist and made a run through the living room to his bedroom.

Antonietta laughed when she saw him run by.

"Matt's done, Samuel," she called. "You boys empty the tub so we can get some clean water in it."

Samuel and Enos each grabbed a handle on the side of the tub

81

and carried it outside to dump out the dirty water. Then they brought it back inside and set it in the kitchen. Antonietta and Myrna took pails of warm water off the stove and dumped the contents into the tub. Then Myrna took the pails and went out back to fill them with water.

"Okay, who's next?" Antonietta called.

Matt pulled a clean set of longjohns out of his suitcase and climbed into them as quickly as he could. Between the warm water and warm air in the house, he was feeling his fatigue. He put the suitcase on the floor, slipped under the covers of his bed, and fell asleep.

He wasn't sure what time it was when he heard a knock at his door. He hadn't bothered to turn on the lights in the room when he came in earlier. He yawned and blinked in the darkness of the room.

He heard the knock again.

"Yes?" he said.

"Dinner is ready," Antonietta said.

"I'll be there in a minute. I need to get dressed. Go ahead and start without me."

"They have. I just want to make sure you get out here before all of the food is gone."

Matt heard a floorboard creak as his aunt walked away.

Groaning, he rolled out of bed. He walked over to the door and hit the button to turn on the lights. He was tempted to forgo dinner, but now that he was up, he might as well eat. Otherwise, he would wake up hungry in the middle of the night.

He lifted his suitcase off the floor and set it on his bed. Then he picked out a pair of pants and a shirt and got dressed. His muscles were starting to tighten, and he moved slowly.

He walked out to the kitchen to see a long table had been set up and was covered with food. Eight people sat along either side eating and talking.

"There's the sleepy head," Enos said. "You must not have worked too hard in Baltimore if you are tired out now."

82

"What were you doing in Baltimore?" Antonietta asked.

"Dockworker," Matt lied.

His aunt nodded. "Well, pull up a chair. You'll have to sit on the end."

Matt found a wooden stool and pulled it up to the table where there was an unused place setting. Antonietta introduced him to her other boarders as they passed him bowls and platters of food. They had chicken, rolls, mashed potatoes, and corn. As he smelled the foods on his plate, his stomach growled.

Matt ate his meal and listened to the miners talking. The topic of unions and strikes didn't come up, but he did hear the black damp mentioned once, safety a few times, and price for tonnage a few times. Everyone seemed more willing to talk about the weather, the upcoming dance at the church, moonshine, and baseball.

Matt participated in the conversations occasionally, but he wasn't familiar with a lot of the things being discussed. Besides, he really just wanted to go back to bed.

He noticed his Antonietta staring at him a few times. She didn't say anything. She merely stared as if she was thinking about something.

After dinner, he went back to his room and unpacked his suitcase. He tucked the pistol under his clean longjohns. He put the ammunition in the nightstand drawer. He also placed stationary and his pen in the drawer.

When he had finished unpacking, he slid the empty suitcase under his bed. Then he pulled out a sheet of stationary and his pen and sat down at the small table next to the window in his room. He wrote out a short letter to his contact at Consolidation Coal. He mentioned that he had found work in Eckhart Mines and had the trust of some of the miners. So far, he had not heard any talk of the union in town or a possible strike. He sealed the letter in an envelope and rather than address it to David Groth at the regional offices for the Consolidation Coal Company in Cumberland, he wrote Groth's home address on the envelope. He didn't want it to be evident that correspondence was being mailed to the largest mining company in the region.

He put the letter under his pistol in the drawer. He would take it into Frostburg on his next trip there and mail it at the post office there. He would also rent a box there to receive mail. Since Eckhart had its own post office, but he didn't want to risk someone remarking that he was mailing regular letters to Cumberland.

Matt flipped off the light switch and climbed back in bed. He thought he might not be able to get to sleep since he had taken a nap. He was wrong about that.

Chapter 10

February 9, 1922

Antonietta sat in her bedroom with the door closed. The furnace had been stoked for the night with coal her brothers brought home from the mine. A lamp was on beside her bed as she rocked in a nearby chair. The chair was turned so that if she glanced up, she would see the picture of Michael from their wedding day.

That picture of them smiling outside the church, standing in their best clothes seemed like a lifetime ago. They were supposed to have had a lifetime together. Then the mine had killed Michael. Just a freak accident. It should not have happened. Rock falls were expected in the mine, but dead spots… It was chance. Almost as if God had reached down and plucked him from the earth saying his time was done. But how could his time have been done? Only a few years married and no children yet. What mark had he left on the world other than with Antonietta? It was her job to remember him. Her job was to try and make sure that no one else died like he did.

While she was happy to see Matt come home, one part of her hated to see him back in Eckhart Mines. She thought that he had escaped. She'd been happy that he left, but now he was back down in the mine, the same mine that had killed her Michael. She'd be cursed if she let such a thing happen to him or her brothers or any of the miners for that matter.

She liked this time of evening when everything had settled down. The wash was done. The dishes were clean. Everyone was in bed for the most part. Nobody was out on the streets.

She had her Bible open and was reading from the Book of Matthew, thinking about the day. She flipped to the story of the prodigal son in the Book of Luke and thought about how it applied to Matt. He had left Eckhart Mines with his inheritance–the pittance that it was–and returned penniless. Antonietta felt that she and her brothers had done a good job of welcoming him back, but then, he hadn't left on harsh terms.

As she read, she heard some noises that stood out because of the silence in the house. She wondered if someone had been out late and just now come in. When the sounds continued, she closed her Bible and stood up walked to the door and listened.

It sounded like moans and muted yelling. Antonietta unlocked her door and eased it open. The kitchen and sitting room were still dark.

She heard the noise again, but it wasn't coming from that direction. It was coming from across the hall in Matt's room. She stepped across the hall and put her ear to the door and heard the noises from inside.

"Matt, are you all right?"

Her only response was more moaning. She knocked on the door. She heard flailing and creaking bed springs.

"Matt, Matt, are you all right? Are you sick?"

Just more moaning.

She knocked on the door harder. "Matt, Matt." She tried the door, and it was locked.

She rapped again. "Matt!"

The noises stopped, and she heard the creaking of the bed springs and the creaking of wood floors. The door opened a few inches.

She saw Matt's face. His eyes had dark circles under them. His hair was mussed.

"I heard you moaning and yelling in your sleep. Are you all right?"

"It's just a nightmare, Aunt."

"It was a harsh nightmare."

"Yes, I supposed it was."

She wondered what kinds of horrors would make someone like Matt so weak.

"Do you often have these nightmares?"

"I can't say for sure, but I think so."

"Would you like some milk?"

He gave her half a smile and shook his head. "No, no. I can get back to sleep fine. I'm tired, but the problem always is staying asleep long enough to get some good rest."

"Would you like to talk about it?"

Matt shook his head. "It's just a bad dream, Aunt. You can't do anything about that."

She sighed. "Okay, then. You know where to find me. You're home now, Matt. Everything's going to be fine. Your family's here. We love you."

"I know that."

He shut the door, and she heard him settle back down in bed.

She walked back into her room, wondering if she'd be able to get to sleep now.

Chapter 11

February 12, 1922

Matt woke up Sunday morning and stretched. Pain shot through his shoulders, and he let out a light groan. He could feel pain in his lower back. He wished that he could soak in a tub of hot water, but the metal tubs in the boarding house weren't comfortable and offered no privacy. He wondered if he could slip away to Failinger's, rent a room, and take a bath in one of the porcelain tubs there.

Matt didn't rush to get out of bed, but instead rolled over and relaxed. It was still twilight outside, but the sun would be up soon.

Knowing that he wouldn't get back to sleep, he slid out of bed. He poured water into the washbasin and splashed some water on his face. That fully woke him up. He performed the calisthenics routine that he had learned in the Marines. Nowadays, it was called the Daily Dozen; twelve exercises performed for roughly half a minute to forty-five seconds each. It worked all parts of the body and helped stretch and loosen his muscles. When he finished, he wiped his body down with a wet cloth.

He dressed in clean clothes. His aunt kept up with the laundry, so he always had a fresh set of clothes to wear each day, although he usually wore coveralls and a flannel shirt for work in the mine.

In the kitchen, he sat down on one of the benches and ate breakfast with his family and the other boarders. He joined in the conversations occasionally, but he listened more with an ear toward any news that he might pass on to his employer. Not that he heard anything worth repeating. Thomas Roswell, one of the boarders, complained that he had a cold, and he kept wiping his nose. Enos looked like he was still half asleep, but Matt suspected that he was actually hungover. Samuel and Myrna were dressed for church and not saying much at all.

As Antonietta and Myrna cleared away the dishes after breakfast, Matt asked, "Where are my parents buried?"

"They have a place in St. Michael's cemetery," she told him. "We held a Mass for them at St. Michael's, and your uncles and I pooled our money together for the first time to get them a stone."

Eckhart had a Baptist and Methodist church, but the Ansaros were Catholic, so they rode the trolley to Frostburg to attend Mass at St. Michael's. The cemetery was about halfway between the church and Eckhart.

"Thank you for that."

She patted him on the cheek. "No thanks are needed, Matt. They were family."

He got a general description of where the stone was located and headed out of the boarding house.

"Are you not going to church?" Antonietta asked.

"No, ma'am, church is not for me any longer," Matt admitted. "Honestly, I find it hard to believe in God nowadays. Maybe someday I'll feel the call again, but not now."

He had started praying daily in the Marines, reading the Bible, and attending Sunday services. Then he had watched the destruction caused by artillery shells as they tore apart soldiers. He had seen children who had starved to death because of the war going on around them. Matt had prayed harder than ever to understand why such useless death was necessary, but he never received an answer. He only saw more death. Mustard gas choked the breath from men and blistered their skin. He didn't stop believing in God. He still read the Bible, but he had come to think that he wouldn't find his answers or peace in a church.

Matt donned his cap and walked up the street toward the church. He was in no rush. In fact, he was happy to stretch out his legs. The cemetery was two blocks off of the National Road on Mt. Pleasant Street. It was filled with a variety of headstones and even a few wooden markers. He found his parents' grave after a few minutes of walking up and down the rows of graves. The granite marker was small and plain, but it had his parents' names carved into it along with their birth and death dates.

Geno and Eliza Ansaro had died within days of each other in October 1918. They had been taken in the great pandemic along with millions of others all over the world. Matt had seen Marines struggling to breathe as they died from the flu, and he was glad in a way that he hadn't been here to see his parents die in that way. He would have been tortured over not being able to do anything. They should have had someone with them, though.

His father had died first, hacking like miners do after years in the mines. Only instead of back dust coming up, it had been blood. His mother had passed away in her sleep three days later after spending a day in a delirium.

He stood staring at the stone, chewing his lower lip. It was hard to imagine his parents not being around, but they had been gone a little more than three years now. They had never had much in their lives, but they had done what they could to make sure he would do better. They had encouraged his dreams.

"I meant to come back," he said.

He would have come back, too. Not to work in the mines. He had planned on taking his parents with him to Baltimore. He could have helped them find work there. He could have gotten his father out of the mines, but even as the war was winding down, he had received a letter from his aunt telling him that the flu had taken both of his parents.

"I wish I could have been here. I don't know if I could have saved you, but at least I would have been able to show you what I have become."

He bent down and plucked some of the weeds that had grown

up around the headstone. Despite this, he was surprised to see how well kept the area was. Some graves were far more overgrown. Matt guessed that it was Aunt Antonietta's doing. It was something that he would take over for her while he was here.

He turned and walked out of the cemetery heading back to Eckhart Mines, but then he paused and changed direction. He walked toward the miners' homes until he found the one he was looking for.

It looked no different than the ones on either side of it. It was a small, square, two-room house. It probably could have fit on the first floor of the boarding house.

He stood on the street staring at the home where he had been born. The midwife had been called there early one morning when his mother went into labor. It was the house where his parents had died, struggling to breathe as their lungs had filled with fluid brought on by Spanish Flu. It was where he'd grown into a man.

All that he had left were the memories. Any sign that his family had lived in the house was gone, probably within days of them dying. Mining companies didn't leave their homes vacant. When one miner died, his family was evicted, and a new mining family moved in with a healthy worker. It was as if they were trying to hide the fact that their workers died. Out of sight, out of mind.

The door to the house opened, and a young woman in her early twenties stepped outside. She wore a calico dress, probably the outfit she only wore on Sundays for church. Although she probably didn't mean it to, it hugged her figure, putting improper thoughts in men's head on a day that they should be concentrating on being on their best behavior. Her light brown hair shone in the sun, and it was tied up with a red ribbon.

She looked over at Matt, and her face went pale. Her mouth opened as if she was going to say something. Matt thought that he recognized her. It wasn't surprising since he probably knew most of the people in town, but some of them were bound to change after five years.

He was about to introduce himself to the woman when a tall man came out of the house holding a young child in the crook of his arm. He set the boy on the ground, and he ran over to walk with the woman.

The young family walked over to him.

"Matt? Is that you?"

The voice froze him in place. He should have recognized the face earlier. Laura was still beautiful, although she had grown into a woman. Her face looked a bit fuller, but it was still Laura Henshaw.

"Hello, Laura."

Matt forced his legs to move. He didn't want to look at her. He wanted to turn and walk away. That hadn't worked for him five years ago, and he seemed incapable of doing it now.

Laura met him halfway. They stood about a foot apart staring into each other's eyes. He wanted to grab her and hug her, but he knew better than to do it.

"You're back. I thought that you had left for good," Laura said.

"I ..." He couldn't think of what to say He could only see her as he had at the end of the school year dance five years ago kissing Russell Sparber and Nico Bartucci, among others. It wasn't one or the other. It had been both of them. Matt just couldn't remember the order. "I have a job in the mine," he finally managed to say.

Laura turned to the tall man behind her. "Matt, this is my husband, Peter Spiker. Pete, this is my old friend, Matt Ansaro."

Old friend.

Were they? Could they be? They hadn't parted as friends, despite courting for a year and talking about marriage.

Matt noticed Pete staring at him and then Laura. Then Matt saw Pete was holding his hand out. Matt reached out and shook it.

"Pleased to meet you," Pete said.

"Likewise."

Laura squatted down and picked up the toddler who was holding onto her skirt. He had his mother's eyes. "And this is our son, Jacob," Laura said.

Matt's breath hitched, and he realized that he had heard Laura wrong. She had meant hers and Pete's son. Not hers and Matt's. Their relationship had never gone far enough for that to be a possibility. He wondered if he might not have a child in Europe, though.

"How long have you been back, Matt?" Laura asked.

"Just a few days. I started working Thursday."

"How is it going so far?" Pete asked.

"I used to work in the mines, so it's not totally new to me, but I've still got aching muscles and blisters," Matt said.

"I don't think that ever fully goes away."

"Are you here to stay this time?" Laura asked.

He stared at her for a moment. There seemed to be more to her comment than the words conveyed, but he wasn't sure what.

"Stay?" Pete said.

"Matt went off to enlist in the war," Laura said to Peter, although she stared at Matt as she said it. "He said that he wasn't ever coming back."

Now Matt understood. "I don't know. I came back because I needed to. I needed the work, and I certainly have that, but it's not work I like. It's not work I'm interested in, and that can be a dangerous thing in the mine if you don't pay attention to what you're doing."

"Don't remind me." Laura put a hand on her husband's arm. "I worry every day that Peter goes into the mine."

Laura set Jacob down, and he started running around his father's legs.

"Jacob looks like he is pure energy," Matt said.

"You don't know the half of it," Laura replied.

Matt squatted down and looked at the little child. "How you doing there?" Jacob stopped running and stared at Matt from behind his father's legs. Matt stood up and said, "Looks like a strapping boy that you're going to have."

"I hope so. He takes after his father in that regard."

"I'm going to go on with Jacob," Pete said. "He won't stay still much longer."

"That's still?" Matt asked.

Pete nodded. He kissed Laura on the cheek. "Catch up when you're finished talking."

He took Jacob's hand, and they walked off toward the church.

Matt watched them go, thinking that he could have been Pete if he had stayed in Eckhart.

"Can I ask you a question, Matt?" Laura said. "I understand you needed work, but why come back here, especially because I know how much that you wanted to get away from here before?"

That gave Matt pause. He was surprised that no one else had asked him about that, but he should have known. He and Laura had spent a lot of time together in those years before he left.

"I needed more than work. I needed to be with family, I guess, to be someplace familiar. For the past five years, it's all been different. Different than I've ever known. Baltimore and South Carolina and Europe. Sometimes it was different from night to night. There's the sense of gravel shifting underfoot when you're climbing a hill, and the dirt starts to give way, and you feel it moving, and you're on the ground, but you don't feel like you're steady. You're solid. That's what it's like, and right now I need that feeling of being on solid ground until I can make my way up the hill."

"Are you sure you're going to go up the hill and not tumble down?"

"I know it. There's no doubt in my mind. This is just a temporary stop. I won't die here. I won't die in that mine. My future lies elsewhere."

"How do you know that?"

"I just do. There's no doubting it. It just is. Like the sun coming up. It's going to happen. I just have to do my best to make it happen, and those times, like now, when it doesn't seem like I'm doing anything to make it happen, I just need to hang on until I can do something."

"It's good that you know that."

"You don't?"

"What is there for me to know? I'm married. I've got a child. My future now is to do the best I can to raise that child and make my husband happy. I guess I'll have more children at some point, and I'll be doing the best I can to make them happy, too."

"But what's going to make you happy?" Matt pressed. It was a question Matt wished he could answer for himself.

"Well, seeing them happy does make me happy."

"But you can't live your life in them."

"I have to, there's not much else to do. I know my numbers. I can read, but I don't have a real education like some others going to the Normal School up the hill. I'm a miner's wife, and there's only so many options for me."

"But what if Peter found other work and he wasn't a miner anymore? Then you wouldn't be a miner's wife."

"But Peter's like everybody else around here. It's his job. It's all he's known. It's his secure footing. He's not looking to move on. He might try to be a foreman or maybe even a superintendent like Joey."

"You mean Mr. McCord?"

"He has me call him Mr. McCord in public, but in private, if it's just the two of us talking, he lets me call him Joey."

"You two talk alone often?"

"Now and then, but I mean, we were friends. He's like you. He knew he was destined for better things, and he's achieved it. We're more than acquaintances now, but I can't rightly say we're friends. He's so much higher than me. Occasionally, when we're in the store, and he's there, we'll talk for a bit, or sometimes I'll see him on the street," Laura said.

"What about us? Are we just more than acquaintances, but no longer friends?"

"You told me you would write."

"And I meant to, but I didn't write anybody," Matt said.

"Why?"

"At first, I was too busy with basic training. I did write some things on the boat because we had a lot of time, but by the time we got to Europe, things got busy again, and I never did mail them. And then, with the war, it seemed like there was nothing I could say that would be worth saying."

"I could think of some things you could have said. I didn't know whether you were alive or dead. All this time, and then I see you standing on the street like a ghost."

"I'm sorry."

95

"I would have gone with you."

Matt shook his head. "Gone where?"

"To war?"

"Where would that have left you? Besides, if I remember right, we weren't talking when I left."

She put her hands on her hips. "And whose fault was that?"

Matt looked away, embarrassed. When he looked back, he said, "I think we both played a part in that."

"I still loved you after all that," she said.

Matt knew what she wanted him to say, but he couldn't. He may have broken her heart, but Matt had also suffered. Although it had ended badly, Priscilla had helped him get past Laura as Pete had helped her get past Matt. He knew that if he reopened that old wound now, it would hurt even worse like it had when Priscilla broke off their engagement.

"You shouldn't have." He tipped his cap to Laura. "You had better catch up to your family, and I need to get back to my aunt's house."

He turned and walked away, hoping that she wouldn't try to stop him because he would have stayed. He was only so strong.

Chapter 12

February 12, 1922

Laura rose in the morning before the sun was up. She needed to get the fire in the cook stove going. Some people had switched to gas, but Eckhart Mines was a coal town, so the miners used coal. It only made sense since the company deducted a weekly charge for coal whether or not the miner used it.

Pete still snored lightly in the bed, and Jacob murmured softly in his sleep, almost like a smaller version of his father.

She picked up the thin robe draped over the chest at the foot of the bed and walked into the other room. She poured a bucket of coal into the stove and got the fire going.

While she was waiting for the stove to heat up, she prepared Pete's lunch. Using some leftover ham from last evening, she made a ham and cheese sandwich. She peeled a potato and cut it into smaller chunks and put it on the lunch pail tray with the sandwich. For some reason, Pete loved the crunch and taste of raw potatoes. Then she sliced a wide piece of apple pie and slid it onto the other tray. Finally, she filled the bottom of the pail with water and stacked the other trays on top.

By the time the lunch was ready, the stove was hot enough that she could cook flapjacks for breakfast. They had three chickens that provided them with eggs. Laura traded the extra eggs to her neighbor for milk from their Jersey cow.

"Peter, time to get up," she called.

She heard a grunt from inside the bedroom. She wouldn't call him again unless she had to. She didn't want him to wake up grumpy. He needed to go to work focused and happy. It was the goal of most miners' wives. They knew the dangers that their husbands faced daily and they did what they could to make sure their husbands could stay focused on their work.

A few minutes later, Pete walked out of the bedroom, pulling the straps of his coveralls over his shoulders.

"Good morning," he said.

She set the plate of flapjacks on the table and then walked over to give Pete a morning kiss. He sat down at the table and started eating.

Although it wasn't talked about often, miners knew the daily dangers they walked into. They had to put any worry to the back of their minds if they were to function correctly underground, but Laura had noticed that Pete made sure to kiss both her and Jacob goodbye each morning and tell them that he loved them. When they had first been married, Peter had just said it to her, and Laura had thought it a romantic gesture. Then when Jacob came along, Peter had done the same thing for him. That's when Laura realized her husband was making sure that if he didn't come home one evening, the last thing he would have told them both was "I love you."

After Pete left for the mine, Laura started work on the various chores that needed doing. One nice thing about living in a small house was that it didn't take long to clean.

She looked over their finances. Things were tight, and the reduced work that was available was not helping matters any. She thought about trying to get a job from time to time, but Jacob was too young. She couldn't leave him for the day, and she couldn't afford to pay someone to watch him.

Still, it wasn't something that she felt comfortable talking to Pete about. He would just worry while he was working, and she didn't want that. A miner who wasn't focused on his work could make a mistake that would kill him.

She took a walk with Jacob for a little while before lunch. He seemed to be growing daily and was becoming a heavy load when she had to carry him around town. She usually made him walk near her.

Laura paused to look in the store windows as she walked up Store Street. She couldn't afford the lovely dresses or toys for Jacob that she saw. Looking was usually enough. If she needed something so fancy, she would find a way to save her pennies until she could.

She was already carrying too much credit at the Eckhart Mines General Store. She didn't like Mr. Portnoy much, but it was the only place that she could afford to buy things sometimes. Not that she could afford it if the cost had to go on the books.

As she and Jacob walked, she thought about seeing Matt again. She had never imagined that she would see him again after he left for the Marines. They had messed things up royally at that dance. Sallie Harcourt had latched onto him so tightly. He had let her kiss him and even enjoyed it. Laura had just wanted to get even with Matt. She couldn't remember the boys whom she had kissed. She knew it was a stupid move later that night, but by then, it was too late. Matt wasn't talking to her, and her reputation had been blackened and stayed that way until she married.

She paused to look at her reflection in the window of the butcher shop. She turned to the left and looked at her profile over her shoulder. She used to think she was pretty. Certainly the boys had or at least they had told her so. Nowadays, she wondered if she was becoming worn down from work and stress like so many of the miners' wives.

She wondered if Matt still thought she was beautiful.

Beyond the surprise of seeing him back in town, he seemed different. It was more than the scar on his neck, though that had been terrifying to see because she could see how close he had come to being killed. No, the last time she had seen him, he had been tired from working full-time in the mine. Now, he had energy, lots of it, but it seemed to keep him on edge like a rabbit ready to bolt at the slightest sound.

She walked into the dry goods store and looked at the shelf of Maybelline make-up the store offered. She picked up a tube of lipstick and stared at the color. She could use it not only to make her lips look red, but they could be shaped into a Cupid's bow like Clara Bow in the movies. What caught her attention was the mascara that would help lengthen her eyelashes.

Then she saw the price on the make-up and sighed. She had wanted to use what little money she had to buy a chicken that she could cook for dinner. She had pasta at home, though. She could cook that tonight.

She carried the make-up to the counter and paid for it. It didn't take all of her money. She would hold onto the rest.

She walked home quickly, anxious to try out her purchases.

When Pete came home from work, she had the spaghetti sauce cooking on the stove, and the smell of oregano and basil filled the air.

Pete walked in, filthy as usual. He stopped in the doorway when he saw his wife. Laura had put on her Sunday dress and her new makeup. He stared at her open-mouthed.

Laura grinned.

"Do you like it?" she asked, holding her arms out at her sides.

Pete nodded. "You look amazing. I recognize the dress." He paused. "Are you wearing make-up?"

"Yes. It's been so long since I've had any."

"What's the occasion?"

"No occasion. I just decided that I wanted to impress you."

"You always impress me the way you juggle everything that you do with the house and Jacob." Pete looked around. "Where is Jacob?"

"He's next door with Mrs. Whittaker."

"Why?"

Laura reached behind her and unbuttoned her dress. Then she let it fall to the floor around her feet. Pete's eyes widened. She enjoyed the way his eyes roved over her body. All her doubts from earlier in the day washed away.

"I thought that I would help you wash off the grime from the mine," she said.

Pete grinned. "You are a vixen. It's not even Saturday."

Laura laughed. "Get in the tub before the water gets cold."

He walked forward and swept Laura into his arms and kissed her. She pushed him away.

"You're filthy," she said.

"That's fine," Pete said. "You wash me, and then I'll wash you."

"In that case..." She pulled him closer, threw her arms around his neck and kissed him.

Pete swept her up in his arms and carried her into the kitchen for a bath.

Chapter 13

February 17, 1922

Joseph sat at his desk in the mine office tallying yesterday's tonnage. He heard the outside door open but didn't look up. He punched more numbers into the adding machine. Whoever it was could wait a minute.

"How long do you plan to keep me waiting?" a man said.

Joseph looked up. An older man stood at the counter. He wore a gray-striped double-breasted suit. His face was soft with jowls starting to sag, bushy white eyebrows, and white hair.

"Father, I didn't know you were coming," Joseph said.

"I'm not here as your father."

Joseph swallowed hard. "Yes, Mr. McCord."

Winston McCord allowed Joseph to address him either as "Father" or "Mr. McCord."

Joseph stood up and put on his suit coat. He walked over to the counter and held out his hand. Winston McCord shook it. They hadn't hugged since Joseph was eight years old.

"What can I do for you, sir? I can show you our production numbers. I was just finishing yesterday's."

Winston inclined his head toward the door. "Let's walk. I don't want the wrong person hearing."

"We can go up to the house."

Winston nodded. "Fine. Fine."

They left the office and headed up Federal Hill. It was cold enough for a coat, but in his rush to accommodate his father Joseph forgot to put his on. His father wondered what they needed to talk about. He obviously didn't want to speak on the phone where an operator might overhear.

"How have you been, Mr. McCord?" Joseph asked.

"I have been aggravated."

"By me?"

"No, by the UMW, but you aren't far behind."

"The Stone Mountain Coal Company made some bad calls last year, and now the industry is paying the price," Winston said.

Joseph couldn't believe his father had just said that. "We broke the union at Blair Mountain."

Winston stopped and stared at his son. "Do you have to have someone wipe your ass after you crap, boy?"

Joseph pressed his lips together to keep from snapping at his father. After all, his father had said he wasn't here as his father but his boss.

"The company won that conflict, but people were killed," Winston said. "The whole situation got a lot of bad press. People sympathized with the miners."

"But they started it."

"Don't interrupt. People don't care so much that miners were destroying company property, which would only drive coal costs up. They think of the company and picture a building. No, people were upset about what happened to the miners. People picture miners, and they don't see the union, they see men. That whole situation in West Virginia has stirred up other miners."

"Not in Eckhart."

"Yes, in Eckhart, and didn't I tell you not to interrupt?"

"Yes, sir."

"Then listen. Consolidation Coal has hired the Pinkerton Agency to help us head off the problem before it becomes a problem."

They reached Joseph's house. He opened the door and let his

father enter before him.

"Maizy," Joseph called.

His cook and maid walked out of the kitchen, wiping her hands on a dish towel.

"Hello, Mr. McCord and...Mr. McCord," Maizy said.

"Can you get me a cup of coffee?" Joseph asked.

Maizy nodded. "Do you want a cup, Mr. McCord?" she asked Winston.

He shook his head.

"Let's go into the library," Winston said.

Joseph found himself following his father down the hallway of his own house. The room had a fireplace and two walls that were covered with shelves and filled with books he had never read. This room still looked as it had when his father had lived it. His father had read the books, but Joseph had never cared for them.

His father took a seat in his favorite leather chair near one of the two windows in the room.

"As I was saying, we're trying to deal with the union without drawing a lot of negative attention. The Pinkertons are sending in undercover detectives to various towns in Western Maryland. Their job will be to find out who the union members are. Your job will be to fire those men who are employed here without making a big deal about it."

Winston stopped speaking and stared at Joseph.

"Oh, may I speak now?" Joseph asked sarcastically.

"Don't be a smart mouth."

Maizy came in and set a cup of hot coffee next to where Joseph was sitting. Then she left quietly.

"You don't need to send any detectives to Eckhart," Joseph said.

"It's not my call. Pinkerton is putting men where they think they are needed. We don't know who they are or even which of our mines they are investigating. They are operating independently. It will help keep the miners from learning about them."

"We don't have a union problem in Eckhart," Joseph said.

Winston shook his head. "Are you truly so foolish? The UMW

is trying to get in anywhere it can. Eckhart is a prime location on the National Road and near the railroad."

"And I won't know who is a Pinkerton and who is not?"

"No, you'll get a call from the company about who needs to be fired or not."

"Shouldn't that be my call? I am the superintendent."

"And you work for Consolidation Coal, Joseph. Don't get above yourself. You are not in charge here. You were given this position because you could take orders."

"I do more than that. I run a good operation for Consolidation Coal."

Winston sighed. "You run an adequate operation. The mines could produce more. You are lucky we don't need more right now. That reminds me. We need you to eliminate the third shift completely."

Joseph had a skeleton crew working third shift in the hopes that he would be able to add men to it.

"That won't make the miners happy."

"Better that than having your miners work less than full time. You can do it gradually and run two shifts heavy until we start eliminating union members."

"I don't like this."

"You don't have to. Just do what you're told."

"Yes, sir."

His father left a few minutes later, barely saying goodbye. Joseph also realized that his father hadn't said anything to him about how his mother was doing. That was how it went with his father. Business was business, and family was family. The two didn't intersect.

Chapter 14

February 18, 1922

Saturdays were half work-days. The miners headed home at lunch, and for most of them, it was bath day. They had the rest of the day and Sunday to relax or do other chores before heading back into the mines on Monday morning.

Matt felt like he must be getting used to going into the mine. He didn't feel so claustrophobic anymore. He wasn't sure whether he was still having nightmares. Antonietta hadn't said anything to him about yelling in his sleep since that first night. His bed sheets were always twisted into balls or thrown off the bed in the mornings, so he still suspected he had nightmares.

Once he washed and dressed, Matt headed off to Frostburg. It felt good to stretch his legs. He dropped his report off in the box for outgoing mail at the post office and decided to stroll through town.

The streets were filled with people doing their shopping. He noticed some miners' wives among them, but mainly it was farmers and businessmen. The miners, for the most part, stayed in their own towns.

Matt thought about stopping in for a drink in Failinger's basement, but it was still too early in the day. Besides that, he hadn't eaten lunch. He was more hungry than anything.

He started looking for a place to eat when he heard a familiar voice shouting over the noise of the town.

"Women are just as capable as men. They have the minds to run a business. Don't they run your households?"

Matt looked around and saw Samantha Havencroft. She stood on a wooden crate, so she was two heads above the most of the people around her. No one seemed to be paying much attention to her as they walked by. They gave her a wide berth, probably afraid that she would ask them a question.

"Women can run businesses, hold elected office, and be college professors," she said.

One man walking near her kicked the crate, and it slid to the side. Samantha dropped a stack of pamphlets she was holding, and they flew into the air like confetti. She started to fall backward. Matt rushed forward to help, but he knew that he wouldn't reach her in time.

With a yelp, she fell, but she managed to grab hold of a nearby streetlight to keep from hitting the ground.

Matt reached her as she was straightening up.

"You don't seem to be drawing much of a crowd," he said. Actually, with her losing her balance and the pamphlets flying in the air, she was attracting a lot of attention.

Samantha glared at the crowd. "Oh, now you want to stop and watch?" she said to the crowd. "You couldn't do that earlier when I was saying something important."

The crowd started to break up and move off. Their expected laugh at Samantha's expense had been thwarted. Matt started gathering the pamphlets off the street.

"They're foolish," Samantha said. "They don't care about what's in their best interests."

"You're wrong there," Matt said. He began trying to pick up some of her pamphlets. "They are very interested in things that will help them, but what they believe that is and what you believe is different. A woman recently told me, 'What good's a right, if my belly is grumbling?'"

Samantha frowned. "Rights are important. Women shouldn't be treated like slaves."

Matt raised an eyebrow. "Slaves? Really? I'm the one picking up your pamphlets while you stand over me."

Samantha sighed. "Okay, not slaves, but they aren't treated equally."

"Samantha, you have your basic needs taken care of. You have plenty to eat and a warm place to sleep. You are educated, so you have skills. Many of these people are missing one or more of those things in their lives. A miner's wife isn't worried about whether or not she can become a coal miner. She's worried about finding enough food to feed her family. She's worried about whether or not her husband will come home from the mine."

"But rights are important."

Matt nodded. "Yes, they are. However, these people are like Esau from the Bible. They are willing to trade their birthright for a meal because they are hungry."

She waggled a finger at him. "And look where that got Esau."

"I'm not saying it's a great choice, but it's a necessary one."

Samantha looked away from him out over the street. When she finally met his stare again, she said, "That makes sense."

"Don't sound so surprised."

She put a hand on his arm. "I'm sorry. I didn't mean it to sound that way."

He passed her what pamphlets he had collected. "So are you finished here?"

She looked around at the crowd that was ignoring her again. "Apparently, I never got started."

"I was looking for a place to eat lunch before you distracted me. Would you care to join me?"

She looked at him oddly. "Can you afford it?"

"I thought with all your talk about equality that you would pay," Matt said innocently.

"Really? Well, I guess…"

Matt started laughing, and she slapped him on the arm.

"I did the inviting, Samantha. I'll do the paying," he said.

"It's just that after everything you told me, I thought you might not have that much money."

"I'm single. I live in a boarding house that my aunt and uncles own, so I think they are giving me a break on the rent. And coal mining is not my only income."

Samantha perked up. "Oh, are you an eccentric millionaire?"

"Eccentric, yes. Millionaire, no."

She took his arm, and they began to walk. "Where are we going?"

"Do you have a favorite place?"

"Failinger's is wonderful, but I only like to eat there for dinner. For lunch, I would recommend Charlie's."

"Then lead the way."

As they walked down the street passing stores doing a brisk business, Samantha said, "So you live with your aunt and uncles. What about your parents? Do they live in Eckhart?"

"They died from Spanish Flu while I was on a ship on my way back to New York from Europe. They were fine when I left France but gone by the time I reached America."

"I'm sorry, but at least you still have family who cares for you. It's good to have family."

"Sometimes. I worry about them. That's why I'm here."

"Are they in trouble?"

Matt shrugged. "Possibly. Do you know about Matewan and Blair Mountain?"

"Who doesn't? That just happened a few months ago." Samantha paused, then said, "Wait. Are you worried about something like that happening here?"

"I don't know, but it's possible. The mines here aren't unionized, and there have been violent strikes here before where people have been killed. I want to make sure my family stays safe. I don't want to lose anyone else."

"So you came back here to watch out for them?"

Matt nodded. "Yes." It was not a lie, but neither was it the full truth.

They reached the restaurant. Matt hesitated, trying to gauge Samantha. When she also paused, he held open the door for her.

She smirked and walked inside.

The restaurant was small and well lit with only half a dozen tables near the front. The kitchen area was in another room behind a pair of bat-wing doors. The floor was white linoleum, although it was somewhat dirty. The walls also were exposed brick were decorated with bright, colorful scenes of Italy.

They took a seat at an empty table.

"The owner's wife is Italian, so there's an Italian influence to the meals," Samantha told Matt.

"I'm Italian."

She cocked her head sideways and raised an eyebrow. "Yes, with a last name of Ansaro, I wouldn't have guessed. I come here for the hamburgers and French fries, but you can also get spaghetti and lasagna."

Matt shook his head. "No, a hamburger and fries sound wonderful. My aunt cooks a lot of Italian dishes. They're wonderful. You should try one. You probably wouldn't want to eat the Italian cooking here."

"Don't tell Mrs. Brighton that. She'll probably come after you with a knife."

They both ordered hamburgers and fries with Coca-Colas. They spent an hour at lunch talking without any hint of tension. Samantha was relaxed so that she wasn't looking to take offense, and Matt was as open as he could be without revealing that he was a Pinkerton agent.

Surprisingly, he even told Samantha about Priscilla after he mentioned that he had been engaged once.

"You can't just say something like that and leave it hanging," Samantha said. "Tell me more. Why aren't you married now enjoying the domestic life in Baltimore?"

"Because I'm not rich."

Samantha's head rocked back. "What?"

"I had a good job in Baltimore, certainly better than being a coal miner. I met Priscilla at a party thrown by a regional manager who was trying to impress some new clients. At first, I thought you looked a lot like her, which may be one of the reasons I was so quick to help you the first time we met."

"And now?"

"You look nothing alike. There's some physical similarity. Your hair color and styles. Your height. The way you both carry yourself. Your eyes are blue, though. Hers are brown. Also, yours get this ... brightness ... in them when you are talking about equal rights. Your cause makes them come alive. If eyes are the window to the soul, then when you talk about your cause, you open your windows."

"Is that the only thing that makes them brighten?"

Matt shrugged. "It's the only thing that I've seen so far, but remember, we've only met three times, and one of those times was in a dark and smoky speakeasy."

Samantha grinned. "I remember, and I will teach you to dance."

"You are welcome to try," he offered.

"So Priscilla and I are different."

"I can tell you more ways if you want."

"No, I believe you. So you two got together at that party."

Matt nodded. "She was the prettiest woman there, and I was feeling cocky, freshly back from the war. The regional manager had me wear my Marine uniform so he could show off his war hero employee."

"Oh, so you're a war hero?"

"No, but he thought so."

"And Priscilla couldn't resist a soldier."

Matt shrugged. "Maybe. I'd like to think she was attracted to me, but given how things worked out, that might have been the problem. When she finally saw past the uniform, she didn't like who she saw."

"That seems doubtful."

Matt snorted. "Looks who's talking. When you first met me, you yelled at me."

Samantha blushed. "I said I was sorry about that."

"I know. Anyway, Priscilla and I saw each other for six months. I felt so lucky. The first sign of trouble was when I met her parents. Her family was a client of my company. They were a couple of steps above me on the social scale and thought their daughter could do better. Priscilla said she loved me, though, and I was so proud that she took a stand for us."

Samantha nodded. "You should have been. She sounds strong-willed."

"I asked her to marry me, and she said, yes. I spent my savings on the ring. We planned the wedding, and then a week from the day, …" He hesitated and press his lips together in a hard line. "… a week from the day, she called it all off. She said that she had met someone else and couldn't marry me."

"That's terrible."

"I found out who it was a couple days later. He came from a wealthy family in Baltimore, and honestly, I don't believe he was better looking than me. I know he couldn't have treated her better than I did. The difference was the money. He had it. I didn't."

Samantha reached across the table and put a hand on his. "You don't know that for sure. Maybe there was another reason, not that it would excuse how she broke it off with you."

Matt frowned and then shook his head to chase away the memories.

"What about you? Any broken hearts in your past?" he asked.

"If there is, I don't know about it. Certainly, no one who wanted to marry me."

They moved onto more pleasant topics and finished the meal. Matt paid the check.

As they stepped back onto cold, windy street, Samantha said, "Thank you very much. I enjoyed myself."

"May I walk you home?"

"Are you worried about my safety walking alone?"

"No, I'm just looking for a reason to extend our time together."

She nodded toward him. "In that case, yes, you can walk me home. I won't be able to ask you in, though."

"I wasn't angling for an invitation."

"I know, but I would have asked you in. The thing is my father would overreact. He would either make you uncomfortable by treating you with suspicion or reading too much into this," Samantha explained.

"Well then, since I don't want to put you or me in that position, I'll say goodbye to you for now."

He shook her hand as she smirked at him. He wondered if she knew what he really wanted to do.

Then she walked off down the street, and Matt found himself thinking, maybe being home wouldn't be so bad.

After dinner, Matt, his uncles, and his aunts walked down Store Hill to the Gem Theater to watch Rent Free, a silent comedy that starred Walter Reid and Lila Lee. Matt had seen the movie in Baltimore, but he still smiled at that story of a painter who moves into an abandoned house to live rent-free until the daughter of the former owner finds him.

After the movie ended, the women went home, but a group of miners walked over to the J. J. Carter's Grocery, Hardware, and Clothing Store and sat on the porch. The store was closed, but one of the miners went around to the back and came back soon after that with a bucket filled with bottles of beer. Either he had hidden them earlier, or someone was running a speakeasy behind the store.

It didn't matter to Matt. He wasn't here find bootleggers. He took a bottle, pulled the cork, and took a swig. It burned his throat, and he spit it out.

"Watch it there!" Tom Henderson called. "You almost hit me!"

"Sorry, I don't normally drink piss," Matt said.

The other miners laughed. "Beggars can't be choosers. It's free beer," Jack Scarpelli said. He was the one who had retrieved the beers.

"There's a reason that it's free."

Jack laughed and chugged his beer. Matt shook his head and hand the beer to Samuel. He pulled his hands back.

"I agree with you. I never drink Jack's homebrew," Samuel said.

Enos took the bottle and drank from it. "I'm not as picky as you two."

"So Matt, what's it like being home?" Mario Tomacelli asked.

Matt shrugged. "Not so much to do as there is in Baltimore."

"You just saw a movie, didn't you? We have dances and places to eat."

"You have one theater. What if I didn't want to see that movie? I had already seen it," Matt said.

"So you're cultured," Jack said. "Too good for our beer and our town."

"Do you think Eckhart is just as good as Baltimore?" Matt asked.

Jack rubbed the back of his head. "I've never been there."

"If you had, I don't think you'd be so defensive. Baltimore has 730,000 people in it. It has a port that receives ships from all over the world. It has buildings that tower over the tallest building in Cumberland. It has all types of restaurants."

"So why'd you come back here?" Jack asked.

Matt paused a moment and then said, "Because my fiancée broke off our engagement, and I didn't want to stay around with all of the memories."

"That's too bad. Was she pretty?"

Matt nodded. "Very."

"I wouldn't mind a pretty woman," Jack said.

"I'm sure any woman who goes out with you is thinking she wouldn't mind a handsome man," Enos said.

Everyone laughed, even Jack.

The conversation continued back and forth like that for an hour. Matt found himself caught up on the things that had happened in town, good and bad. The coal mines had helped bring electricity to Eckhart Mines, although to help them, it just happened to help the residents, too. He learned who had married whom, and the people who had died. Matt was surprised when the miners talked about Joey becoming the superintendent. No one really liked him, but they all agreed that he was a fair boss.

At one point after Tom Henderson complained about the dropping wages for the third time in an hour, Matt asked, "Have you ever thought about doing something else?"

"Why would I do that?"

"Because you are complaining a lot about your pay. You could find a better paying job that isn't so dangerous and allows you to see the daylight."

"You tried to leave, and you wound up right back here where you started," Tom said.

"Not by choice, and I won't stay here forever."

Tom finished off his beer. "I've been a miner all my life. I come from a family of miners. It's what I know. I've got coal dust in my blood."

"So has my family, but they also own a boarding house, and Enos wants to run a taxi someday."

That started everyone laughing again. "I wouldn't get on the road if I knew Enos was driving a car. I'd be afraid for my life," Mario said.

The group started drifting apart a few minutes later. As they walked back to the boarding house, Enos grumbled about how he would make an excellent taxi driver.

Samuel said to Matt, "Some people don't want to change, Matt. They complain about things like Tom does, but if it truly changed, they would complain about that."

"You and Enos aren't afraid of change, though."

"I'd like to think not."

"Then what do you want to do beyond mining?"

Samuel was quiet as he walked and Matt began to think that he wasn't going to answer the question. Finally, he said, "I'd like to earn enough to have a house of my own, although I'd still run it as a boarding house. Then maybe one day, I would have enough to own a hotel."

"Really?"

"Does that surprise you?"

Matt shrugged. "I'm trying to picture you in a suit greeting people who come to stay in a hotel."

"You doubt I could?"

"It's not that. I'm just trying to picture you dressed up with your mustache trimmed and hair slicked back. I bet Aunt Myrna would like seeing you like that."

Samuel smiled. "What about you, Matt? What is your dream beyond Eckhart?"

Matt couldn't tell him that he was already living one dream beyond Eckhart, but Matt wasn't sure being a Pinkerton was his ultimate dream.

"I want to be a police officer," he admitted.

"You didn't see enough danger in Europe that you want more?"

"Being a police officer isn't about being in dangerous situations, although it's probably less dangerous than mining. It's about helping people and protecting them. That's what I want to do."

"That's a good dream to have."

Matt nodded. Of course, he was already doing that in a way, but the people he was helping and protecting just didn't realize it.

Chapter 15

February 20, 1922

The Maryland State Normal School had opened in Frostburg in 1902 with the mission to train future teachers. In its twenty years of service, the school had seen enrollment increase from fifty-seven students to roughly seventy-five.

Samantha's father and nine other professors taught the classes. Her father was also in charge of the Model School and its faculty where another 150 or more elementary students attended. They were educated by students from the college as a practical application of the teaching methods they learned.

The Normal School's two-year program provided instruction in Latin, mathematics, history, rhetoric and literature, natural and physical sciences, drawing, music, calisthenics, psychology, philosophy of education, philosophy of school management, pedagogy, observation, practice work and primary manual training. It was everything a well-rounded teacher needed.

At eighteen years old, Samantha was finishing up her second year. She wasn't sure where she would go when she graduated. She had wanted the education, but she didn't know if she wanted to be a teacher like her father.

She sat in her natural and physical sciences class as Professor Hughes returned the biology exam the students had taken the day before. He walked along the aisles of desks placing each student's test in front of him or her.

As he laid Samantha's test in front of her, he said, "Nicely done, Miss Havencroft."

She glanced at the test and saw that she had received an A.

"Thank you, Professor," she said.

He continued down the aisle, and Samantha picked up the test to look at it more closely. She read through each question wondering if she had truly earned her A. The true-and-false and multiple-choice questions were easy. Either she got the right answer or not. It was the open-ended questions where the teachers had more leeway in their grading. Samantha knew that the sciences were not her strongest subject. If she had been Samantha Smith, would she have still earned an A?

The professor finished returning the tests and glanced at the clock on the wall.

"That is all our time today. I want you to review your tests this evening and find the correct answers to the questions that you missed. I will see you all tomorrow."

The students started closing their books and stacking them into a pile. They stood up and walked into the hallways of Old Main where most of the classes at the Normal School were taught. Samantha's literature class was on the second floor, so she headed for the stairs. Vernon Mitchell was suddenly walking beside her.

Where had he come from?

"Good morning, Samantha," he said.

The young man behind her had thick wavy hair and sea-green eyes. He was a handsome man who knew it.

"Good morning, Vernon." She quickened her pace and hoped that wherever he was going, it wasn't on the second floor.

"How would you like to go to a movie tonight?" he asked.

"I have to study."

"Study? You're a straight A student."

"And the reason for that is because I study," Samantha told him.

"How about this weekend then? We could go to the movies

and dinner."

Samantha stopped walking and turned to face Vernon. He was also a senior, although he was nineteen years old. He was also a head taller than Samantha.

"Vernon, I've told you before that I don't want to see you anymore," she said.

"Why not? We had fun when we went out. We got along great together."

Samantha's eyes widened. "I don't know what date you were on, but it didn't go so great."

They had gone to dinner in a restaurant in Frostburg, and Vernon had spent the meal talking about himself. Samantha had wanted to go dancing afterward, but Vernon had taken her home where he spent most of the evening chatting with her father and virtually ignored her.

"Why not?" Vernon asked.

"All you wanted to talk about was yourself."

Vernon crossed his arms over his chest. "I wanted to give you the chance to get to know me."

Samantha nodded. "I got to know you all right, and I know that we wouldn't work out."

"How can you say that? Your father approves of me."

"Well then, maybe you should ask my father out. I met someone else whom I actually like," Samantha asked.

She was talking more loudly than she wanted to, but she was getting angry with Vernon for continuing to press the issue after she said, "No."

She turned to go, but Vernon grabbed her by the arm and pulled her back around. "Whoever he is, he can't be as good a match for you as me."

Samantha stared at Vernon and frowned. If she hadn't been holding her books in her free arm, she would have slapped him across the face.

She said through clenched teeth, "Take your hand off my arm."

Vernon looked at his hand as if he didn't know what he had

done. He let go and stepped away from Samantha.

"If you touch me like that again, I will tell my father," she said.

This was one time she didn't mind using her father's name because she knew that it carried weight with Vernon, and he might actually listen and leave her alone.

She turned and walked up to the second floor, happy to leave Vernon behind. She went into her literature class with Professor Smythe and took her seat.

The class was reading *Tamerlane and Other Poems*. When it was initially published in 1827, the author had been listed as "a Bostonian." This later edition had the author's name listed. It was the first book published by Edgar Allan Poe. Samantha didn't care much for Poe's short stories, but she was fascinated by his poems. She loved the imagery and rhythm.

After her literature class, she had a lunch break. She didn't have an appetite for lunch, so she ate an apple and a biscuit while sitting on a bench in the quad. It was a sunny day and unseasonably warm, so she enjoyed the beautiful weather while she could.

Despite the weather, Samantha felt surprisingly sad. At first, she thought it might be that she somehow felt guilty about her confrontation with Vernon, but she tossed that idea aside when she remembered his behavior.

She wasn't the only one on the quad this afternoon, but she was the only one alone. The other students were in couples or groups. Samantha didn't have anyone at the school whom she could call a friend. She wasn't sure if it was because she didn't know how to make them or if she was afraid to trust them because they would turn out like Vernon. One of the things that she liked about Matt was that who her father was had no bearing on Matt's opinion of her.

She remembered her dinner with Matt and how at ease she had been with him. She smiled at the thought and then wondered what would happen this summer.

She would graduate from the Normal School and then what? It would be time for her to leave Frostburg, but where would she go?

Baltimore might be nice or maybe Washington D.C. Her interest in politics might come in handy there.

She wondered if Matt would want to come with her. Washington had no coal mines, but there would undoubtedly be work for him there. He had found work in Baltimore that wasn't in a coal mine.

Across the quad, she saw her father walk out of the athletic building and start along the path to Old Main. How much longer would he stay here? He was getting older now, and he had no one to look after him.

Should she stay in Frostburg to look after him? He wasn't an invalid yet. Maybe she was just trying to find an excuse to remain. That thought startled her.

Why would she want to stay here?

Chapter 16

February 21, 1922

Matt climbed into the coal car with his uncles to take the man-trip to their work location. He was surprised to find that a knot didn't form in his stomach. His muscles still tensed up, but at least he wasn't afraid.

That didn't mean that the ride to the face was any smoother. Sitting on the hard bench in the coal car, Matt felt every bump go right up his spine.

"We're going to blast a new section out this morning," Samuel said. "So stay on your toes. There might be a lot of loose rock."

Matt felt a chill that didn't come from the cold air in the mine. Rock falls had killed a lot of miners, and as with most accidents in coal mines, there were few ways to predict where and when they would happen.

Enos lit the carbide lamp on his helmet. It gave off an orange glow that lit the way ahead for a short distance. The headlamp had an upper and lower reservoir. The carbide was placed in the lower tank and water in the upper. By opening a valve, water dripped onto the carbide. The resulting reaction created a gas that burned, providing a bright, broad light. Carbide lamps also had reflectors behind the flames to focus the light forward. Miners would often use their picks to carve a shelf near where they were digging. They could then take the carbide lamps off their helmets and place them on the temporary shelf.

Matt caught the smell of alcohol on Enos's breath and said, "Best not breathe on that carbide Enos, you'll cause an explosion."

Enos leaned in close and told him, "Ha! Ha! Ha!" emphasizing the hard H so that he exhaled on Matt.

Matt lit the carbide on his headlamp, and it began to cast a circle of light in front of him. Some miners were switching to battery-powered headlamps. They offered brighter light, but one advantage of carbide was that the flame changed color if the air got bad.

When they reached the face, they set to work setting timbers along the tunnel edge. They would have to place more as the mine shaft moved deeper into the mountain. The timbers helped stabilize the ceiling of the tunnel. Between the picks and explosions, plenty of vibrations could jar loose rocks, and falling rock killed more miners than other hazards in the mine.

Matt, Samuel, and Enos hammered on the ends of the augers to drill into the face. Once the bit set in the rock, they kept turning the crooked handle around and around to dig into the areas around the coal seam. When the drill holes were five to six feet deep, they began turning the handles in the opposite direction to back the augers out of the hole.

Next, they used a long copper needle to tamp a black powder cartridge into the hole. Because the company made the miners pay for dynamite, most of them made their own charges by pouring black powder into a rolled up newspaper. Dirt was tamped in around the needle to fill in any open space. The needle was pulled out leaving the powder cartridge at the back of the hole and a small path open to it.

Matt had his uncles tell him where to drill. He had been so long out of the mines that he had lost the skill of knowing where to dig. He still handled the auger pretty well, though. He could get it to dig into the earth with relative ease.

He had to trust in his uncles' skill that they had used the right amount of black powder in the charges. If not enough black powder was used, the resulting chunks of coal would be too large to load in the coal car, and the miner would have to break them down into smaller pieces, which would take time away from loading the cars and earning money. Use too much powder, and you wound up with too much slack, which was fine coal waste that a miner wasn't paid for. A large explosion could also weaken the ceiling, increasing the chances of a cave in or rock fall.

Samuel inspected Matt's work at drilling his hole, nodded, and gave him a squib. This was a tube of fine powder with a twist of sulfur-impregnated paper on one end that roughly resembled a bottle rocket used by youngsters during the Fourth of July holiday.

Matt was surprised to see Samuel inspect Enos's hole, too.

"Well, what did you expect? I've worked down here nearly as long as you have," Enos said when Samuel nodded his approval.

"I'm just double-checking," Samuel told him as he handed his brother a squib.

When all the squibs were inserted, Samuel said, "Ready?"

Matt and Enos nodded.

"Fire in the hole!"

The men lit the ends of the squibs and then scrambled to put some distance between themselves and the face. The paper burned slowly, but the powder in the squib sent the flame back to the powder charge with a "rocket" effect.

The sound of the explosion sounded muffled and far away, but it loosened the coal around the auger hole. It also stirred up coal dust in the air and filled the tunnel with black powder smoke. The bad air in the tunnel after an explosion could give a miner a headache.

While they waited for it to settle, Matt kept his hand on the wall, feeling for vibrations that could indicate the explosions knocked something other than coal loose. His throat burned from a temporary lack of oxygen because of the smoke and dust. Eventually, the ventilation fans cleared the air easing the pain in his head somewhat. Sometimes miners waited until the end of their shifts to set their charges. That way, the air would be clear for the next day's work. Samuel insisted that you dug when you could, and if you needed to blast, you did that whether it was morning or afternoon.

Once the fans had cleared up the air, Matt, Samuel, and Enos used their picks and shovels to free the coal and load it into the coal car. However, Matt wondered if Enos was suffering from bad air. Every time he swung his pick, he wobbled as if he might fall over.

Samuel finally took it from him and made him sit down.

"You idiot, you knew you had to work this morning," Samuel said.

"I was working," Enos said.

"You were either going to fall over or wind up hitting someone with that pick, and I don't want it to be me."

"Is he drunk?" Matt asked.

"More likely, he's hungover. You can't say anything about it, or he'll lose a day's pay, maybe more," Samuel said.

Matt and Samuel tried to separate coal from rock and ash before tossing it in the coal car. It took time away from digging, and their lighting wasn't the best. Even though the coal breakers on the surface did much the same thing, it was expected that the miners would sort their own coal or have their pay docked. Consolidation Coal had a reputation for being picky about their coal. They wanted it as clean as possible.

Enos stood up after a few minutes and began helping. "I can do this. The smoke made things worse. I'm not sober, but I can work," Enos said.

Samuel nodded and continued working.

It was dark when the Ansaros came out of the mine. During the winter, miners only ever saw the sun on weekends and during lunch. Miners in the deeper mines might not even come outside for lunch. It made the name Sunday all the more appropriate to them.

As Matt walked up the street toward the boarding house, he saw Laura standing on her stoop and Jacob playing in the yard. She looked at all of the miners searching for Peter. She waved to Matt, and he waved back.

"Anything happen today?" she asked.

That was the question every miner's wife wondered throughout the day. It was a question whose answer could change lives.

"Everyone is coming home. I don't even think there were any injuries, at least none that I heard about." Laura smiled. "I suppose Peter will be along shortly.

"Do you two wait for him every day?"

Laura came down off the stoop and walked over to the fence.

"If the weather is bad we wait inside, although judging by how quickly Jacob gets dirty, he likes to play in the mud."

Jacob spun in circles until he fell over dizzy. "Boys are like that," Matt said.

"Do you have children?"

Matt snorted. "I'm not even married."

"The single women around here will like to hear that."

Matt shrugged. "I've had a mixed experience with that so far."

"Oh, really?" Her eyebrows raised. "You've been back less than a week. Who have you met?"

Matt wasn't about to tell Laura about Calista. He was sure that she wouldn't approve, and it wasn't his proudest moment.

"I met a girl ... I guess that she would prefer to be called a woman ... who is interesting. Her name is Samantha Havencroft."

"I don't know her."

"She lives in Frostburg. She's not from a mining family. She goes to the college."

Laura stared hard at him. "Oh, so you found yourself a smart woman?"

Matt blushed. "I don't know about that. The first time I met her, she screamed at me."

Laura grinned. "I'm sure that you deserved it."

"I wouldn't say that. I was just trying to help her."

"Always the gentleman."

A voice behind Matt said, "Hello."

He turned around and saw a tall miner walking toward them along with Enos. They were having a conversation that involved a lot of hand gestures Matt couldn't interpret.

"Peter!" Laura exclaimed. She reached across the fence and hugged him and then tried to brush the coal dust off of her dress.

"Da!" Jacob chimed in as he ran to the fence.

"Peter, you remember Matt from the other day, don't you?"

Peter shook Matt's hand. "The hometown boy returned."

"That's me. Well, I guess I'll let you get to your dinner. Me, I'll be last in line for a bath tonight."

"But it's only Tuesday."

"Well, Aunt Toni takes the proverb, 'Cleanliness is next to godliness' as the eleventh commandment. It was good seeing you again, Laura."

"You too, Matt. Goodbye, Enos."

Matt turned and headed up the hill with his uncle. As he walked past the company store, he saw Joey standing on the porch smoking a cigar. If it hadn't been for the smoke coming off the tip of the cigar, Joey could have been mistaken for a statue.

"Mr. McCord," Matt said, touching the brim of his hard hat with his fingertips."

"Matteo, I see you didn't take long to renew your acquaintance with Laura Spiker."

Matt stopped walking "She's a friend."

"I remember that the two of you used to be more than that."

Matt nodded. "Used to be, but I'm sure you know she's married now and has a child."

"I do, which means that you ought to stay away from her."

Matt took a deep breath to bite back his sharp comment that he had in mind. Instead, he said, "Why is it any concern of yours, Mr. McCord?"

"I am just trying to keep things running smoothly in Eckhart."

"And me talking to an old friend disrupts that?"

"You talking to an old girlfriend could."

"I have no animosity toward Laura or Peter. I'm glad that they're happy."

"Stay away from her, Matteo."

Matt's face flushed. Was Joey saying he and Laura were having an affair? Did Joey think himself so powerful that he could control the lives of everyone in Eckhart Mines?

"When I'm in the mine, Mr. McCord, you are my boss, and I'll listen to you. After hours, I am my own man, and if I choose to be friends with a woman, married or otherwise, it's no concern of yours unless she happens to be your wife, family, or mistress. Is she any of those, Mr. McCord?"

Joey pulled his cigar from his mouth and said, "No."

"Well then, I don't see that we have anything to discuss."

"If you're so interested in stirring up trouble at my mine, Matteo, I don't need you here. You're fired."

"What?" Enos said.

That was unexpected. Matt couldn't lose this job. This was where he needed to be to accomplish everything that he wanted to do.

"You can't do that," Matt said.

Joey blew out a smoke ring. "I think we've established that I can." He jabbed his cigar in Matt's direction. "I want you out of my town."

"Your town?" Matt looked at him and shook his head slowly. "You may be older and have a position of importance, but you're still that petty, scrawny boy who believes himself so much better than everyone around him."

"I don't believe it. I know it. I am in charge of this mine and, by extension, this town," Joey said, his voice rising to a near shout.

Matt realized that Joey truly believed what he was saying. He saw himself as far superior to anyone in this town.

This was going from bad to worse. Joey was on the verge of bringing about a total failure to Matt's assignment. He not only wouldn't find out the union members for Consolidation Coal, but he would also cause his uncles to lose their jobs. Joey could even blacklist the family so that no one would stay in the boarding house. Joey was a king of a little kingdom, and he was exercising his power.

"Well then, I guess it's a good thing that I don't live in a company home," Matt said.

"Perhaps not, but your uncles work in the mine, and none of the other mines will hire you if I say not to," Joseph told him.

Matt launched himself at Joey, ready to plunge his fists into the man's soft flesh, but Enos grabbed him and pulled him back.

"Don't Matt, it will make things worse," Enos said.

Matt tried to squirm free, but his uncle had one hand on the back of his shirt and the other hand on Matt's arm.

"Worse? How much worse can it get!" Matt shouted.

"Worse. Trust me."

Joey nodded. "Listen to your uncle, Matteo. Touch me, and I'll have you arrested. Then I'll fire your uncles, too."

Enos dragged Matt away, never letting go of his nephew.

Joseph tossed the cigar stub into the street and went back inside the store to warm up. Portnoy saw him and shook his head.

"Do you have something to say?" Joseph asked.

Portnoy turned and walked into the back room mumbling something that sounded like "ass."

Damn Matteo for coming back! Joseph could deal with a miner husband. After all, he was the mine superintendent, but Laura had had a relationship with Matteo. That gave him a step up over Joseph.

He sat down at his desk to finish a few more letters and reports that he needed to go out with tomorrow's mail. He worked at it for half an hour and then pushed everything aside. He couldn't concentrate on what he needed to say.

He put on his coat and started to head outside when he heard the front door of the store open. Peter walked in.

"I need a can of carrots," he said.

Portnoy took the can off the shelf and brought it over to the counter. He told Peter about the price, and Peter tossed a few coins on the counter. Joseph stepped into the store as Peter turned to leave.

"Good evening, Mr. McCord," Peter said.

Joseph smiled broadly. "Hello, Pete, what brings you up here? Laura was just in the other day."

"She needed a can of carrots for a recipe."

"Ah." Joseph nodded as he sucked on his cigar.

"At least you have the money," Portnoy grumbled behind him.

"What?" Pete said, looking over his shoulder.

"Ignore him," Joseph said. "By the way, I didn't know that you were friends with Matteo Ansaro."

Pete looked confused for a moment and then said, "Matt Ansaro? He's an old friend of Laura's."

Joseph chuckled. "I grew up with them. They were a lot more than friends, as I recall."

"What's that mean?"

Joseph shrugged. "Just that they used to see each other, and there was talk of them getting married before Matt went off to join the Marines."

"Laura never said anything about that."

Joseph nodded. "Probably because she had a hard time getting over him, and now he's back and a war hero and everything."

Pete looked at the floor, his face turning red. Whether it was from embarrassment or anger, Joseph couldn't say.

"I have to get home. Laura is waiting for this." He held up the can.

"Have a good night, Pete."

"You too, sir."

Pete left. When Joseph turned, he saw Portnoy staring at him with a frown on his face. Of course, with Portnoy that wasn't unusual.

Enos led Matt up Store Hill to the back of one of the larger houses. It was two stories with a peaked roof and no porch just a cement stoop.

"Where are we going?" Matt asked.

"Just follow me," Enos told him. "You need to calm down. I've never seen you so angry before."

Matt shook his head. He had lost control when it looked like everything he had returned to Eckhart Mines to do was going to fall apart. He felt at that moment, he could have killed Joey or seriously hurt him.

Enos knocked on the door. A woman answered. She was rail thin with squinting eyes.

"Hi, Marie," Enos said. "Matt here has had a bad day. We can use something to calm him down."

Marie opened the door wider and let the two of them inside.

Enos nudged Matt through the door and into the kitchen of the house. When they were inside, Marie closed the door and opened the door to the basement staircase, which was behind it.

Matt and Enos went downstairs, and Matt found himself in a speakeasy. I was dark and smelled of damp and earth. The basement had been converted into a saloon with half a dozen tables and a bar along one wall. Matt and Enos sat down at a table. A few moments later a man walked over. He was bald, although he wore a thick, drooping mustache.

"Do you have anything good tonight, George?" Enos asked.

George shook his head. "Maybe this weekend. Right now, it's just the 'shine from the mountain."

Enos nodded. "Bring us a bottle and two glasses then."

When George left, Enos said to Matt, "You lost control back there."

Matt slouched in the chair and stared at the table. "I know."

He had to find a way to fix this quickly.

"What would you have done if I hadn't been there?" Enos asked.

"I would have beaten him," Matt said quietly.

"And that would have ended with you in jail."

Matt sat forward and rested his forearms on the table. "It would have been worth it."

Enos shook his head. "No, it wouldn't have been."

George returned with the bottle and two glasses. Enos took out his wallet and paid for the booze. Then he poured them each a drink.

Matt swallowed his in a gulp and regretted it. It tasted foul. Enos didn't seem to mind, but then, he was probably used to it.

"If you're going to be a miner, Matt, you've got to get used to taking orders. I'm surprised you didn't learn that in the military."

"I got into trouble a time or two because of that, Enos, and I don't want to be a miner. This is just temporary for me."

"It's over for you if Mr. McCord blacklists you."

That was true. Matt had to think of a way to fix this. He couldn't beg for his job back. Joey would enjoy the show and still not rehire him. Matt had to find another way.

"I'll have to figure something out," Matt said.

"Good luck with that." He raised his refilled glass and downed another shot.

"Why do you think he fired me?"

"You heard what he said."

Matt shook his head. "But Laura and I aren't carrying on. We just talk when we meet."

"Laura's a pretty woman."

"What that got to do with anything? She's not Joey's wife."

"Doesn't mean that a man can't be jealous."

They stayed until they had finished the entire bottle. Matt had four shots, and Enos finished the rest. Enos could barely walk out of the house. Matt supported him and led him up the street to the boarding house.

His mind was a muddle of thoughts. He had to find a way to get rehired and quickly.

Chapter 17

February 22, 1922

Matt waited until breakfast to tell his family that he'd been fired from the coal mine. It also meant that he had time to clear his head of moonshine and think up a way that he could head things off before Joey went too far and blacklisted his family.

Once everyone had settled down to eating, Matt said, "I have some news that you all need to know." Everyone paused in their eating to look at him. "Joey McCord fired me."

"What!" Samuel said. A couple of people gasped. Antonietta closed her eyes and almost seemed to be praying.

"Why did he fire you?" Samuel asked.

"He saw me talking to Laura Spiker and didn't like it."

Samuel's eyes widened. "That's it?"

"I was there," Enos said. "That's what happened."

"He told me to stop speaking with her, and I told him what I do on my own time is none of his concern," Matt said.

Samuel nodded slowly. "True, but he wouldn't have liked hearing it."

"What will you do?" Myrna asked.

"Well, he nearly knocked Joey's block off," Enos said.

Myrna put her hands on her mouth. "You didn't!"

Enos grinned. "No, I stopped him, but it wasn't easy. Matt

could probably be a boxer if he wanted. He's strong and quick."

"If Mr. McCord blacklists you, you won't be able to get a job in any Western Maryland mine."

"Thank the Lord," Antonietta said.

Matt glanced at her. He knew where she stood on all of this.

"I am hoping that Joey cools down and comes to his senses," Matt said.

"It sounds like you need to cool down as well," Samuel said.

Matt shrugged. "I won't deny that, but Joey also threatened to fire you and Enos, too."

Samuel glanced at Enos, who nodded.

The other boarders stayed out of what was obviously a family conversation, although they would no doubt talk about in the mines today.

"I talked with a lawyer that I met in Frostburg," Matt lied. "He said that he thought he could help me since I didn't do anything wrong. He is going to go to Cumberland and talk to the man in charge of Western Maryland's Consolidation Coal mines."

"That's Joey's daddy," Enos said.

"Then I wouldn't hold out much hope," Samuel said.

"It's all I've got right now," Matt said.

"I think you should take it as the blessing it is and find yourself a job in a store or even the tire company in Cumberland. Anything would be better than the mines," Antonietta said.

After the men had left for the mines, Matt dressed in the suit that he had worn when he arrived in Cumberland. When he left his room, his aunt stopped what she was doing and stared at him with her hands on hips.

"Don't you look handsome?" she said.

"Thank you."

"Where are you going dressed like it is Sunday?"

"The lawyer I told you about wants me to go with him to see whoever he needs to talk to at Consolidation Coal."

"Are you sure this lawyer knows what he's doing? What's this lawyer's name? I've never heard of the main office changing something that the local superintendent decided."

Matt shrugged. "I don't know what will happen, but I'm will-ing to try."

Matt walked over and hugged his aunt. "I don't know how long I will be."

Then he walked outside and over to the National Road where he caught the Cumberland and Westernport trolley to Cumberland. He tried to rehearse what he would say in his head as he stared out over the landscape. He was going to be walking on a razor blade during this meeting. If he said the wrong thing, he might wind up making matters worse. It was the only thing he could think of do-ing, though.

He got off the trolley in Cumberland and went into the Liberty Trust Bank to retrieve his badge from the safe deposit box. He walked down Baltimore Street looking for the office of the Consol-idation Coal Company. He found the building and stepped inside. At the front desk, he introduced himself as Jason Cameron of the Pinkerton Detective Agency and asked to see David Groth, who was the man to whom he had been sending his reports.

The man came from his office and met Matt at the front desk. He was a tall, thin man who was nearly bald even though he couldn't have been more than thirty-five years old. They shook hands, and Matt showed him his Pinkerton badge.

"I don't believe that we've met, Mr. Cameron," Groth said.

"I manage the agents in the field in this region if they need as-sistance," Matt lied.

"I see."

"Is there somewhere we can talk?"

Groth looked concerned, but he was smart enough to know that he didn't want to get into a discussion about undercover opera-tives out in the open.

"Let's go back to my office," he said.

They walked down the hallway to a windowless office. It was stark with no pictures on the walls, just a desk, two chairs, and a filing cabinet. They sat down in the chairs.

"It has come to my attention, Mr. Groth, that our detective in

Eckhart Mines was fired without cause. He needs to be rehired without the superintendent knowing who he is," Matt said.

"Why is that? It would be much easier if I could just tell our mine superintendent there that the man is working for us."

Matt shook his head. "No, for some reason, this superintendent has taken a dislike to our man there, and if he knew our detective's true reason for being there, the superintendent might expose him to the miners to let those men get rid of him."

Groth's brow wrinkled. "That seems unlikely."

"How likely is it that a company would hire undercover detectives to spy on their employees?" Matt countered.

"Can't you just put another man in Eckhart Mines?"

Matt shook his head. "It took us a while to get our man in there in the first place. Perhaps, we could get another man in there, but it would take some time. Meanwhile, who knows what would happen. This man knows the area. He grew up here. He's a trusted miner. He is making inroads already into finding out where the UMW is going to meet and being part of that meeting. He is a valuable asset that we don't want to waste him. Not too many of our men have experience mining, and even fewer are from this area."

"I can appreciate that," Groth said.

"I figured that you would understand. Also, when the union troubles start, Frostburg will be neutral ground for the UMW to meet. The coal companies don't have much influence there. Having a detective in Eckhart puts us close to Frostburg. If the union wants to cause trouble for the coal companies, they could do worse than disrupt traffic along the National Road or the Cumberland and Pennsylvania Railroad."

"So what is it that you are asking me to do?"

Matt took a deep breath. This was where he would succeed or fail.

"Call your superintendent. Explain to him that word has reached the office that firing a miner without cause might actually inflame union troubles in his town, and since it was done without cause, the miner needs to be rehired."

Groth shook his head. "We don't interfere with a local superintendent's decision to hire or fire someone."

Matt leaned forward. "But you can. You have the authority."

Groth rubbed the side of his face. "Is it true what you said about the union troubles?"

Matt nodded. "It might very well be. It just won't be the way he thinks. You have to understand, from everything we have learned so far, coal mines all over the country are powder kegs ready to explode. They are just waiting for someone to light the fuse. Your superintendent probably realizes this, and he will think that it's connected to that, but the actual problem it will cause is to interfere with your ability to head off union problems."

"What is the assessment of the situation that you are hearing from your detectives?"

Matt leaned back in the chair and rubbed his chin. "The union is making inroads among the miners because of what happened at Blair Mountain. Coal miners are concerned and sensitive to the littlest changes. Not only have we heard complaints about reduced wages and reduced hours, but we also hear rumbles about the increases in pay deductions or even the lighting in the mines. After what happened last year, everyone is looking for problem signs and seeing them." Groth nodded as Matt spoke. "The area is primed to explode. It's just a matter of where the fuse is going to be lit. Not only does this firing hurt our investigation, but it also creates a source of irritation for the miners."

Groth held up his hands in surrender. "Fine. I'll take care of it, but please inform your employer that we need to see results. Our purpose is to head off strikes and violence. If either happens, the situation will get bad quickly and spread."

"Yes, I am aware of that, and we hope to achieve the same goal because if violence does spread our detectives will be in the middle of it. We don't want to see them die."

Matt stood up and shook Groth's hand. Now he needed to wait and see.

Chapter 18

February 22, 1922

Joseph walked up Federal Hill to his home. He paused on the front porch and turned to look over the town. He had grown up in Eckhart Mines, but now it was *his* town. He kept the coal production numbers where they should be, and even a little bit better, despite the reduced hours that he was working with. The union wasn't in town, or if it was, it was afraid to make itself known.

His professional life looked bright, so why did he hesitate to go inside and enjoy the fruit of his labor? It was because it could feel empty. Yes, he knew Maizy lived there, and the reason he had invited her to be a live-in cook and housekeeper was so that he wouldn't feel lonely. It didn't work. Maizy didn't avoid him, but she didn't go out of her way to be around him.

Joseph wasn't the only single man in town, but the miners had friends and family with them to keep company. Joseph had neither. He was the superintendent of the Consolidation Coal Company mine in Eckhart. He couldn't befriend a miner and have him expect Joseph to show him favoritism.

No, Joseph had a singular duty, and he needed to bear it alone.

That didn't mean he couldn't marry or take a mistress. One or both needed to be the right woman, though. A wife should advance him socially and bear his children. His mistress should keep him happy. Ideally, they should be one and the same. Ideally, but not likely.

Joseph thought he had found one of the women in his life. Laura Spiker was married, but she definitely seemed interested in him. He had been interested in her for years since she had first kissed him five years ago. Of course, she had kissed a lot of other boys that night, but it had been Joseph's first kiss, and he remembered it. Then Matteo had gone off to join the Marines, and Joseph had thought he had a chance with Laura. Joseph's father had sent him off to school in Baltimore before Joseph could tell Laura how he felt. Joseph had liked the women there, but he had always remembered that kiss he had shared with Laura. When he had returned home to take over the mine, once again, he thought that he would have a chance with her, only to find out she was married.

He heard the telephone ring inside the house. He went inside just as Maizy answered it.

"Mr. McCord just walked in," she said. She held the earpiece out to Joseph. "It's your father, Mr. McCord."

Joseph tried not to hurry over and take the earpiece from Maizy. He held it up to his ear and spoke into the mouthpiece. "Hello, sir."

"Joseph, what are you doing up there?"

"What do you mean?"

"I mean I got called into the office of Vice President Richard Trimble. He told me that you had fired a miner without cause yesterday."

"I have cause." What was this about? Why would the Consolidation Coal vice president care if one miner was fired? He never had before.

"Not enough you didn't. Don't you think we have enough to worry about with the unions without you going and giving them a cause to complain? I was told, in no uncertain terms, that you are to rehire that miner immediately."

"What? Since when does the company tell superintendents who to hire and fire?"

"They don't, and the fact that they are telling you to rehire this miner means that you screwed up."

"I did not."

"Don't argue. Just go out and rehire him. I don't care what he did."

"What if I don't? It's not right. It will make me look weak in front of my men."

"You don't have a choice, Joseph. If you don't, Vice President Trimble will chew my ass out, and I will gladly give him you in my place. After he is done with you, you'll be out of a job quicker than that miner was, and that miner will still have his job."

"Fine."

Joseph hung up the phone; slammed it down is more accurate. Embarrassed, he looked around. Maizy had wisely chosen to disappear back into the kitchen.

He could ignore his father, but there would be consequences.

What was so important about Matteo that he needed to be rehired? He was a good miner, but not the best. He was a veteran, but so were other men in the mines. Somehow after only working in the mine for a couple weeks, Matteo was protected from firing.

Matt arrived home before the end of the day shift at the mines. He changed out of his suit and went out to the living room. He sat down on the sofa to read the newspaper that he had picked up in Cumberland. It wasn't something that he often got to do.

"How did your meeting go?" Antonietta asked.

Matt closed his newspaper. "I think it went well. No promises were made, but I think that something will happen. I probably won't hear anything until tomorrow."

Antonietta shook her head. "Honestly, I wouldn't count on anything changing. The mining company doesn't care about a single miner. That's why the union makes sense. It's not the company versus single miners. It's the company versus thousands and thousands of miners banded together."

Matt wondered how true that was. Did the union put miners on equal footing with the mining company or was the goal to put the union in control of the company like the company controlled the miners now?

His uncles and the other boarders came home shortly after that. It wasn't a night for a full bath, but it still took a few minutes for the miners to scrub their hands and faces clean with Lava soap.

As Enos walked by in his longjohns, he said, "Well, there's the slacker pretending to be sick."

"I'm not sick," Matt said. "It's just that I worked so hard that I decided that I needed a day off."

"Any word about getting rehired or at least not blacklisted?"

Matt shook his head. "Not yet."

Enos nodded and headed up the stairs to his room.

"Word was spreading today about why Mr. McCord fired you," Samuel said.

"Was it the truth?"

"As far as I know."

"How quickly is it spreading?"

Samuel shrugged. "I don't know, but it was probably fast."

The story would spread and be exaggerated. Even if it weren't, it would weaken Joey's position with the miners, and he wouldn't like that. Too bad. That was Joey's problem for overreacting. Matt had another concern beyond his family.

"How did Pete take it?" Matt asked.

"I haven't seen Pete. He works in a different area."

Matt shook his head. "Joey is a fool."

"Maybe, maybe not. What is whispered, and very carefully, is that some people think Joseph McCord takes too great an interest in Laura Spiker."

"Well, he knew her when we were kids."

Samuel nodded. "Yes, but he also knew some of the other miners' wives and some of the miners when they were all younger, but Laura is the one he seems to speak to when she is in the store or passing on the street. She's the one he watches from the porch on the store."

"Are you saying…"

Samuel held up a hand. "He's never said or done anything inappropriate, mind you. The question is: Is it because he's afraid or that she would tell him no?"

"And she would tell him no," Matt said quickly. "She's married and in love with her husband."

Samuel motioned for Matt to calm down. "I'm not saying that she wouldn't, Matt, but you've been out of the mines for a while, and you were young when you worked in them before. You haven't been back long enough to hear the stories that I've heard from miners. Mine superintendents and company store managers hold a lot of power in a company town and not just over the miners but everyone in the town."

Then he turned and walked upstairs.

Matt shook his head. No, Laura would not cheat on her husband. Then he paused. That wasn't what Samuel had been suggesting. He'd said superintendents had a lot of power they could exert on people in town, and that included miner's wives. Joey wouldn't do something like that, would he? Hadn't he tried something similar when he fired Matt? Joey had used his power to try and make Matt do what he wanted.

Matt grabbed his coat and walked out onto the porch. Dusk had arrived, and the shadows stretched long across Eckhart. He sat down on the porch swing and began moving back and forth, trying to calm down. He didn't like the thoughts that Samuel had put into his head about Laura. He could tell himself that they weren't true, but then, he knew what she had done after she had caught him kissing another girl years ago.

He looked out over the street. He could see the lights coming on inside houses and plumes of smoke rising from the chimneys. A few people passed by on their way to and from Store Hill.

Matt also knew how faithful Laura had been before he had messed things up. That is how she seemed now. She was happy and in love. If Pete were as good a man as people thought, Laura wouldn't betray him. Pete wouldn't make the same mistakes that Matt had.

If she had a choice in the matter.

One shadow stopped nearby, and Matt saw the lit tip of a cigar glowing in the dark. It was Joey.

"Good evening, Joey," Matt said.

Joey walked up to the porch, but he didn't come up. "It's Mr. McCord to you."

"Not if I'm not your employee."

Matt wasn't sure why he was trying to goad Joey, except that Samuel's insinuations about Laura still rankled.

"That's why I'm here," Joey said. "I've had time to think things over, and you are a good worker. Consider yourself still on the payroll."

Matt was tempted to say something smart-mouthed, but his professionalism took over. His trip to Cumberland had been successful, and now he needed to close the deal. He needed to go back into the mine.

"Thank you, Mr. McCord," Matt said. "I will be back to work in the morning."

"Good."

Then Joey turned and walked away.

Chapter 19

February 23, 1922

Matt scrubbed all of the coal dust off of himself on Thursday after he returned to the boarding house, and then he shaved in his room. It was something that he only did a few times a week when his whiskers made his face itchy.

He dressed in a clean set of clothes and grabbed his coat as he headed out the front door to catch the trolley at Kelly's Pump.

"Dinner will be in a few minutes," Antonietta said when she saw him come out of his room.

"I won't be staying," Matt said.

"Where are you going?" She leaned closer. "And you shaved."

Matt paused in the doorway. "Yes, I did shave, and I'm going into Frostburg."

"In the middle of the week?" Most miners reserved their trips into Frostburg for Saturday when they had more time and money.

"It seems like the best time to go."

"Are you going to meet a woman?" Antonietta asked.

"Yes." He paused and then added, "Hopefully."

Enos hurried down the stairs. "I heard that. Great going, Matt. Is she pretty?"

Antonietta narrowed her eyes. "Hopefully?"

"I don't actually know how to get in touch with her."

"Well, that doesn't seem like a serious relationship then."

Matt sighed. He needed to get to the trolley stop. "I never said that it was. I only met her last week."

"And where are you going to try and find her?"

"Failinger's."

"The hotel?" Enos slapped him on the back. "Good job!"

Matt shook his head. "It's not like that."

Antonietta said, "It had better not be."

"I'm going to the restaurant. It's where I first met her," Matt told his aunt.

"The restaurant or the bar?" Enos asked.

"Bar?" Antonietta said.

"Come on, Toni, most people know there's a bar in Failinger's basement," Enos said.

Antonietta stared at Matt. "Is that where you're going?"

Matt put his coat on. "Right now, I'm going out the door." He kissed his aunt on the cheek. "I will be back later."

"You had better not be drunk. One drunk in the house is bad enough," she said as she swatted at her youngest brother with a dish towel. Enos just laughed and dodged out of the way.

Matt jogged over to Kelly's Pump and caught the next trolley to Frostburg. He would have walked, but he didn't want to work up a sweat. He got off on Main Street and walked into the hotel.

Matt walked to the doorway of the restaurant and looked inside. The headwaiter walked over.

"May I help you, sir?" he asked.

"I'm looking for Samantha Havencroft," Matt said. "She's an attractive blonde about twenty years old."

"We have a few blondes here this evening, but I'm afraid that I can't help you."

He walked Matt over to an empty table and seated him. Since Matt had enjoyed the steak last week so much, he ordered it again. It was a treat because his aunt hadn't cooked beef since he had moved in.

He watched the crowd move around as he waited, scanning each face, hoping to see Samantha among them. He knew it was a

long shot to come here, but he had hoped that she might be a crea-
ture of habit and visit every Wednesday night. He should have realized that Samantha wouldn't do as he expected.

He did see Calista, though, working the room. She looked inviting in a tight-fitting white dress that helped her stand out in the
dark restaurant. When she noticed him, she walked over.

"Hello, Matt, remember me?" she asked.

Matt stood up and kissed her hand. Calista actually blushed a bit.

"I doubt that I would forget you. Would you like to join me?"
He pointed to the empty chair.

"Is that an invitation for later?"

Matt was glad it was dark because now he could feel himself
blushing.

"No, just an invitation for company. I will buy you dinner if
you like. No strings attached."

Calista sat down. "No, thank you, but you could buy me a
drink. That's why I come here."

Matt waved the waiter over, and Calista ordered a scotch. The
waiter knew Calista, so he knew Matt wasn't a revenue agent trying to trap him.

She leaned forward on the table revealing her cleavage. "So, if
there's to be no repeat of last week, that would mean you are either
feeling guilty about last week, you don't have the money, or you
found someone else." She paused. "Well, you obviously have the
money. You're here and bought me a drink. You didn't strike me
as the guilty type the last time we were together."

"You don't know me."

She arched an eyebrow. "Then you are feeling guilty?"

Matt shook his head. "Not over that, at least not in the way
you're talking about."

Calista smiled and nodded. "So you have found someone."

"Maybe."

"We don't need to be exclusive. I certainly won't be. It doesn't
bother me."

"It does bother me. I'm not that kind of person."

Calista patted his hand. "See? I knew that."

Matt chuckled and shook his head.

The waiter brought Calista her scotch, and she held it up to Matt. "A toast to your new possibilities."

Matt tapped her glass with his.

"So do I know this woman?" Calista asked. "Is she the one you were talking to last week?"

"As a matter of fact, she is. I was hoping to see her here to-night."

"She comes in a couple times a week, usually by herself. Sometimes she is escorted, but never by the same man twice. Good luck changing her."

"You don't think I can?"

Calista shrugged. "I hope that you can. I still believe in love."

"Do you?"

Calista touched her hand to her chest. "Not for me, but if others find it, best of luck to them."

"Why not you?"

"Look at what I do, Matt. I'm not the marrying type."

"But you were married."

"That was years ago."

"And what if you met someone ... special? Would you be willing to marry then?"

Calista shook her head. "It won't happen, and I'm fine with that."

She finished her drink and then left to move around the room, searching for eligible men. Matt ate his meal and then walked back to Eckhart Mines alone. He hoped the night air would clear his mind, but he was disappointed that he hadn't seen Samantha. It had been a long shot, but he didn't know what else to do. Maybe it was a sign. If they didn't find each other, then they just weren't mean to be together.

Laura finished the last of the dishes from dinner and dried her hands on a dish towel. She walked over to where Jacob sat on the floor and picked him up.

"It's time for bed, big boy. Give your daddy a kiss," Laura

said. She lowered Jacob to where her husband in a worn green armchair so that the boy could kiss and hug his father goodnight.

Then she carried him into the other room in the small house and put him in the trundle bed next to her and Peter's bed. She sat beside his bed for a while, making sure that he calmed down and actually went to sleep. When he finally stopped wiggling around, she crept out of the room to read a little bit before she started to get things ready for tomorrow.

With a sigh, she sat down in her rocking chair across from Peter.

"Why didn't you tell me about Matt?" Peter asked.

"I introduced the two of you," Laura said. "What else did I need to tell you about him?"

"That he is an old boyfriend of yours."

"Because he is an *old* boyfriend of mine from five years ago. Last week was the first time that I've seen him since that time."

"I heard the two you almost got married."

"I wouldn't say almost," Laura said.

"Did you talk about it?"

"Yes, but we weren't even eighteen at the time. We talked about a lot of things that didn't happen. He left town to join the Marines."

"And now he's back," Pete said.

"And now I'm married," Laura said quickly.

Pete closed the newspaper that he was reading and stood up. Without a word, he walked into the bedroom.

Laura was tempted to follow him, but she knew that they would probably get into an argument if she did and she didn't want to wake Jacob.

Now, who would be telling Peter stories about her and Matt? All that had happened so long ago. They were both so different now than they had been back then. There was nothing romantic between them. Matt was just an old friend.

Why did Pete have to be jealous?

Chapter 20

February 25, 1922

Samantha stepped off the trolley at the Kelly's Pump stop and looked around Eckhart Mines. Despite it being so close to Frostburg, she had never visited here before. She had only driven through it on her way to Cumberland. She had thought that it would be easy to find Matt because it was a small town. However, seeing all of the houses on the hillside, she realized that although it was smaller than Frostburg, it still had a lot of homes.

Matt said he lived in a boarding house. That would be one of the bigger homes. It narrowed things down somewhat, but it was still a daunting task.

She started walking up the street. She saw a man coming from the other direction and asked him if he knew Matt Ansaro. He shook his head and kept walking. The next man she met said, "I know an Enos Ansaro."

There couldn't be that many Ansaros in Eckhart Mines. "Do you know where he lives? He may know Matt."

"Sorry, Missy, I've only ever seen him at the mine or in the woods enjoying a pint of moonshine with friends."

Samantha sighed and kept walking. She decided that she would ask a woman this time. A woman would be more helpful anyway. She saw a young woman taking advantage of the warm day and hanging laundry on a clothesline.

Samantha walked up the fence and called, "Excuse me."

The woman finished hanging up a shirt and walked over to the fence.

"I'm trying to find where Matt Ansaro lives. Can you help me?" Samantha asked.

The woman smiled. It was a sweet smile that lit up her whole face and showed how beautiful she was.

"Yes, I know where he lives. Are you a friend of his?" the woman asked.

"I guess you can say that. We've only met a few times, so I guess we're more like friendly acquaintances."

The woman extended her hand. "I'm Laura Spiker. I'm an old friend of Matt's."

Samantha shook Laura's hand. "I'm Samantha Havencroft."

"Oh, he mentioned you when we were talking one day."

Samantha smiled. She wondered if it made her look as attractive as Laura. "Really?"

"He said that you yelled at him the first time you met."

Samantha's smile disappeared. "I don't think that he'll ever let me forget that. Men!"

Laura laughed. "Don't worry. He wasn't angry about it or anything like that. In fact, I think it made him curious about you."

"He better be careful then, or he'll get a lot more curious."

Laura laughed again.

"What do you think of Matt?" Laura asked.

"He's very nice and different from most men that I've met," Samantha admitted.

"Is that all?"

What did Laura expect her to say? Samantha barely knew Matt.

"I don't want to get pinned down to one person," Samantha said.

"But you came down from Frostburg to see him. So I would guess you think he's more than nice."

Samantha didn't answer, but she could feel herself blushing.

"Matt is more than nice, Samantha, and he deserves someone

special, but a miner's wife is not an easy life," Laura told her.

Samantha held up her hand. "Who said anything about marriage? I don't want to get married. Not to Matt, not to anyone."

Laura stepped back. "Sorry, I didn't mean to offend you. Matt lives in his aunt's boarding house. It's two streets past the general store. Turn left, and it's the third house on the left."

"Thank you."

"The miners work a half day on Saturday," Laura said. "He should be home by now. My husband is."

Samantha said goodbye and headed up the street. Now she was nervous about seeing Matt. Did he really think that she would marry him? They had only met three times. She was tempted to turn around and head home, but perhaps she and Matt needed to clear the air about marriage before things went any further.

As she walked through town, Samantha was amazed at how small some of the houses were. They were nicely kept but so small that they weren't much larger than cabins. At least the house where Matt lived was a reasonable size, but since it was a boarding house, it must have a lot more people living in it.

She walked up onto the porch and knocked on the door. A middle-aged woman answered the door. Samantha could see similarities to Matt in her face and guessed that she must be Matt's aunt.

"Hello, I'm looking for Matt Ansaro," Samantha said.

"Come in," Antonietta said. "I'm his aunt."

Samantha stepped into the room. It was clean with plain furniture. Pictures clipped from magazines hung on one wall, and a photograph that looked like a wedding photo of Antonietta hung on the opposite wall.

"You're not from Eckhart, are you?" Antonietta asked as she examined Samantha in her dark skirt and light-blue sweater top that reached her hips.

"No, ma'am, I live in Frostburg."

"And you know Matt?"

"We've met a couple times. Why do people seem surprised at that?"

"Well, Matt has been back in town less than two weeks for one

thing, and you've already met a couple of times. Also, and I mean
no offense, but you don't look like you associate with too many
miners."

"I don't. In fact, I think Matt may be the only one I've ever
met, and he doesn't look or act like I imagined a miner would."

"Then you should see him when he comes home from the mine
all covered in coal dust and mud." Antonietta paused, and then
asked, "Did you meet him Wednesday night?"

Samantha shook her head. "No, I was doing some work at
home."

Antonietta nodded. "That may be why he looked so sad when
he came home."

"What do you mean?"

"Oh, he dressed up nicely after work on Thursday and even
shaved. He went into Frostburg, but he didn't stay out too late.
And he wasn't smiling when he came home."

"I didn't know."

"No reason you should. Let me see your hands, young lady."
Samantha obediently held her hands out. Antonietta took them in
hers. "Feel the difference? You've got soft hands, dear. You aren't
used to working."

"I work very hard. I have my studies and my campaigning."

"Do you now?" Antonietta arched an eyebrow. "Let me go get
Matt."

Antonietta walked down the hallway to Matt's door and
knocked on it.

"Yes?" he said from inside.

She heard him moving around as if he was hurriedly putting
something away.

"There's a young woman here to see you," Antonietta said.

The door cracked open, and she saw Matt's face.

"Young woman?"

"Samantha Havencroft."

Matt smiled. "Oh!"

"I don't like her," Antonietta whispered.

"Why not?"

"She's probably never worked a day in her life. She can't understand what your life is like. Her hands are soft."

Matt sighed. "She is used to working, Aunt, just not physical labor. Not everyone works that way."

"Well, if she's going to be a miner's wife, she had better learn to work that way."

"Who said anything about her being a miner's wife?"

Antonietta snorted. "Go out and meet her."

Matt walked out to the living room and saw Samantha in her short dress that quickly identified her as someone not from Eckhart Mines.

"Matt," she said with some relief.

"Aunt," Matt said. "You didn't even offer her a place to sit?" Matt motioned to the couch. "Let's sit down." Samantha took a seat on one end of the sofa and Matt sat on the other. "Not that I'm not happy to see you, but how did you find me?"

Samantha smirked. "Apparently, I'm more resourceful than you. You said you lived in a boarding house with your family. I just asked around. What did you try?"

"What do you mean?"

"Your aunt said that you went to Frostburg looking for me Wednesday, but you didn't find me."

Matt glanced at his aunt. She lifted her chin a bit as if daring him to say something to her. Then she sat down in the rocking chair.

"I went to the …" He glanced at his aunt again and decided he didn't want to mention the speakeasy. "…place where we met the first night I was in town. I didn't see you, but I asked about you. I guess no one knew your name."

"That's surprising."

"Why's that? Do you go there often?"

"Yes, but that's not why they should know my name. Not my first name, maybe, but my last name is well known in town. My father is the president of the college."

Antonietta stopped rocking in the chair.

"What?" Matt asked.

"You didn't know that?" Samantha asked.

"Why should I have? The day we met was my first day back here in five years."

Samantha laughed. "I thought it was odd that you didn't mention anything about the college other than to ask about my classes."

"I thought you were a student."

Samantha nodded. "I am, but that doesn't mean I can't be the daughter of the president, too. I just don't bring it up."

"No, I guess you wouldn't." He glanced at his aunt and then took Samantha's hand. "Let's take a walk."

They stood up. Matt took his clean coat off the coat rack by the front door.

This wasn't going to work out. Even if he weren't a coal miner, she would have been out of his class. He had learned his lesson with Priscilla. He should find someone in his own social class, but Samantha was the woman he was interested in getting to know better.

"Can you show me the coal mine? I have always been curious as to what one looks like," Samantha said.

They stepped out onto the front porch and started walking down the street.

"You should have told me your father was the president of the college," Matt said.

"I just did."

"I mean before now."

"Why?"

"Why? Because a woman like you doesn't belong here with a man like me," Matt said, surprised that she didn't understand.

"It doesn't matter to me that you're a coal miner, Matt."

Matt nodded. "With most women, I would doubt that, but not you. I truly believe that it doesn't matter, but it will matter with your father."

"I doubt that you'll be surprised if I tell you that my father and I don't see eye to eye on most things." Samantha laid a hand on his arm. "Matt, it doesn't change anything. My father doesn't really approve of the life I lead anyway. This will just make him think that he's right. I don't care because I'm happy."

"Really?"

"You don't believe me?"

"I believe that you are happy right now, and as much as I would love for that to continue, I'm not sure what you realize getting involved with me would mean. Look at my life. I'm a coal miner. I spend my days in the dark. I am also filthy most of the time."

"You sound like you're trying to scare me off."

"I don't know what I'm trying to do. I don't quite understand things now. When I thought you were just a student or a shopkeeper's daughter, that was something I could see working. Now I'm afraid that I might pull you into something you will regret, and I wouldn't want to do that."

"Matt, we're not talking about marriage. We're just dating. The purpose of it is to find out if things between us are worth a lifetime commitment. If they aren't, then we'll go our separate ways."

"You make it sound easy."

"For me, it has been, but I see your point. You're thinking about what happened with Priscilla, right?" Matt nodded. "Well, I don't know what will happen between us, but I can promise you that if it ever gets to the point where you propose, and I accept, I won't be backing out of it. Other than that, we'll have to see how things go. Can you accept that?"

Matt considered it. What she said was reasonable, which he should have expected from her, but it still scared him. He didn't want to feel like he had felt when Priscilla left him.

He nodded. "Let's see what happens."

They stopped walking at the mouth of the mine. Since it was Saturday afternoon, the area was deserted. Samantha stared into the dark hole.

"Can we go in?"

Matt shook his head. "It's considered bad luck for a woman to go into the mine. Besides, your dress would be ruined in minutes, and your shoes aren't made for walking along an uneven mine floor."

"Are you telling me that mine is sexist?"

"I'm just telling you what miners believe, and if they see a woman in a mine, they will expect something bad to happen, and it often does, not because the woman was in the mine, but because that's what they expect."

Samantha looked left and right. "There's no one around right now, though."

"Saturday is a half work day. Everyone has gone home."

"Good."

Samantha took off running into the mine. She went in about thirty feet or so and then turned around and ran back out.

"Are you crazy?" Matt nearly yelled.

"No, and nothing bad happened either," she told him.

"Look at your dress." The edges were coated in black coal dust. It wasn't ruined, but it would take some scrubbing to get clean. "I hope that no one saw you."

Samantha laughed. "Everything will be fine. You'll see. We have to fight stereotypes." She stared down the dark shaft. "How do you see? I don't see any lights, and it was getting dark even the little way that I went in."

"We have lights on our helmets. We also have some battery powered lights in the main work areas, but it is pitch black without them. You get a hundred feet or so in there, and you will see the light from the mine opening, but it won't reach you."

"And you're in there all day?" Matt nodded. "I don't think I could stand it. Why do you do it?"

Matt hesitated. She deserved to know the truth about him, but this was not the place to do it. It was one of those things that would have to wait until he knew where their relationship was actually heading.

"My family are all miners. It's what I grew up seeing them do so it's what I figured grown men did for work."

"But you went into the military."

"And that was worse than mining. I mean, I know now that we're at peace, military life wouldn't be like it was, but two years at war made me come to expect certain things even if they aren't totally correct."

"So you are going to stay a miner for the rest of your life?"

Matt shuddered. "I hope not. It's what I need to be doing right now, but someday, I see myself going back to Baltimore or at least Cumberland."

"Really?"

"You sound surprised. When you finish school here, where will you go?"

Samantha shrugged. It was an indecisive gesture that Matt hadn't seen her do before, mainly because he had never seen her hesitant. "I don't know what I'll do. I would like to be a college professor, but I will probably only be hired as a school teacher."

"When has something like that ever stopped you from going after what you want?"

Samantha laughed. "You're right. I'm going to be a professor when I graduate."

They continued to walk around Eckhart; not holding hands but walking shoulder to shoulder and talking. Matt pointed out the places where he had played as a kid, although he didn't go far into the woods because Samantha wasn't dressed for hiking.

He pointed out the house where he had lived with his parents. Laura was outside taking down the dry laundry, folding the clothing, and laying in it a wicker basket.

"That's the woman who finally told me where you lived," Samantha said. "She said she was a friend of yours."

"From before I moved away." Matt waved to Laura, and she walked over the fence.

"I see that you found, Matt," Laura said.

"He's been walking me around the town," Samantha said.

"Get him to take you for ice cream," Laura said. Eckhart Mines had an ice cream parlor that was popular in the summer.

"It's a little cold for that still."

Laura shrugged. "Maybe, but it is my favorite treat. I don't care what time of year it is. Did Matt tell you there's a town dance at the Literary and Sporting Club Hall next week?"

Samantha swatted Matt's arm. "No, he did not, and Matt

knows that I love to dance."

"And you know that I don't," Matt said.

"He thinks he looks like a grasshopper jumping back and forth," Laura said, laughing.

"Can we go, Matt?" Matt cast a frown at Laura. "You don't have to dance. We'll go, and I'll dance with everyone else."

"Then why do you need me there?"

"Are you ashamed to be seen with me?" Samantha asked.

"No, it's not that, but if you're not even going to dance with me..." Matt started to say.

"Was that an invitation?"

"It sounded like one," Laura said.

"Oh, yes, Matt, I'd love to dance with you. It will be fun," Samantha told him.

Matt looked bewildered. He wasn't sure what had happened, but apparently, he had agreed to take Samantha to the dance and dance with her. Only he couldn't remember actually saying that.

He got Samantha away from Laura as quickly as he could, and he walked her out to Kelly's Pump to wait for the next trolley.

"Don't look so glum, Matt. The dance will be nice," Samantha said.

"I know it will be because you will be there. It will probably remind me of you at Failinger's."

"Except no booze."

"I wouldn't be so sure," Samantha told her.

The trolley came and stopped near them. Samantha looked at him, then gave him a quick kiss and jumped aboard.

Chapter 21

February 28, 1922

Antonietta baked lasagna on Tuesday evening. It was Matt's favorite dish when his aunt cooked it. She knew just how to season it so that he tended to overeat. When he finished the lasagna and handmade rolls, he started back to his room, but Samuel stopped him.

"Grab your coat, Matt," he said.

"Why?"

"We need to go into Frostburg tonight. An organizer is going to make a pitch for us to join the union."

That was not something Matt really wanted to hear. He needed to keep his family away from the union not encourage them to join.

"I didn't know you were interested in being union," Matt said.

"Consolidation Coal has cut our rates, and there's a lot of safety issues with the mine that are going to get someone killed if we aren't careful. I want to hear what the UMW can do about it."

Matt took his clean coat off the hook and followed Samuel and Enos out of the house.

"Are we the only ones going?" Matt asked.

"Others will come later," Enos said. "We need to spread out when we leave town, or the wrong person will notice too many people heading into Frostburg on a weeknight."

The three of them hiked up the road to Frostburg, and Samuel led them to the Junior Order of United American Mechanics Hall. The room was filled with miners, many of whom Matt didn't recognize, so he assumed they were from other coal towns along Georges Creek. It was standing room only, but that meant there were only 150 people or so.

"Not too many people here," Matt said.

"He's been holding meetings for a week," Samuel said.

A few additional union members wouldn't make much of a difference, but if this organizer was pulling in this many people each night, it meant hundreds of miners were showing an interest in the union. It was bound to get enough members to start making a difference or causing problems in the area.

Matt took a seat between his uncles on a bench. He wished that he could take notes, but that would draw too much suspicion. He would have to try and remember as many names as he could.

Maryland miners were generally happy with their working conditions, but the layoffs and wage reductions since the end of the war had made them nervous. The mine owners seemed just as nervous. They may have won the battle at Blair Mountain, but the sheer number of miners across the country meant that they could be overwhelmed if the miners worked together.

The union organizer was a man named Harvey Thomas. He was dressed in a pinstripe suit, which Matt saw was a mistake. The man looked like a mine owner. He certainly didn't look like a miner or someone who could represent miners. However, his half-hour pitch made some excellent points. Miners would always want to earn more, and the union would have to increase their wages more than their dues would reduce them. He also talked about improving the safety in the mines, despite that some of the measures would undoubtedly bankrupt some of the smaller coal mines. In fact, Matt wondered if these men would support the union if they knew how many miners would wind up losing their jobs because of the cost of the things that union wanted.

When the talk finished, some of the men were quick to sign up to be a member of the United Mine Workers.

Matt looked at Samuel, "What do you think, Uncle?"

Samuel tugged at his beard. "I like what I heard."

"Damn right," Enos echoed.

"Are you going to join then?" Matt asked.

Samuel shook his head. "Not right now. I still want to mull things over a bit. If I join now, it's a risk with no promise that any of the things the union is talking about will happen."

"Well, I'm going to sign up," Enos said.

He stood up and moved to join the line of miners waiting to become union members.

Matt frowned. What should he do now? His own uncle was joining the UMW. Matt was supposed to report him. It was exactly what Matt hadn't wanted to happen.

When Enos returned from signing up to become a member, Matt was surprised to see a bottle in his hand. Enos waved it around.

"A little signing bonus from the UMW," he said as he took a swig. Well, that ensured Enos would be happy with his decision ... at least for now.

"Stick it in your coat, Enos," Samuel said. "It's time to head back.

The Ansaros left the meeting hall and ambled toward Main Street. It was cold out even with their coats on.

"You picked a bad time to come home, I guess, Matt," Samuel said. "There's talk of a national strike. The UMW is eager to gain back the advantage it lost with that massacre in Blair County last year, and the coal companies are feeling cockier than ever. And to top it all off, coal demand is dropping. There's too much production."

"Will Eckhart survive?" Matt asked.

"Survive? Sure. We're on the National Road. We're close to Frostburg and not too far from Cumberland. We'll survive, but will we survive as a coal town? I don't know. We're not Consolidation's biggest operation."

"Maybe that's a good thing."

"For young men like you, and even Enos, it probably is. Me?

I've been a miner for more years than you've been alive. It's all I've ever known. I'm not sure what I would do or what I could do if I weren't a coal miner."

Eckhart Mines wouldn't be the first coal camp to fade away, and it wouldn't be the last. The difference was this was Matt's hometown. He wanted to see it survive.

As they walked by an alley, they heard a sound and paused. Matt tried to stare into the darkness, but the streetlights didn't reach that far.

"Just a rat," Enos said.

They heard the sound again. Matt knew it wasn't a rat. It sounded like a moan.

"Somebody's back there," he said.

They stepped into the alley. "Hello," Samuel called. "Who's there?"

A person had to be careful in Frostburg nowadays. More than one person had been jumped and beaten by thugs.

The moan turned into a sob, and it was high enough that Matt knew it was either a woman or a child. He wished they had brought a lantern with them. He saw movement ahead of him, but couldn't make out what it was in the darkness.

"Help me, please," a woman said.

Matt and Samuel rushed forward. They found a woman sprawled on the ground between an empty crate and a rain barrel.

"What's wrong, ma'am?" Samuel asked. "Are you hurt?"

"He hit me," the woman said. "He didn't have to do that."

Samuel helped her to her feet, but when she kept stumbling, he lifted her up and carried her back to the street.

Matt froze when he saw her. It was Calista, but she had been beaten. Her face was beginning to bruise, and one eye was swollen shut.

"Calista."

Calista's head lolled to the side, and she stared at Matt with her uninjured eye. "Matt?"

"Yes, it's me." He took her hand in his, and she winced. "Who did this to you?"

"Matt, Matt, it was horrible. I didn't do anything wrong. He didn't have to do this."

Matt saw a car coming up the street. He stepped into the middle of the road and waved the car down. He ran up to the driver's window.

"I've got a hurt woman here," he said. "Can you take us to the doctor?"

"I don't know where any doctor lives, but I can drive you to the hospital," the man said.

Matt turned to face Samuel. "Bring her over here, Samuel."

Matt opened the rear door of the car so that Samuel could slide Calista into the back. She moaned as she settled down onto the seat.

"Do you know her, Matt?" Samuel asked when he backed out of the car.

"Yes, I met her a few weeks ago when I first came to town. I'll go with her to the hospital. You and Enos can go home. I'll get home when I can."

Matt ran around to the other side of the car and climbed into the back with Calista. He lifted her head so that she could rest it on his lap. He rubbed a hand on her cheek. It was cold. How long had she been outside without her coat? She could have frozen to death.

He shrugged out of his coat and draped it across her.

"What happened to her?" the driver asked.

"Not sure. We just found her in that alley. Someone beat her up pretty badly."

"Matt," Calista said.

"I'm here, Calista. We're taking you to the hospital."

"I didn't do anything wrong. He was too rough. He liked hurting me."

"Who?"

"He didn't give me his name. If he had, it would have been fake. They're not all like you," she said, shaking her head.

Matt stroked her hair, trying to soothe her. He needed better light to see how severely she had been beaten.

"What did he look like, Calista?" he asked.

Calista sobbed. "He was mean, Matt, so mean. I wouldn't have gone with him if I had known how mean he was."

"I know." He smoothed her hair back and then hugged her.

"He was big. Taller than you. He wore this big bowler that made him look taller. He was well dressed. I thought he was a gentleman." She grunted as if she was in pain and clutched at his arm. "He was not a gentleman. He had a thick, brown beard and mustache, oh, he had a scar over one eye that split his eyebrow."

The car pulled to a stop, and Matt looked up. They were outside the small two-story Miner's Hospital.

"Thank you, mister," Matt said to the driver.

"I've got a wife and daughter," he said. "I wouldn't want to see this happen to them."

Matt got out of the car and went around to the other side to help Calista out. He scooped her up in his arms. She draped her hands around his neck and laid her head against his shoulder.

He walked into the hospital holding her. When the nurse on duty saw them, she rushed over with a wheelchair.

"What happened?"

"She was attacked and left in an alley," Matt said.

He set her gently into the wheelchair. The nurse got behind her and started pushing her down the hallway. Matt moved to follow.

"You'll need to wait here, sir. The doctor will examine her and treat her."

Matt started pacing back and forth in the lobby. What kind of person would do this to a woman? But, of course, he knew. He had seen this happen to women like Calista before. For some men, passion was violent. Calista was lucky. She could have been killed.

The nurse came back a few minutes later.

"How is she?" Matt asked.

"Are you her husband?" Matt shook his head. "Just an acquaintance."

"Well then, she'll have to tell you. It's not for me to say."

"But she will be all right?"

The nurse nodded. "Certainly. There was nothing life-threatening. She will just need a couple days here and a lot of rest."

"Good. Good. Listen, give her whatever she needs and send all of the bills to Matt Ansaro. That's me. I'm staying at the Starner Boarding House in Eckhart Mines."

The nurse nodded and wrote the information down. Since she wouldn't let Matt see Calista, he headed back toward Eckhart. He wished that someone would jump him. He was brewing for a fight. Really, he only wanted to fight one person, though.

He would have to watch for the man with the bisected eyebrow.

His aunt was waiting for him when he got home.

"Your uncles said that you found a woman who had been attacked in town." Matt nodded. "Will she be all right?"

"The doctor said, 'yes,' but I didn't get to see her."

"And you know her?"

"We've met a couple times. Her name is ... Jenny."

"Did she tell you who did this to her?"

"She didn't know his name."

Antonietta shook her head. "What is this area becoming when an innocent woman gets attacked on the street?"

Matt wasn't about to tell her that while Jenny might be innocent, Calista was far from it. He kissed his aunt on the cheek and headed back to his room.

"Matt, are you going to join the union?"

He stopped and turned around. "I don't know. It sounds good, but it hasn't done a lot for the miners yet. It's always the things they don't tell you about that are the things that help you make your decision."

"Such as?"

Matt shrugged. "That's the problem. You don't know until you find yourself in a situation where the union won't or can't help you."

"I think you should join."

"Really? Why?"

"One of the things the union fights for is safer mines. If the mines here had been safe, Michael might still be alive."

Matt nodded. "I understand that, but they can fight for it all they want. The more important thing to consider is can they get it?"

165

He went into his room and started to undress. Then he stopped and sat down in the chair in his room and wrote down the names of the miners he knew from the meeting. He left his uncles' names off the list. When he had written down eight names, he read over the list and crossed off three of the names. Those men had been at the meeting, but they hadn't joined the union. He should add Enos's name to the list since he had joined, but Matt just couldn't bring himself to do it.

He pulled out another sheet of paper and wrote out a report about where the union meeting was held, how many attended, how many appeared to join the union, and what the organizer said. Then he added the names of the men he knew had joined the union.

He folded the letter and sealed it in an envelope. He would mail it after work tomorrow.

Chapter 22

March 1, 1922

Joseph walked from the office into the Eckhart Store to pour himself a cup of coffee. Portnoy must have been somewhere off in the back because the store was empty. Joseph stepped out onto the front porch to sip his hot coffee. The morning was sunny, and it was actually warm out. He wanted to enjoy the pleasant weather while he could. It was still early enough in the year that things could turn very cold again quickly.

Frostburg, although not named for the cold, had seen snow in June. Light snow, granted, but snow nonetheless.

Joseph saw the trolley making its way down the National Road on its way to Cumberland. A few people, mostly miners' wives, moved around outside. The miners were underground until this evening.

He looked down the street and saw Laura playing with her son in their front yard. He couldn't remember the boy's name. She chased him around, and he screamed with delight. After a few moments of running hunched over, she stopped. She put her hands on her hips and leaned back, arching her back, which pushed her breasts out. Joseph froze and forgot to swallow his coffee. Then Laura relaxed. She ruffled her son's hair and looked over at Joseph. She waved to him. Had she known he was watching her?

Joseph had known Laura since they were ten years old. He had actually known her before Matteo had. She was just as beautiful now as she had been then, although now she had a woman's figure, which she had just shown off.

What Joseph remembered the most about Laura, though, was that she had been kind to him when the other miners' children had avoided him because his father had been the superintendent. She had talked with him, walked with him, and played with him. She didn't pick on him because he was smaller than the others. They had been friends.

Then she had met Matteo.

Joseph had thought that he had planned for every eventuality, but now Matteo had returned. Joseph had tried firing Matteo, but that hadn't worked. Joseph had a rival. He couldn't afford to dawdle any longer. He needed to take actions to put himself in the right position when the opportunity arose, and it would. He had no doubt about that. If there was one thing that he knew how to do, it was how to get what he wanted.

He carried his coffee back into his office and sat down at his desk. He pulled folders from the pile on his desk and began perusing the reports they contained. He looked through the production numbers for the miners. Then he looked over the mine condition reports and the reports that showed where the coal veins showed promise. He scribbled notes on a sheet of paper that he referred to occasionally. It took an hour before he thought he had an answer to two problems.

He put the reports away and then walked down to the mine. He found Tom Gianconne in the equipment shed. He was tallying the weights from the latest cars that had come out of the mine.

"Tom, I've got some changes I want you to make tomorrow," Joseph said.

Tom stopped what he was doing and walked over to Joseph. "Yes, sir, Mr. McCord, what do you need me to do?"

"I want you to move Peter Spiker and Matteo Ansaro from where they are working now to Tunnel No. 7. Matteo is ready to take on a partner, and Peter also needs one, so let's get them working that tunnel. It has shown some promise."

"But it also needs a lot of shoring up, and it's a very wet area," Tom said.

It surprised Joseph that his foreman knew that without referring to a report. Then again, Tom had written the report.

Joseph nodded. "I know. I have read your reports, which were thorough, but given the cutbacks that headquarters has forced upon us, we'll have to wait for those two to pay off the tunnel's promise before we commit resources to it."

Tom hesitated. "What if something happens to them before then?"

That was why he was having Tom deliver the news to Matteo and Peter. Joseph didn't want to be associated with what would be an unpopular decision.

"Your reports didn't say that the danger was imminent. Did you sugarcoat the report?" Joseph asked.

"No, sir," Tom said quickly.

"Then the tunnel will be safe enough until we can decide on whether the effort is worth it. Start them tomorrow."

Tom stared at the ground. "Yes, sir."

Joseph clapped Tom on the shoulder. "Good man. I knew I could depend on you."

Joseph headed back to the office smiling. He didn't see how he could lose now. One way or another, his problems would be taken care of.

Matt trudged out of the mine with Enos and Samuel at the end of the day. It seemed wrong to call it a day since he saw so little of the sun.

Enos managed to stay sober for work, but Matt had seen him sipping from a flask on the man-trip out of the mine.

When Enos had seen him watching he said, "It's to wash the coal dust out of my throat."

Matt hadn't said anything. His uncle drank a lot, but he wasn't sure if he would call Enos an alcoholic or not. Matt could understand wanting to forget things. Different people had different ways of accomplishing that. Matt liked fighting. During a fight, he only thought of avoiding being hit and how to land his next punch. Was drinking any better than fighting as a way to cope with life?

Matt climbed out of the coal car and headed to the equipment shed to hang up his medallion so that everyone would know he was out of the mine.

"Matt, tomorrow, I'm going to have you working in Tunnel No. 7," Tom Gianconne said.

Samuel stepped up beside Matt. "Wait a minute, Tom, that section of the mine is in poor shape," he said.

"Yeah," Enos said. "Why are we being pulled from an area where there's still plenty of coal left to get?"

Tom shook his head. "You and your brother are staying in Tunnel No. 5. I'm just moving Matt."

"Well, you can't let him work in the tunnel by himself."

"He won't be," Tom said. "Peter Spiker is in a three-man group. I'm moving him off of it to work with Matt."

"I don't like it, Tom," Samuel said. "It's reckless to put them in that tunnel. You know that. Are you going to shore it up and pump it out?"

Tom sighed. "Look, it is not my decision. Matt and Peter are working that tunnel tomorrow. If it starts to show promise, we will make the necessary improvements to continue working it."

Samuel jabbed a finger in Tom's face. "This is wrong, and you know it."

"It's not my decision to make. Take it up with Mr. McCord if you want."

Tom turned and walked away.

Matt had to admit that he felt an uneasiness about this decision, too. It wasn't that he knew that section of mine because he didn't, but something felt wrong. It might have something to do with working with Laura's husband, but that didn't seem like an important enough reason to worry.

It wasn't like he had much of a choice. If he wanted to work, it was going to have to be in Tunnel No. 7.

He listened to Samuel complain about the decision all the way home. His uncle definitely thought that it was the wrong choice.

Matt washed up at the house. He didn't take a full bath. He just used a rag and Lava soap to clean himself and wash his hair.

He shoved the letter he had written last night into his pocket and headed out to the National Road to catch the last trolley into Frostburg. He got off as close to the post office as he could. It was closed, but there was a slot for outgoing mail. He pushed his letter through it and then headed toward the hospital.

Miner's Hospital had been built with the help of the State of Maryland in 1912. The legislature had contributed $25,000 to the construction with the stipulation that the board of directors include a coal miner and a coal mine operator among the people who made up the board of directors. The inclusion of coal mining representatives led to the hospital's name.

Calista was conscious when Matt walked up to her bed, but her bruises had darkened to black and purple. Not only was her left eye swollen shut, but the left side of her face was swollen. It gave her a lopsided appearance.

She lay in the women's ward. It was a smaller ward since most of the hospital's patients were miners who had been injured in one of the area's mines. The room had six beds, but only two were filled.

Calista smiled when she saw him. Her skin tone–what wasn't darkened by bruising–looked good. The cold hadn't caused any permanent damage.

"How are you feeling?" Matt asked.

"I hurt all over. When it gets too bad, they give me a painkiller, but that puts me to sleep," she said.

"That's what you need now. Lots of rest."

He pulled a chair over and sat down next to her bed.

"Have you thought any more about what happened to you?" Matt asked.

"That's all I've been thinking about. It gives me nightmares."

"Can you tell me anything else about who did this to you?" Calista shook her head slowly. It looked like it might hurt her. "Where did it happen?"

"I met him in the speakeasy in the basement of the Cloud Hotel. He seemed nice enough and was dressed like a shopkeeper. I thought it would be a good night, but he didn't just want to have sex with me. He wanted to hurt me while he was doing it."

"I'm sorry."

"Don't pity me, Matt," she said sharply. "I've been hurt before, but usually it's accidental. Some men talk like they want to hurt you, but that's as far as it goes. Some men will slap you because it helps them somehow. I don't like it, but I've never been afraid before. I was this time. I felt like he wanted to hurt me more than have sex with me."

Matt had known men like the ones Calista had mentioned. Usually, they were men whom the brutality of war had unleashed something in. Some even bragged of their cruelty as if it marked them as more manly.

"Is there anyone I should let know that you're in the hospital? Parents? Children? Friends?" Matt asked.

Calista frowned. "No. My parents live in Pittsburgh. I don't have any children, and I wouldn't want any of my friends to know I'm here."

"How did you wind up in Frostburg if your parents live in Pittsburgh?"

"My husband was a miner in Pittsburgh, but he decided to try his luck in Maryland because he heard that Maryland mines paid better and were safer. So we moved here before the war, and it was better for a while, but then he went to fight in Europe and never came back."

"I'm sorry."

"Don't be, Matt. I knew what I was doing. I didn't get tricked into this life. I know the risks, and despite what you see before you, I'm usually very good at avoiding them. I'm doing what I needed to do when I couldn't find a job. It's no worse really than some miners' wives have to deal with even when their husbands are alive."

Matt had heard rumors of mining companies providing pleasure women to their miners or forcing women to trade sex for extensions on rent or credit at the company store. The mines weren't the only places he had heard of such things either. Other businesses that dominated a town sometimes abused that power.

"Have you stopped looking for a job?" he asked.

"Yes." She paused. "Don't try and save me, Matt. I make more money doing what I do than I could at a factory or store."

Matt sighed and didn't press the point.

"Well, like I said earlier, you need to rest so you can get better."

She shook her head and then winced from the pain. "I can't. I've got to get out of here."

"You can't go back to work in your condition. You need someone to watch out for you until you're ready to get back on your feet."

"I can't afford to stay here. I don't have any savings. I make enough to live on, but that's it. If I'm not working, I'm not earning."

Matt put his hands on her shoulders and gently pressed her back down on the bed.

"Don't worry about that. Your hospital bills have been taken care of," Matt told her. "You just need to get better. You can leave when the doctors say you can leave and no sooner."

"Am I a charity case for the hospital?"

Matt shook his head. "No, you are a patient, and they'll treat you like a patient. You just need to get better."

She stared hard at him. "You're not telling me something."

Matt grinned, hoping that he was charming enough to keep her from pressing the issue. "There's probably a lot that I'm not telling you, but nothing that will hurt you if you don't know it."

He spoke with Calista for a little while longer. Then he said goodbye and headed into town. He stopped in at the diner where he and Samantha had shared lunch and took a seat near the front window so that he could look out onto the street. He watched the people walk by. It was getting dark out, so it was hard to make out faces. Shadows hid people's faces from him ... and their eyebrows.

Matt had thought that he was looking for Samantha, hoping that she would join him for dinner. Just now, he realized that he was searching for a man with a bisected eyebrow and a bowler hat.

He ate his meal, barely tasting it as he watched the street. He knew it was a long shot, but he was still angry that he didn't see the man who had beaten Calista.

He paid his bill and walked back toward Eckhart.

As he walked, he found himself thinking about his uncles. He wondered if he had made the right decision returning to Eckhart Mines. Enos had joined the union, and Antonietta supported his decision. How long would it be before Samuel joined? He naturally favored the protections that the UMW promised. When that happened, Matt would be in an awkward position. As soon as he did his job and wrote their names in a report, his bosses would know that Matt lied to them.

He watched a trio of college boys walking toward him on the sidewalk. They were walking shoulder to shoulder, forcing people to stand next to the buildings or walk in the street as they passed. Matt walked down the middle of the sidewalk.

Funny, how he considered them boys. They were only a couple years younger than him if that. They hadn't gone to war, though. They hadn't grown up in coal mines. They lived in a different world than Matt, one that caused them to seem younger than him although they were the same age.

The boys laughed and were bragging about something. They were drinking out in the open. They weren't drunk, but it certainly wasn't smart to flaunt Prohibition so openly. They would force the police, who could overlook private offenses, to take action against a public one.

Matt pushed between them, refusing to step around them.

"Hey, watch where you're going," one of the boys said.

"Look at this guy's neck," another one of the boys said. This young man was as tall as Matt but heavier built. "It looks like someone rubbed a cheese grater over it."

Matt stopped walking and turned to look at them. Usually, he would walk away. He had learned to ignore comments about his scar. He wasn't in the mood to be forgiving tonight, though.

"Take a look, if you want, but it will be the last bit of fun you have this evening," Matt said.

174

He stared at the boy in the center. He would be the leader of the group, and he was the one who had made the comment about Matt's scar. He was also the one to step towards Matt.

"You're right, Roger, it does look like someone ran a grater across this guy's neck, but you can't tell the difference between it and his face."

Matt brought his knee up into the youth's crotch. With a gurgling yell, the boy gulped and dropped to his knees. The boy named Roger swung at Matt. He ducked, and the boy's punch carried his body around. Matt gave him a shove, and he fell over the boy on the ground. The third boy punched at Matt, but Matt moved so that he took the blow on his shoulder and not his face. It was a solid punch that forced him back a step.

Roger scrambled to get back on his feet. The third boy swung again. Matt blocked the punch and jabbed at the boy's nose. It didn't break, but Matt bloodied him. Then he kicked Roger to keep him down on the ground.

Matt stepped back and spread his legs apart. Then he raised his fists.

"Now I'm ready to ready to fight," he said.

The boys stared at him. Roger and the first boy got to their feet. They faced Matt, although they didn't look cocky any longer.

"Let's go, boys, before the police get here," Roger said.

The trio looked at each other, and then as if on signal, one of the policemen blew his whistle. The three boys turned and ran off.

Matt looked at the crowd around him. Most of them were laughing and smiling. They started to break up, and Matt just walked away with them. The police wouldn't find anything but some blood on the bricks.

Chapter 23

March 2, 1922

When the coal car stopped, Matt climbed out along with Peter Spiker. The two had barely said half a dozen words to each other on the way to the tunnel. It wasn't too unusual. The encroaching darkness felt like a real weight pressing down on a man and filling him with a sense of despair. At least, that is how it felt to Matt and judging by the quiet among the other miners on the coal cars, they felt the same way.

Matt felt his boots sink into the mud when he climbed off the car. He set a hand on a nearby support and gave it a shove. It wobbled.

"We shouldn't be down here," Matt said.

"Don't have much choice," Pete replied.

They started down the short tunnel. Matt's boots made sucking sounds as they pulled free from the mud with each step. They had to bear walk because of the low ceiling.

Pete stopped and leaned in close to the tunnel wall, so the light from his headlamp concentrated in a small circle. "There's coal here."

"But there's too much water. This tunnel should be drained if they want to work it properly."

With electricity now in the coal mines, electric pumps kept the water out of mines. Consolidation Coal also built the Hoffman

Drainage Tunnel in 1903 not far from Eckhart. Its design allowed the coal mines in the area to drain naturally. Although it cost $300,000, it saved even more on maintenance and equipment.

Matt and Peter reached the end of the tunnel and settled down to start their work. They fell into a silence that was only broken by their picks striking the wall. They worked the morning through, and when they stopped for lunch, they had to sit on the rails because they were the closest thing to a dry place to rest.

"So how long have you and Laura been married?" Matt asked, trying to start a conversation. He didn't feel like spending the day not only in darkness but silence, too.

"We got married in 1918."

"You weren't afraid of being drafted and having to leave her?"

"Once I met Laura, I knew that I wanted to marry her. I didn't want to wait on maybe being drafted," Pete said.

Matt couldn't argue with that. "She is a great woman, and your son is a cute tyke. I wish that I could say that I knew right away that I wanted to marry someone. Even when I finally asked someone to marry me, it wasn't immediate."

Pete stopped eating, suddenly interested. "So you're married?"

"No."

"But you said..."

"She threw me over for a rich guy shortly before our wedding."

"Sorry about that."

Matt shrugged, not that Pete could see it in the dim light. "It hurt. It still hurts sometimes. I made a bad decision. You don't have to worry about that. You chose well. Laura won't treat you like Priscilla did me."

"Then why didn't you marry her? Laura, I mean."

"Because back then I kinda treated her like Priscilla treated me."

"I wish I could say that I'm sorry."

"You shouldn't." Matt paused. "I will tell you this, though. If you hurt her, I will make you sorry."

Things went better after lunch. Once breached, the barrier between the two men began to crumble. Matt told Pete about Baltimore, and Pete told him stories about growing up in Vindex in Garrett County.

The only time they stopped talking is when they were concentrating on setting charges. Neither one wanted to make a mistake with that, especially in a tunnel that didn't seem particularly safe. They started hammering on the ends of the augers to drill into the face. They kept turning the crooked handle around and around to dig into the mountain. When the holes were five to six feet deep, they began turning the handles in the opposite direction to back them out of the hole. Pete ran fuses into the holes.

"Set," Pete said.

Matt nodded.

Pete took out his matches and lit one. He laid it against the fuse.

"Let's go," Pete said.

They hurried away, not running but moving at a quick pace. They wanted to be far enough away in case the explosion sprayed debris or brought the roof down.

Pete tripped and went sprawling.

"My foot got stuck in the mud," he said.

Matt grabbed him under the arm and pulled him to his feet.

"We're lucky the rest of you didn't get stuck," Matt said.

They hurried away as the powder exploded with a dull, "Whumpf!"

The face cracked and a few pieces fell loose. They would have to dig out the loose coal and dump it in the coal car.

"We shouldn't be down here yet, now with this mud," Matt said. "If you had gotten stuck closer to the face, you might have been hurt."

"It's the job."

"We aren't paid to die," Matt said. "We're paid to mine coal."

Antonietta opened the door to Matt's room and carried in her wicker laundry basket. She set it on the bed and then turned to open the top drawer of Matt's bureau. She pulled the shirts off the top of the pile of folded clothes in the basket and laid them in the basket.

While laundry came with the price of rent, she only put Matt's and Enos's laundry away after it was dried and folded. They were family. Samuel's wife put his clothes away. With her other boarders, Antonietta laid the clean laundry on their beds.

She searched the drawer for the pistol, but Matt must have moved it, knowing she would be putting his laundry away. Hopefully, he wasn't carrying it with him. That would be asking for trouble, even in a rough town like Frostburg.

She shut the drawers and turned around to get the laundry basket off the bed. She saw a wadded up piece of paper next to the wastebasket. She bent down to pick it up and toss it in the basket. Matt was as sloppy as a teenage boy.

She unwadded the paper just to make sure that it wasn't something important. She read the list of half a dozen names. Most of them she recognized as miners in town. It didn't seem vital, so she wadded up the paper again and tossed it in the basket. She grabbed the laundry basket and headed across the hall to her room.

When Peter walked into his house after work, Laura frowned at him. She still wasn't happy about his jealousy about Matt. It was nice to know that Pete loved her, but he should know by now that she was faithful to him.

"You're dirtier than usual," she said.

"I'm working in a wet tunnel now with Matt," Pete said.

"So did you two get in a fight or something?"

Pete shook his head. "No, we actually had a pleasant day or at least as pleasant as things can be in a coal mine."

"So then why are you so dirty?"

"We were trying to get away from a blast, and my foot caught in the mud. I fell, and Matt helped me get away," Pete told her.

Laura laughed. "Well, thank heavens. Now, strip down, so you don't track mud and dirt over the rug."

Pete started to unbutton his shirt.

"Do you know Matt has been inside a real castle?" Pete asked.

"Was that during the war?"

Pete nodded. "Yes, he said it was beautiful and far bigger than even the Queen City Station. It was filled with furniture and paintings that are hundreds of years old."

Laura blinked and drew back. "I can't imagine that. We'll be lucky to make our furniture last twenty years."

"Me either."

Pete finished pulling off his shirt and tossed it in the clothes basket. Then he undid his belt and started pulling off his pants.

"So why are you so chummy with him now?" Laura asked. "I thought you were jealous of him."

She could see her husband blushing through the layer of dirt on his face.

"I was, but I realized that he is ... not jealous ... but he wants what we have. He wants a wife and children."

"He's young. He can still have that."

"Sure, but he doesn't have it now."

"So you won't get mad if you see me talking to him?" Laura asked.

"Maybe. I don't know. If I do, I'll get over it. I do know he regrets leaving things the way he did with you."

Laura shrugged. "I was upset when he left but not broken hearted. Honestly, I was still a bit mad at him. Then I met you a few months later, and I wasn't even upset."

"Awww..." He leaned forward to try and hug his wife, but Laura jumped back.

"Don't you dare! Not until you wash up!" Laura shouted.

"If you loved me, you would."

"You used that excuse to get me to kiss you the first time."

Peter grinned. "It worked then."

He went to the sink in the kitchen. Laura had already filled it with warm water. He scrubbed himself as clean as he could. By the time he was cleaned and dressed, Laura had dinner of vegetable soup and fresh bread on the table.

Matt nearly turned around and went back into Frostburg when he saw Samantha's father's house. He suddenly had flashbacks to meeting Priscilla's parents. It hadn't gone well. This house must have been four times the size of his family's boarding house. He stood at the front gate staring at it and wondering why two people would need such a large house.

Matt had considered telephoning Samantha, but he wanted to see her in person and spend time with her.

He took a deep breath, let it out, and walked up to the door and rang the bell. An older man with broad shoulders and an erect stance answered the door. Matt assumed it was Samantha's father because she hadn't mentioned anything about being so well off that they hired servants.

"I'm here to see Samantha, sir," Matt said.

The man looked him up and down without changing his expression. "May I ask what this is about?"

"I'm not here for any particular reason, sir," Matt said. "She's not expecting me. I thought she might like to go to dinner or simply take a walk this evening." He really just wanted to talk to Samantha for a while because he thought that it might help him think clearer.

"Samantha and I ate dinner earlier."

From upstairs, Samantha called out, "Father, who is at the door?"

"A gen...a young man to see you," Mr. Havencroft said. He stared at Matt's scar. "Are you a veteran?"

"Yes, sir."

Mr. Havencroft nodded. "You were fortunate."

"It depends on how you look at it."

"Some scars cannot be seen," Mr. Havencroft said almost to himself.

"Yes, sir. Are you a veteran?"

"I fought in Cuba. My father sent me. He forced me to go actually. He agreed to pay for my education, but only if I served. He said it was a matter of family pride that our family had fought in every American war since the War of Independence."

"That's a proud lineage to have, sir."

Mr. Havencroft nodded. "Terrifying, though. I sometimes wonder if my father knew what he was sending me into. He never talked about his own experiences in the Civil War."

"It's difficult to speak of such things."

"Impossible, more like it."

Samantha came down the stairs wearing a navy blue dress and heels. "Matt, I didn't know it was you."

"That's fine, I was talking with your father," Matt told her.

She walked up beside her father and stared at him. "Really?"

"Yes, your father and I have something in common."

"What is that?" Samantha asked.

Mr. Havencroft shook his head slightly.

Matt paused for a moment and then said, "Our appreciation of you."

Samantha looked back and forth between the two men, but she didn't say anything.

"Your father said that you had eaten," Matt said. "Perhaps, you would like to take a walk. It is surprisingly warm this evening."

Samantha smiled. "That would be lovely. Let me get some appropriate shoes for walking and a jacket."

She hurried back upstairs, leaving Matt alone with Mr. Havencroft.

"Thank you for not saying anything," the older man said.

"Certainly. Doesn't Samantha know that you're a veteran?"

"No. At first, it was because it had never come up, but if you know her well, you know that if I tell her now, she will pester me with questions."

Matt nodded. "And complain that women don't run the wars."

Mr. Havencroft laughed. "Yes, you do know my daughter."

Samantha came back down the stairs with her coat on. She took Matt by the arm, and they started down the walk as Mr. Havencroft went back into the house.

"My father seems to like you," Samantha said.

"I don't know if I'd say that, but we have an understanding."

"So why did you come by this evening?"

"I wanted to see you, but I also thought I'd ask you if you would like to go to Cumberland Saturday afternoon."

"Really?"

Matt nodded. "Yes, I have an errand that I need to take care of in the city, but I thought we could see a show and eat dinner or whatever you might want to do."

Samantha squeezed his arm tighter. "That would be wonderful, Matt, but can you afford it?"

"Yes, in fact, the errand I need to run is to the bank."

"Why don't you have an account here in town?"

Matt hesitated. He was so tempted to tell her the truth, but instead, he said, "I set up this account when I came from Baltimore and haven't needed to close it."

"What time should I be ready?"

"I can be here by 1:30."

"Then I have a surprise for you. I can get father's car and drive us into Cumberland. That way, we won't have to wait around for the trolley."

"Then maybe we should forget about Cumberland and just drive along the National Road until we can't go any further," Matt suggested.

Samantha sighed. "You joke, but some days I would do just that."

"So would I. Do you ever feel that you don't fit in?"

She laughed. "Have you met me?"

"What do you do to keep from going crazy?"

"Who says I haven't gone a bit crazy? I keep trying to get a world that doesn't care to agree with me," Samantha said.

"Then why do it?"

"Just because something won't happen doesn't mean it's not worth doing. Why do you feel like you don't fit in? You're back with your family."

Matt nodded. "I am back with them, but they look at me like I'm still eighteen years old. They don't know me anymore. They don't know what I've been through and what my life is like."

"Are you afraid they might not like you if they did know?"

Matt looked away. He couldn't bear to face her. "I know they wouldn't."

Samantha put a hand on his cheek and turned his face so that Matt was looking at her. "They're family, Matt. They will forgive you."

Matt shook his head. "I don't have anything to forgive. My life is different from what they think. There are things I have done and things that I need to do that they wouldn't understand."

"Have you told them?"

Matt shook his head. "I can't."

"Then you might be underestimating them."

"No, you don't understand. I literally can't tell them what is happening. That is part of the problem."

Samantha stopped walking and turned to face him. "Can you tell me?"

Matt thought about that. If there was anyone he could tell, it was Samantha. She didn't live in Eckhart, and she had no connection to coal mining. Should he burden her with his secret, though?

"I can't tell anyone at least not right now."

"Don't you trust me?" Samantha asked.

"Yes, very much so, but I just can't tell anyone right now. It's not my choice."

They started walking again and did so in silence. He had come tonight because he wanted to talk to Samantha and he had done the exact opposite.

"Are you mad at me?" he asked.

"I'm trying not to be," Samantha admitted. "I believe that I can trust you, so now I need to prove that."

"Thank you."

"Will you ever tell me?"

"When I can, you will be the first person I talk to."

Chapter 24

March 4, 1922

Samantha drove the Nash down Federal Hill, moving to the side to allow a westbound trolley to pass her at one point. She watched the people in Eckhart Mines pause to stare at her. Cars were still a novelty in the area. People either used the trolley or walked where they needed to go. For long trips, they took a train.

The other thing that was unusual was that people didn't often see a woman driving. Samantha waved to the women she saw, hoping to give them a bit of inspiration that it shouldn't be unusual to see a woman driving a car.

She stopped the car in front of the boarding house. Matt was sitting on a rocking chair on the porch. He stood up and hurried down the stairs to the car.

"This is a beauty," he said.

"Father indulged himself when he was hired as the president of the Normal School and bought this," Samantha told him.

Matt walked all around the car taking in all of the details. All Samantha knew about the car was that it had very little protection from the elements. It had no windows on the side to keep out the rain and cold. This was the first time since last fall that she had even thought about driving it.

"Would you like to drive us to Cumberland?" she asked.

Matt shook his head. "I haven't driven in over a year. Priscilla's family had a car that I drove us around in once or twice, but I usually just took the trolley where I needed to go."

"Well then, get in, and I can drive."

Matt opened the door and slid into the passenger seat. He watched her carefully as she put the car in gear, and they turned around to head back to the National Road. They took in the sights as they drove through LaVale and then the Narrows. They retraced the path Matt had taken when he had first arrived back in Eckhart Mines.

They talked about what they saw, how Cumberland compared to Baltimore, the mountains, and other casual conversation that two people who were getting to know each other share.

As they came into Cumberland on Mechanic Street, Matt directed Samantha up Baltimore Street until he saw the Liberty Trust Bank. He pointed it out to her, and she found a place to park nearby.

"Do you want to come in with me?" Matt asked.

She shook her head. "No, it's a nice day. I'll wait here for you."

"I'll try to be quick."

He got out and hurried into the bank. He walked over to an open window and asked to check the balance in his account. He had made arrangements to have his pay forwarded to this bank by a wire transfer. It appeared correct, and he withdrew fifty dollars from it. Part of the money would pay for his excursion today, but most of it would go toward Calista's hospital stay.

Then he asked to get access to his safe deposit box. He took the box into the same room where he had gone to add his items to it, but this time, he opened it to remove something from it. He looked through the papers and items until he found the picture of Priscilla. He slid it into his jacket pocket and closed the box.

When he climbed back into the car beside Samantha, they continued up Baltimore Street to the Queen City Station. Matt had decided that he was going to take the opportunity with Samantha to do something that he had always wanted to do.

They went inside and were seated at the restaurant. It was a large room that doubled as a ballroom. During special events, the tables in the middle of the room were removed to allow for dancing. About half of the tables were occupied with diners, but Matt couldn't have said whether they were residents or travelers on the Western Maryland Railroad.

The waiter handed them with menus. Matt ordered fried chicken with green beans. Samantha ordered a salad and soup. They had to settle for iced tea to drink because of Prohibition.

Once the waiter left, Matt said, "I want to show you something."

He reached into his pocket and took out the picture. He slid it across the table to Samantha. She looked at it without picking it up.

"This is Priscilla," Matt said.

"Oh!" She picked up the picture and studied it. "She's quite attractive."

Matt nodded. "I was in love with her. I was going to marry her."

"You've told me that. Why is the picture all creased?"

Matt hesitated. "That is part of the reason that I wanted you to see the picture. Even though I was in love with her, and she broke my heart, I couldn't let go of her. Lord knows that I tried. All of those creases are from the times that I wadded up the picture and threw it away."

"And since you still have the picture, you must have pulled it from the trash every time," Samantha said. "You must have loved her a lot not to be able to give up on her after she broke your heart like that."

Matt sighed. "I suppose. Sometimes, I wonder if everything that happened between us wasn't for the best."

"How so?"

"It's just a feeling that I get." Matt shrugged. "I don't know. I did want to show you something, though."

He took the picture from her hand. Then he took a matchbox from his pocket, struck one of the matches on the side, and held it to the edge of the photo.

"What are you doing?" Samantha said sharply.

Matt looked at the burning photo and dropped it into the ashtray on the table.

"I decided that it was finally time to give her up for good, and I wanted you to see it because you're the one who has convinced me that I could move past her," Matt said.

A few people at nearby tables looked at the flame in the ashtray, but it soon died down.

The waiter brought their meals a short time later, and they began eating.

"How long has it been just you and your father?" Matt asked at one point.

"My mother died when I was young. I was only six."

"And your father never remarried or thought about it?"

"I can't say whether he ever thought about it or not, but no, he never did remarry. He threw himself into his work. I had a governess when I was young, but we moved around every few years as my father tried to move up in the ranks of academia. That meant he had to find a new nanny every time we moved."

"It sounds like you might have been lonely because moving around that much also meant that you had to make new friends with every move."

Samantha nodded quickly. "Yes. I don't think my father ever understood that because he never seemed to have close friends himself."

"Aren't you and your father close? He seems protective of you."

"We're close, but he doesn't approve of my positions about women's equality. He thinks it hurts his professional reputation."

"I wonder if my parents would approve of my decisions sometimes," Matt said.

"Were you close?" Samantha asked.

Matt nodded. "It was sad coming home and not seeing them in their house. They died from the Spanish Influenza in 1918, so they never got to know that I made it through the wall all right. I was on a ship on my way to New York."

"What happened?"

Matt looked at the table. Samantha deserved to know what had happened, at least some of what had happened.

"I received a field promotion in early 1918, so I was one of the company officers leading the Marines who took part in the St. Mihiel Offensive in August and September. Things got pretty bad at times. You might be firing at one person while some other soldiers would be aiming at you, and you wouldn't even know it. Things were just that confusing. You almost had to forget about trying to stay alive to live."

"That doesn't make sense," Samantha said.

"If you thought about living too much, about all of the places someone could be hiding and firing at you, you would freeze up. There were just too many places. And if you froze up in one place, you were a sitting duck."

It didn't matter anyway. You might plan out the perfect advance that kept you safe from enemy fire while allowing you to fire on them, only to be killed by an artillery shell fired from a mile away.

"In my case," Matt said. "I actually saw the German aiming at me. I tried to swing my rifle around and fire, but he fired first. The bullet hit me right in the chest."

"How are you still alive?"

"It struck dead center in a pocket watch that I had. My father had given it to me before I left Eckhart Mines. I was going to give it back to him with the bullet sticking out of it to show him how he had saved my life, but he died before I could." Matt's voice trailed off as he remembered his father handing him the watch. It had a picture a picture of Geno and Maria Ansaro inside of the cover. Matt's father had told him to keep it close to his heart so that his parents could help protect him. That's what Matt had done, and his parents had kept their promise and helped.

"Matt?" Samantha said.

Matt blinked away the memory. "Sorry, I kind of drifted away there."

"Is all this too hard to talk about?"

"Some of it."

189

She laid her hand on his. "We don't have to talk about it. I understand."

Matt shook his head. "I've started, and I should finish. There's not much more. While I was stunned and laying on the ground wondering why I wasn't dead, an artillery shell exploded nearby. If I had been standing, I think I would have been killed." He snorted. "If I had been lying an inch or the two to the side, I would have been killed. The shrapnel hit me in the shoulder, neck, and chest, but the neck wound was the worst. I survived but only barely. I underwent more than one surgery as they kept having to repair blood vessels. I spent the rest of the war in a hospital."

"You were very lucky."

"I know, but I still have bad dreams about it all."

"I can understand that you would. It's horrible."

"Not nearly as horrible the way I described it. Believe me, being there was even worse."

"I know I keep saying this, Matt, but I'm sorry."

"Me, too. The worst part is that sometimes I think that the Matt who I was did die out there on the battlefields in France, and the person who came back shares his name, but that is all. We don't look the same. We don't act the same. We don't think the same."

"Is that a bad thing? The person I see before me is a good person."

"Maybe." He looked off to the side. "Sometimes, I even wonder about that, but people around here were expecting Matteo Ansaro, and they got Matt Ansaro. That's one of the reasons that I stayed away for so long."

"Your aunts and uncles didn't strike me as disappointed in you."

"Not yet, anyway."

They finished their lunch. Matt looked around and then stood up.

"Feel like taking a bit of a walk or are you too full?" he asked.

Samantha stood up. "If you can walk, so can I. Where are we going?"

Matt lifted a finger and pointed upward. He took her by the hand, and they walked to the lobby and stopped at the front desk.

"We'd like to see the cupola," Matt told the desk clerk.

"It's closed," the neatly dressed young man told him.

Matt slid a fifty-cent piece across the countertop. "Find someone with a key."

The man picked up the silver coin and dropped it into his waistcoat pocket. Then he smiled broadly at Matt and Samantha.

"I just happen to have the key right here," he said. He pulled it out from behind the counter and passed it to Matt.

As Matt and Samantha walked to the stairs that led to the cupola, they continued to talk. Matt asked about Samantha's schoolwork, and she told him that she worried that she was getting higher grades than she deserved in her classes.

"You know that you work hard in your classes, right?" he asked.

"Of course."

"Then what's the problem?"

"I may not deserve the grades that I'm getting."

"But if you are good in your classes, then you may deserve them, and knowing you, you probably do deserve them."

Samantha slid her arm through his and smiled at him. "Thank you for that."

"Besides, you're always complaining how the odds are stacked against women. Enjoy it when the odds are in your favor."

She tried to pinch him on his arm but was surprised to find his muscles so tight that there was nothing to grab. Instead, she dug her fingernails into his arm. Matt winced, but he didn't say anything.

"Jeez, Matt, I think I might have broken a nail on your arm," she said.

"And that is my fault?"

"Of course," she said with a smile. "You're a man."

Matt used his key to unlock the hatch into the cupola. He pushed it back and climbed up inside. Then he stepped back so Samantha could follow him.

Matt worked his way around the widow's walk, trying to see how far he could see in every direction. Perhaps he could have seen further from Lover's Leap in the Narrows, but that almost seemed too high up. This was just the right height. It lifted him above the city while not taking him away from it.

"It's gorgeous up here," Samantha said from beside him.

"I always wanted to come up here when I was younger," Matt said. "Now I can say that I did and that I wasn't disappointed."

"I think I could stay up here all day. It's a little cold, but it's worth it. It seems so peaceful."

"That's what I was thinking." Matt took off his coat and slid it around her shoulders. "That should help you stay warm."

As he tugged the jacket snug near her neck, Samantha rose up on her toes and kissed him deeply. With his hands trapped between them, he couldn't move them to pull her closer. He leaned in and enjoyed the kiss, hoping that it would continue for a long time.

Samantha finally pulled back. "Now you have something to remember with this view."

"What view?" he said with a smile.

He lowered his hands, slid them around her waist, and kissed her again.

"What view indeed," Samantha said when they parted.

Their drive back to Eckhart Mines was filled with a light-hearted talk from two people that were much more at ease around one another.

As Samantha drove the Nash into town, Matt was surprised to see so many people outdoors. Yes, it was a Saturday evening, but these people seemed to be standing around in clusters. Then he saw the sheriff's car.

"Stop here," Matt said. "Something's wrong."

Samantha pulled over and parked the car. He climbed out and looked around. He saw Laura and Pete standing outside their house and walked over to them.

"What's happening?" he asked.

"The company fired five miners," Pete said.

"Why?"

"They joined the union."

192

"How'd the company find out?" Matt asked, but he knew. He'd been worried this might happen.

Pete shrugged. "Someone must have said something to the wrong person."

"Who got fired?"

"Max Smith, Harvey Brant, Bob Connelly and his brother, Beau, and George Pearson."

That was just what Matt had been afraid of. They were all of the miners from his report that he had sent in last week. He was the reason that the miners had been fired.

He walked further up the street where he saw a sheriff's deputy standing inside the fenced yard of one of the company homes. As he got closer to the home, he saw two men carry a chest out of the house and set it on the street outside the fence. Then a third man came out holding a rocking chair. He also set it at the edge of the road.

"How long has this been going on?" Matt asked one of the spectators.

"All afternoon. This is the last house."

"Do these families have other places to go?"

The man shrugged. "Do they ever? Some will have family hereabout, but they won't be welcome if their people are in coal towns. These men are blacklisted. They will not find a job in this area."

If they couldn't work in the mines, then these men would have to find other work. That was no easy thing to do if you had been a miner all of your life. If they couldn't afford a non-company house in Eckhart, they would have to try Frostburg or Cumberland. There would be more job opportunities in those towns, too.

Matt walked down the street and paused in front of an uncomfortable looking deputy. The man held a rifle, but the barrel was pointed at the ground. He stood inside the fence of one of the company houses. A man, woman, and three children stood in the road on the other side of the fence. The woman and one of the children were crying. The other children of the family looked stunned.

Two men carried out a chest and started swinging their arms as if to getting ready to toss it over the fence. The wife yelped and put her hand to her mouth. The deputy noticed what the men were about to do. He opened the gate.

"Just set it outside the fence," he said.

"It's on company property. We can do what we want with it," one of the men said.

"I'm here to ensure this happens in an orderly way," the deputy said. "Set the chest outside of company property."

The men sighed and carried the chest outside the fence. Rather than setting the chest down, though, they dropped it. Then they grinned.

The wife buried her face in her husband's chest and cried harder.

It wasn't as bad as it could have been. The deputy was actually fair about things. In a true company town, it would have been mine guards doing the evicting, and they wouldn't have cared about what got broken or ruined if it wasn't company property. They would have thrown things out into the road.

Samantha squeezed Matt's hand. "This is horrible, Matt."

Matt nodded silently. What could he say? This man was one of the names he had put on his report to the company.

"What happened?" Samantha asked.

"He joined the union."

"Is that so bad?"

Matt stared at her, surprised. "The union and mining companies are enemies, and the miners caught in the middle."

The evicted miners' lives had just taken a significant turn for the worse, and it was his fault.

Chapter 25

March 10, 1922

During the next week, miners found themselves talking less to each other. No one knew who might betray them or what would constitute a firing offense by the coal company. Matt didn't hear anything about union meetings, although he saw the union recruiter once when he went into Frostburg to see Samantha. However, the man did not show himself in Eckhart as far as Matt knew. The recruiter must have been traveling to all of the mining towns along Georges Creek to recruit miners.

Near the end of the first week after the firings, the miners began talking among themselves a bit more. The one word that Matt heard the most, although never in the mine, was "strike." Some miners suggested a national strike was coming, others talked about a local strike, and still others worried how they would get by if a strike was called.

A few miners were attacked in Frostburg. It was unsure whether it was related to the union problems, but most people assumed that it was because the three miners who had been beaten up in three different incidents had all spoken out against joining the union. However, other people had been attacked during the week as well, and they weren't related to coal mining in any way. Frostburg had a reputation for being virtually lawless. Prohibition was rarely enforced, which attracted rough men who were often violent.

Then one evening, Enos didn't come home with Matt, Samuel, and the other miners who lived in the boarding house.

"Where's Enos?" Antonietta asked, leaning out from the doorway and looking toward the corner of the house.

"Don't worry, Toni," Samuel said. "He came out of the mine with the rest of us. He's not hurt."

"There are other ways for him to be hurt. It doesn't have to be in the mine. Miners are being attacked in the streets."

"Not here they aren't." He stripped off his shirt to begin his bath.

The men washed up and came to the dinner table. Antonietta and Myrna laid out a meal of ham, cornbread, and applesauce.

The conversation around the dinner table in the boarding house was still reserved. Matt figured that it was because not everyone was family. While family could be trusted, strangers might be spying on you. Of course, what Matt's family didn't know was that one of their own was spying on them.

During the meal, Matt noticed that Samuel kept looking at Enos's empty place and then at Antonietta. They knew something more than they were saying, and that worried Matt more than if they hadn't known anything.

He went into his room after dinner and lay on his bed with his hands behind his head staring at the ceiling. It had been more than a week since Matt had filed a report with Consolidation Coal. He needed to write something. What would he say? They wouldn't care about the sadness that they had caused. They only wanted to know if anyone had joined the union or was talking about striking. The company would probably be happy that they had quashed conversation among the miners.

Someone knocked on the door to his room.

Matt sat up. "Come in."

Samuel opened the door. He waved Matt over. "Get your coat. I'll need your help probably."

"What's wrong?" Matt asked as he stood up.

"Your aunt is getting worried. We've got to go find Enos."

Matt walked over, and he and Samuel headed out the front door.

"You know where's he's at?" Matt asked.

Samuel nodded. "Most likely."

They walked through town. Samuel carried a lantern to light the way. He veered off the road and headed up a path that led up the side of Big Savage Mountain. Matt followed his uncle, although he had no idea where Samuel was heading. He hoped that he didn't plan on marching over the mountain to Mount Savage or Zihlman.

They walked for about ten minutes before coming upon two men sitting on stumps along the side of the trail. The only way that Matt knew they were there was because he saw the tips of their cigarettes glowing in the dark.

One of the men turned on a flashlight and shone it in Samuel's and Matt's faces. Matt heard a gun cock, and he stopped walking.

"What are you doing here?" one of the men asked.

Samuel held up his arm to shield his eyes from the light. "Harvey, it's Samuel. I know it's dark, but with that flashlight, you ought to be able to recognize me."

"Yea, I see you, Samuel," Harvey said. "Who's that with you?"

"It's my nephew, Matt. He works in the mine now."

"OK, what do you want?"

"Is Enos here?"

"Yea, but he ain't going to be walking down the mountain too easily," the faceless voice said.

Samuel shook his head. "I expected that. We're going to get him. That's why I brought Matt with me."

"OK, go ahead up."

Samuel started walking, and Matt followed him. He realized that they were heading towards a still. The men on the stumps were guards watching for law enforcement or revenue agents.

In another five minutes, Matt and Samuel came into a large clearing that was lit by a fire and several lanterns. Matt saw a barrel of corn mash and boiler with copper tubing sticking out of it. It was a large boiler, maybe 200 gallons. This was no small operation. A dozen men sat around the clearing. They talked, made jokes, and drank. Every so often, one of the men checked a bucket beneath the end of the copper tubing to see how quickly it was filling with moonshine.

"For men who want to keep this place hidden, they aren't too quiet," Matt whispered to Samuel.

Samuel nodded. "That's why they have guards on the trails that lead here. If trouble heads this way, the guards will let them know."

Enos sat on the ground leaning against a tree with his legs spread out in front of him. He held a quart jar of moonshine in his lap. He joked with a man sitting next to him.

Samuel walked over to his brother. "Enos, it's time to go home."

Enos looked up. His eyes were red and heavy-lidded. He shook his head. "I'm tired. I'm done with the mine."

"What are you going to do if not mine coal?"

"I don't know. I'll find something." He paused and then smiled. "I'll be a taxi driver."

"We don't have a car, and we don't have the money to buy one yet. We would have a lot more money saved up if you didn't waste so much on moonshine. That stuff will blind you if you aren't careful."

Enos snorted. "Sometimes I just don't care, Samuel. Look at what they did to those guys last week just because they wanted to make a better living for themselves."

"Those men knew the risk when they joined the union. They'd have to be crazy not to after last year."

"But I joined the union with them, and I was the only one who didn't get fired," Enos said loudly. "Why? It's not fair. I should have been fired."

"You want to be fired?"

Enos shook his head lazily. "Yes. No. Maybe."

Samuel grabbed his brother's face and tried to get Enos to focus on him. "Enos, this is the only job you've got right now. The whiskey is talking, and you sound like a fool."

"No, it's not the whiskey. I'm telling you how I feel."

"Come on home, Enos, and we'll talk about it in the morning."

Enos pulled free from Samuel's grip and swung his head back and forth in a broad, exaggerated arc. "No, we can't talk about this kind stuff in the mines. Someone will hear us."

"Someone might hear you now and report you."

"Well, if they did that, then I could report them for moonshining."

Samuel sighed. "Enos, Toni's worried. Let's go home. You've had enough to drink, especially on an empty stomach."

Enos groaned.

Samuel looked over at Matt. "Come, help me. We're going to have to drag him down the trail."

Matt and Samuel stepped up on either side of Enos. They each grabbed Enos under an arm, and they lifted. Enos was a strong man but not unusually large, so he was easy to lift. Enos's feet were on the ground, but he was putting very little weight on them. Matt and Samuel had to virtually drag him down the trail back to Eckhart.

"How often does he do this?" Matt asked.

"It used to be not that often. Just a few beers after he finished his shift once or twice a week. Lately, it's been more and more. He usually just drinks in his room. He just does not like his life," Samuel told him.

"Do you like yours?"

"Can't say that I do, but I'm sure there are worse ways to earn a living."

"There are better ways, too."

"Until I figure out one of those ways, I'm kinda stuck here," Samuel said.

Antonietta met them at the back door to the boarding house. She frowned when she saw her brother's half-conscious state. Then she swatted him with her dish towel.

"You're a fool, Enos Ansaro," she said. "One of these days something will go wrong. You're going to drink a bad batch, say something stupid to the wrong person, or get caught in a raid. Then what's going to happen to you?"

"I'm no good, Toni," Enos murmured.

"I didn't say that. I said that you're a fool, but you're plenty good. Get to bed. You're going to feel it in the morning."

Enos was still in no condition to walk, so Matt and Samuel took hold of his hands and feet and carried him upstairs to his room on the third floor. They pulled off his dirty clothes and let him fall into the bed.

Matt went back to his room. It was getting late, and he needed to get some sleep since he had to get up early. He didn't envy Enos when his alarm clock went off in the morning.

Matt stripped off his shirt and folded it. Then he laid it back in the drawer.

He heard a knock and opened the door. Aunt Antonietta was standing there.

"How's Enos?" Matt asked.

"He's snoring in his bed. I need to talk to you."

Matt stepped back and opened the door wider. Antonietta came inside, and Matt closed the door. She paced the floor as Matt watched her.

"I was putting your laundry away a couple weeks ago, and I found a piece of paper on the floor. It looked like it was meant for the wastebasket, so I picked it up to throw it away. Then I happened to read it."

She stopped pacing and looked at Matt. His chest suddenly felt tight, and he could feel his cheeks flushing. His aunt knew. He had been careless, and she had found out.

"That sheet of paper had five names on it, and every one of the men named lost his job last week."

Matt didn't say anything. What could he say?

"Why did you have those names, Matt?" Antonietta asked, her voice shaky and uncertain. She was afraid to hear the answer.

He tried to think of a lie that might be believable, but nothing came to mind. Antonietta stared at him, expecting an answer.

"I was taking notes about the union meeting that Samuel, Enos, and I went to."

"Why would you do that?"

"I wanted to remember the promises being made by the UMW man."

"Really?" Matt nodded. "Then why wasn't Enos's name on the list? Why weren't there any notes? Why were there any names at all? How would knowing who had joined the union help you remember promises made?"

"Those were people I could ask."

Antonietta slapped him across the face. Matt staggered back a step more shocked than anything.

"You're spying for the mine. You're spying on your own family!" she shouted.

Matt rubbed his cheek, more stunned than hurt.

"I'm trying to help you."

"Help us? How? How would Enos and Samuel losing their jobs help us? Did you tell the company Enos had joined the union?"

"No."

Antonietta shook her heads as she raised her hands in the air.

"I can't believe you, Matteo. You're family. We took you in without question, and this is how you treat us?"

"I'm trying to help you."

"You said that before, but I don't feel helped. I feel betrayed. That mine killed your uncle, my husband, and you are helping it continue running like that."

Matt shook his head. "I am not."

"I should tell everyone that you're a spy. They'll run you out of town," Antonietta said.

"You can't."

Antonietta put her hands on her hips and glared at him. "Why not?"

"Because my job is on the line, too."

His aunt put her hands on hips and glared at him. "I could care less if Consolidation Coal is angry at you because you got discovered."

"It's not that. Why do you think I'm here in Eckhart?"

"To spy on us. That much is obvious."

"But why Eckhart? My boss isn't a fool. Do you think he

would send me back to my hometown to spy on my family and friends?"

That stopped Antonietta short. She stared at him, and Matt decided he better try to explain before she exploded on him again. He couldn't believe that she had hit him. She had never even swatted him when he was a boy.

"I work for the Pinkerton Detective Agency, and we were hired by Consolidation Coal to spy out union activities. When I heard that the assignment was in Western Maryland, I knew that you all might be in trouble. I don't want any of you hurt."

"You've got an odd way of showing it," Antonietta muttered.

"I knew I could help protect you all, but only if I could be here to control what information Consolidation Coal heard. I also knew my boss wouldn't send me back to my hometown. He would have sent me to some other town where Consolidation Coal owned a mine, so I told him that I was from Vindex. I told him I knew this area, and I knew where some of the trouble spots might be. I was allowed to select where I would come. I chose here so I could protect you from what happened to those other men."

"They lost their jobs because you betrayed them." Matt looked at the floor. That much was true, and he would never forget it.

Antonietta was starting to work up her anger again.

"I know, and I regret that," Matt said. "I had to tell Consolidation Coal something because I'm not the only spy out this way. I don't know who they are, but I know they are throughout the Consolidation mines. I had to report as much truth as I could. They will only keep me here if I'm useful. If I hadn't reported anything, I might have been moved elsewhere, and someone else put here. I chose to leave Enos's name off the list so he wouldn't get in trouble, and I was right to do it."

Antonietta started pacing again. "I don't like this, Matteo. I don't like this at all. What sort of life do you have lying so much?"

"I usually like what I'm doing because I do help people," Matt admitted.

"That's not what you're doing now."

"I am. I'm just not helping everyone."

Antonietta shook her head. "No, you're not."

"What are you going to do?" Matt asked. "Are you going to tell Enos and Samuel?"

Antonietta threw her hands in the air. "I don't know. Does anyone else know that you're spying?"

"My boss knows where I am, but even Consolidation Coal doesn't know that it's me in Eckhart. They only know that the Pinkertons put someone here."

"I have to think about this."

"I understand."

"I'll let you know what I decide."

He looked at his feet. It shamed him that his aunt was angry with him, but he couldn't do anything about it. "Yes, ma'am."

She left him alone in his room, and Matt sank into the chair next to his bed. He doubted that he would get much sleep tonight.

Chapter 26

March 11, 1922

Pete stood in line with the rest of the miners who slowly filed into the mine office to receive their pay for the week. Once they received their money, they headed out through the general store where many of them would have to make a payment on their accounts from their already meager earnings. Portnoy usually stood behind his register calling out the names of miners' names who owed money when he saw them pass through the store.

Even before he entered the office, Pete could hear miners arguing with the paymaster. He could imagine what it was because it was always the same arguments. Either they were disputing the tonnage that they were credited with, or they were complaining about the myriad of deductions. Consolidation Coal deducted for the cost of a doctor whether or not you saw him. Of course, this had been useful when Laura was pregnant. She could see the doctor regularly to ensure everything was going as it should, and Jacob had been born healthy.

The company deducted rent for housing. They deducted the cost of sharpening tools. They deducted the cost of coal used to heat the home. They deducted the cost of the powder and supplies that the miners used in their work.

Between the low pay and the deductions, it wasn't surprising that some men with larger families found themselves with nothing to take home, which only forced them to go deeper in debt to the store.

Pete had grown to hate this life more year after year. He wished that he could find other work like the tire plant in Cumberland. He had been too busy with Laura's pregnancy and work when the Kelly-Springfield Company hired initially, and he had missed his opportunity. He kept listening for another round of hiring there, but he couldn't get away during the week even if he did hear about an opening. He couldn't afford to miss work. It would only put them further behind.

As Pete moved into the office, he could understand what was being said. He'd been wrong. This was something new. The company had lowered how much it was paying per ton. Sidney Bloom, the paymaster, was having to answer the same questions over and over again. He didn't set the tonnage rate. He could only pay what the company allowed him to pay.

Pete noticed more than one man walking away empty-handed. How much lower was the new tonnage rate?

He stepped up to the counter and said, "Pete Spiker."

Bloom thumbed through his pile of pay slips and pulled one out. He slid it across the counter to Pete. He saw the total was more than twenty-five cents a day less than it typically was. He looked at the tonnage wage.

"Five cents less!"

"I don't set the rate," Bloom said automatically.

"Well, then why don't you reduce the amounts you are taking out? You're still taking out the same amount for home coal, I see, even though that same coal is worth less."

"You can either sign for your money or not, Spiker. If not, then you can argue with Mr. McCord and me about it for the next week and still not get any more."

"Pretty soon it looks like I'm going to have to be paying you."

Bloom showed no expression. He'd been hearing the same things for the last hour and was probably numb to it.

Pete signed his pay slip and handed it back. Bloom wrote out a receipt and counted out the money due Pete. Pete took the small pile and slid it into his pocket. Then he walked into the store.

The line at Portnoy's counter was much shorter thankfully. He gave Portnoy a dollar bill and the change from his pay to put in his account. This particular bill would be paid off in three weeks if he and Laura didn't add anything to it, which was doubtful if the tonnage rate stayed so low.

He and Laura now had four dollars to get them through the week.

Pete headed for the front door, but he paused to shove his remaining dollars back into his pocket. When he looked up, he noticed Mr. McCord standing on the porch. Pete was going to talk about the new tonnage rate when he saw Joseph staring at something down the street as he smoked a cigar.

Pete shifted his position so that he could see down the street more. He was curious what could hold the mine boss's attention to intensely.

It was Laura.

She ran around the front yard playing with Jacob and waiting for Pete to come back with his pay.

Someone moved past Pete and went outside. Joseph McCord didn't even glance in the man's direction.

Pete walked outside, across the porch, and down the steps to the street.

"Pete."

Pete stopped and turned to face Joseph. "Hello, Mr. McCord."

"How are you doing? How is the family?" Joseph asked.

"We'd be doing a lot better if the company hadn't cut the tonnage rate."

Joseph frowned and nodded. "I understand. Coal isn't bringing in as much as it used to. The less that we can sell the coal for means that there's less money to pay the miners."

"Yes, sir."

He sounded sincere, but Pete knew, as a supervisor, Mr. McCord had to have some say in the matter. He couldn't press the issue, though.

"How are things in the mine? I heard that you are partnered with Matt Ansaro."

"We are getting along."

"Really? Did he stop paying attention to your wife?"

Matt wasn't the one whom Pete had noticed paying attention to Laura.

"There's nothing to worry about there. They're good friends," Pete said.

Joseph started to frown. He caught himself, and then said, "Well, I'm glad to hear it. Have a good day."

Pete nodded. "You too, sir."

He walked down the street. Laura saw him and waved. She opened the gate and Jacob ran toward Pete. Pete squatted down, opened his arms, and scooped up Jacob. The boy laughed and hugged his father.

Then Pete reached Laura. He kissed her and then gave her a hug. As he did, Pete looked over his wife's shoulder. He could see Joseph McCord watching them from the porch of the store.

"Let's go inside," Pete said.

Matt helped Calista ease out of the hospital bed. She tried to wave him off. He came to help her home today, although she was determined to do things on her own.

She had spent the week in the hospital recovering from the severe bruising. The doctor thought some of her ribs might be cracked, but they couldn't be set. She would just have to endure the pain until they healed. Her tight dresses might actually help hold her ribs in place.

"I'm not an invalid, Matt," she told him.

"Indulge me."

"Indulging men is my specialty," she said with a grin. Then she winced as she stood up.

She walked slowly, but he didn't notice any sign of pain in her steps. Matt stood next to her, close enough to catch her if she fell. She had assured the doctor that she felt fine. In fact, after a week in the hospital doing nothing, she was anxious to be out.

"My neighbors probably think I'm dead," Calista said.

"Then won't you surprise them?"

Matt had paid the hospital bill with the cash he had withdrawn from his bank account in Cumberland.

He and Calista walked up the hill from Miner's Hospital to the National Road and then crossed the street and started down Water Street. Calista lived in a small house at the edge of town that Matt guessed was smaller than a miner's house. It wasn't much more than a shack really.

"What will you do now?" Matt asked as he stopped at the front door.

She arched an eyebrow. "What do you think I'll do? I still need to make money."

Why couldn't she see that this was her chance to start over? She was smart. She could get a job in town if she wanted to. She was pretty. She could marry again.

"You could get a job in a store," Matt suggested.

Calista shook her head. "Once. Maybe. Too many people know what I do here. What do you think would happen when my boss found out?"

"Maybe nothing." Even Matt wasn't convinced by his denial. A shopkeeper wouldn't want word spreading that his clerk was a prostitute.

Calista laid a hand on his arm. "Matt, you have to realize that you're an odd duck."

He nodded. "More so than you realize."

"I know you're not some preacher trying to save my soul, and you're not like any coal miner I've known. I wish I knew why you're doing this."

Matt couldn't tell her even if he were of a mind to. He didn't know why he was helping her.

"Does it matter?" he asked.

She blushed. "I've learned that when men are nice to me, they are usually angling for a free evening."

He wished he could explain things to her. It went beyond what he had seen with the women in Europe, and it wasn't that he felt sorry for Calista. He wanted to do some good for someone, and it seemed less and less likely that it would be his family.

"You can come in if you'd like," Calista said. "It's not much."

She unlocked the door and swung it open. It smelled musty inside.

"Thank you, but no," Matt told her.

Calista nodded. "That's right. You have a woman who you're interested in now." Matt nodded. "She doesn't have to know." Calista wiggled her eyebrows.

"I would know."

Calista grinned. "Just checking to see if I had worn you down yet."

"I was tempted."

She rose up on her toes and kissed Matt on the cheek. "No, you weren't, but thank you."

Calista unlocked the door to her home and went inside. Matt headed back toward Main Street.

Chapter 27

March 13, 1922

The Consolidation Coal Mines in Eckhart had switched over to using electric engines to pull the coal cars through the tunnels since the war. The company found it cheaper since they didn't have to maintain a herd of ponies and pay the men and boys who cared for them. A few ponies and mules were still kept for use in case the power failed, but it now required far less to maintain them. Matt still remembered the mine ponies from when he was a kid, and he and Pete talked about them as they were carried deep under the earth on a clanking coal car that drew power from an electric line along the ceiling of the mine. The line occasionally sparked, and Matt wondered what would happen if it sparked in a pocket of methane. The resulting explosion could bring down the roof of the tunnel.

"I thought that I would be a pony driver when I was younger," Matt said. "I sort of looked forward to it."

"I always felt sorry for the mules and ponies," Pete said. "Some of the ones in the larger mines never saw the light of day. They lived and died underground."

"The same could almost be said for miners," Matt told him.

"But we have a choice, don't we? It's not always a good choice, but we are allowed to make it," Pete said. He rubbed his chin and stared off to the side.

"Are you all right, Pete?"

He sighed and said, "Yeah, I'm fine. I've just got stuff on my mind."

"Like what?"

"You grew up here. Did you ever hear any stories about unusual deals being made?"

"What do you mean?"

Pete leaned closer to Matt and said, "Where I grew up, we heard stories from time to time about mine superintendents taking advantage of women."

Samuel had suggested the same thing.

"What? Wait a minute, is Laura hurt?"

Pete put a hand on Matt's arm. "No, she's fine, but I'm a little worried about her. I saw Mr. McCord staring at her oddly yesterday."

"Oddly?"

Pete nodded. "You know how you stare at a beautiful woman. Well, McCord was doing that and ignoring everything around him."

This sounded too much like Samuel talking.

"Well, you married a beautiful woman, Pete."

Pete smiled and nodded. "I know, but seeing him do that made me uncomfortable. It made me think about the stories I've heard about mine superintendents, and I owe the store money."

Matt's eyebrows raised. "Oh. Joey McCord is not my favorite person, but I can't see him doing something like that. He might try sweet talking her into something, but Laura can handle herself where that is concerned."

"I guess so," Pete said.

"You're not getting jealous of him, are you, Pete, because you don't need to worry about Laura in that way. She loves you."

"I'm not jealous of him, at least not with Laura. It's just that watching him made me really uncomfortable. I felt dirty without even being in the mine."

The coal car stopped at the layoff and Pete and Matt, and other miners climbed out of the coal car. They walked with their tools down the tunnel where they would be working today. The car driver moved onto the next layoff.

Empty coal cars waited to be filled at the end of the temporary tracks. When all the miners were dropped off, the electric engine would return to the surface to disconnect the cars that carried men and start making the rounds to pick up filled coal cars and pull them to the surface.

Outside the mine, the coal was taken to the sorting area near the tipple. The miner's medallion on the car told the mine supervisor which miner got credit for the load. If the coal was too dirty, or rather, if it had too much rock mixed in it, the check also let the supervisor know who to yell at. Larger coal operators along Georges Creek, notably the Consolidation Coal Company, would dock miners' paychecks for dirty loads.

Matt's first coal mining job had been as a sorter. He and other young boys sorted the coal from the rock and slate even more than the miners had done before shoveling it into the coal cars. Any slate, bone, and stone had to be removed from the coal so that it would be clean. Basically, a customer paid for coal not the rest of the stuff around the coal. If there weren't enough coal in each ton, the coal wouldn't burn efficiently, and the customer wouldn't be too happy. So the coal needed to be "cleaned" before it was loaded into the tipple and then railroad cars.

Cleaned coal was weighed at the tipple and then dumped into a chute, which dumped the coal into railroad cars. The railroad cars sat on a short spur of the Cumberland and Pennsylvania Railroad that connected to the main line.

Matt and Pete worked hard through the morning, each filling a coal car. They didn't say much because Pete still appeared worried about Joey McCord's intentions toward Laura. Matt wondered how much was true and how much was Pete's imagination.

Joey and Laura certainly knew each other, and she was definitely a beautiful woman. Men would pay attention to her, but would one become obsessed with her?

Matt sat down on a chunk of discarded stone when the whistle sounded for lunch. Pete shuffled over next to him and dropped to the ground. Matt could do for a nap, but he needed to eat more. He needed the energy to get him through the afternoon.

Matt pried off the lid of the round pail using his fingertips. He pulled out the ham sandwich that one of his aunts had made him this morning. It was wrapped in butcher's paper. He unwrapped it and took a bite. The paper kept him from having to hold the sandwich with his filthy hands.

"What do you got?" Pete asked him.

"Ham with mustard."

"Lucky you. I've just got lard and bread. We don't have much left over now that they have cut the tonnage rate. If I could just pay off my account at the store, I might have a little money to get ahead."

Matt held his sandwich out to the miner. "Here. Let's trade."

Pete shook his head. "I wasn't begging."

"I know that, but Aunt Antonietta will have chicken tonight. I'll be fine until then."

"Are you sure, Matt?"

Matt nodded, and they traded sandwiches. Pere tore into the ham sandwich with relish and Matt wondered how long it had been since the man had eaten meat with his meal.

"This is mighty nice of you, Matt," Pete said.

"I wasn't that hungry anyway."

They ate quickly and drank some water to wash it all down. The whistles sounded throughout the tunnels. Matt dropped the lard sandwich into his lunch pail and jumped to his feet. He and Pete picked up their picks and went back to work. They drilled holes and set charges. Then they backed off to light the fuses.

As they started to walk away, Pete's face suddenly went pale, and he collapsed. Matt rushed forward and grabbed him by the arms to pull him away. He rolled Pete onto his back and sat him up. Then he began pounding him on the back trying to get him to breathe.

Pete had walked into a pocket of methane, and the black damp had nearly gotten him.

Pete started coughing and held up his hand to signal to Matt to stop. Matt did, but he still held him upright.

"How do you feel?" Matt asked.

"Like you might have broken my ribs with that pounding you gave me," Pete said.

"Be glad that it wasn't my fist. Are you going to be all right?"

Pete nodded. "I just need some fresh air."

"That's in short supply down here obviously. Do you want to go out for a while?"

Pete nodded. "I don't want to, but I probably better."

"Let's get to the layoff. I'll call for a driver."

"You two can't have filled that car yet," Harv Mason said when he stopped in front of Matt. "I just left it there before lunch."

"Pete walked into the black damp. He's all right, but he needs to get outside for a little while to clear out his lungs."

"Okay, climb in one of the empties," Harv said without hesitation.

Then Matt climbed into the empty car with Pete. While he might have gotten away with continuing to work alone, he wasn't going to chance it knowing there was at least one pocket of methane in that tunnel.

As the car rolled along, Matt heard Pete coughing.

"Are you sure you're all right?" Matt asked.

Pete nodded. "I just need some fresh air."

The sun outside was bright and the temperature pleasant. Matt hopped out of the coal car and then helped Matt over. The foreman saw them and walked over.

"What are you two doing up here?"

"The black damp nearly got Pete."

"Damn! We've been having trouble keeping the No. 3 mine fan running. It must have shut down again. I'll get someone back out there."

"Wait, why didn't you say anything to us about a problem with the fan?"

"Because it didn't concern you," Tom Gianconne said.

"Obviously, it did. If we had known that the fans were acting up, we would have been watching for problems."

"You can't see the black damp, Ansaro. That's the point."

Matt glared at Tom and clenched his fists. Then he took a deep breath and opened them. He turned and walked back to Pete.

"You don't look happy," Pete said.

"Tom's an asshole."

Pete chuckled, but it turned into a cough. Matt put a hand on his shoulder and sat down beside him.

"Don't tell Laura about this. She'll just worry," he said.

"She should. That tunnel we're in is not the safest place to be or hadn't you noticed?"

"Everybody knows that tunnel is the worst one in there. It was closed for a while."

"Why did they reopen it?"

"Only Mr. McCord could tell you that."

Matt shook his head.

"Thank you, Matt. You saved my life in there."

Matt smiled and slapped Pete on the shoulder. "That's what partners are for." He laid back on the ground and closed his eyes. "Let me know when you're ready to go back inside."

Chapter 28

March 18, 1922

Samantha drove her father's Nash down the National Road and into Eckhart on Saturday evening. She stopped in front of the boarding house and climbed out of the car.

She wore a light blue dress that somehow showed off her figure, although it hung loosely so that she could move while dancing.

Men passing on the street paused to stare. Samantha wasn't sure if she should be happy or mad that most of them were staring at the car rather than her. They circled the car and looked in the windows.

"She's a beauty," one man said. "Can I look at the engine?"

Samantha shrugged. "I guess so."

The man lifted up the engine cover. The Nash was like a magnet that pulled in even more men. Now no one was even paying her attention.

"Don't feel insulted."

Samantha turned around and saw Matt standing on the porch wearing tweed pants and a matching vest, a white shirt, and black tie.

"I bought this dress just for this dance, and none of them even gave me a second glance," Samantha said.

"You said the world is better off without men."

"Yes, but I wanted to torture them with what they're missing," Samantha said, grinning.

"Well, I think you look beautiful, and I'm happy that they're more interested in the car. That just means that I've got you all to myself with very little competition."

Samantha smiled and patted him on the cheek. Then she took his arm, and they walked down to Store Hill and over to the Literary and Sporting Club Hall where the town dance was being held. Some of the miners' wives had spent the day decorating it with bunting and colorful tablecloths. The line of tables at the far end of the hall was filled with small sandwiches, punch bowls, and cups. A line of chairs ran around the outside of the room, leaving the center open for dancing.

People crowded the room. The ones in the middle of the room danced while the clusters of people who were talking sat in chairs or stood at the edges of the room. Women wore their most beautiful dresses, and men wore their Sunday suits if they had one. A four-member band had set up on one corner and was playing dance music.

Samantha grabbed Matt's hand and pulled him out onto the dance floor.

"I knew I would get you to dance with me eventually," she said.

Matt felt awkward on the dance floor as if everyone around him was staring at him. He tried to mimic the moves of the other men who were dancing, but he felt like he was just flailing his arms and high stepping.

Samantha, on the other hand, seemed to move fluidly through her dance moves. She was elegant and energetic. He smiled to watch her dance.

The song ended, and the band took up a slower tune. Samantha moved into Matt's arms, and he put one hand in hers and another on her hip.

"Don't be nervous," she said. "I won't bite."

"That's not what's making me nervous. I'm trying to concentrate, so I don't step on your toes."

217

Samantha laughed, and Matt couldn't help but smile. It was an infectious sound that he loved hearing. It seemed to lift a weight off his shoulders.

When the song ended, the pair moved to the refreshment table for some punch. Antonietta was standing behind the table serving.

"Are you going to dance, Antonietta?" Samantha asked.

She shook her head. "I haven't danced since before my husband died."

"I'm sure Matt would dance with you if you'd like."

Antonietta chuckled. "It was a miracle that you got him to dance with you tonight, and I think one miracle is all we can hope for."

"I'm not that bad," Matt said.

Antonietta patted his cheek as she passed him a glass of fruit punch. "Of course not, Matteo, now go sit down with your punch. You need your rest. I have a feeling that Samantha is going to wear you out this evening."

As they walked over to a pair of empty chairs, Bradley Smith, a young miner Matt knew from school, stopped Matt.

"Do you think there will be more firings, Matt?" he asked.

"Why are you asking me?" Matt said quickly.

"I don't know. I'm just trying to make small talk."

Matt shook his head. "Think of something different to talk about. You'll depress everyone here."

"Well, we are depressed or at least worried," Bradley said. "No one knows how the company found out those miners had just joined the union. Until we do, anyone who joins might get fired."

"It has always been a risk to join the union, Bradley. Nothing has changed."

Matt and Samantha walked over to the chairs and sat down.

"What was that about?" Samantha asked.

Matt explained the situation between the union and coal company to her as she sipped her punch.

"The union sounds like a good thing for the miners," she said when he finished.

"It can be. The problem is that when it grows to the size of the

UMW, it is essentially a big business using the same sort of tactics that it complains about the mining companies using."

Matt pointed across the hall. "There's my Uncle Samuel and his wife."

Myrna held onto Samuel's arm as they walked across the floor. Samuel was dressed in a white shirt and black pants. His blue tie looked as if it was choking him.

Myrna sat down next to Samantha. "Hello, I'm Matteo's aunt, Myrna Ansaro." She shook Samantha's hand.

"I'm Samantha Havencroft."

"You seem to have made Matteo very happy."

"Myrna!" Samuel said. "Don't embarrass the boy."

"Too late," Matt muttered.

Samantha laughed and patted him on the arm. "It's all right. You've made me very happy, too."

Matt just smiled.

"Samuel, when are you going to ask me to dance?" Myrna asked.

"In a minute, in a minute, I need to get used to this," Samuel said.

"What is there to get used to?" Samantha asked.

Samuel's eyes widened. "Dancing."

"I can tell you are related to Matt. You sound like him, but he managed to dance."

"Damn Prohibition," Samuel muttered. "I could use a drink." Then Samuel realized what he had said and shook his head. "Pardon my language, ladies."

Myrna stood up. "I should say so."

She walked off to join Antonietta at the refreshment table.

Samuel sighed and sat down on the chair that Myrna had left. He didn't talk to Matt or Samantha. He just listened to the music. Eventually, Samantha noticed Samuel's foot begin to tap in time with the music. He stopped when he noticed it himself and looked almost ashamed.

"What's the problem, Samuel?" Samantha asked.

He blushed. "I'm not much of a dancer. I never had much time or call for it."

"I think your wife knows how good a dancer or not that you are."

Samuel snorted and nodded his head. "Yes…she does. She's the only woman I've danced with in the past seven years."

"Well, if she still wants to dance with you knowing that, dance with the lady."

Samuel frowned as he thought over what Samantha had said. Then he stood up, took a deep breath, and walked over to Myrna. Samantha watched him say something to her. He took her hand, and they walked out into the middle of the room to start dancing.

"That was very kind of you," Matt said.

She smiled. "You know me and dancing."

A young man whom Matt didn't know walked over and stood nervously in front of Samantha. He swayed back and forth slightly, looking everywhere but at Samantha.

"Would…" He cleared his throat. "Would you like to dance?"

Samantha looked over at Matt. He smiled and shrugged.

"Go ahead, I know how much you love it," Matt said.

She kissed him on the cheek. "Don't worry. I know who I came to the dance with."

"Yes, but I also know you're of an independent mind, so coming to the dance with me wouldn't bother you too much if you saw a better opportunity."

Samantha stood up. "I don't think I will, as far as better opportunities go."

She took the young miner's arm and walked out onto the dance floor with him. As awkward as he seemed, he was actually as good a dancer as Samantha.

Peter and Laura came off the dance floor. Laura sat down beside Matt. He was surprised to see that she was wearing make-up, which she rarely did.

"Hi, Matt," she said.

Peter shook Matt's hand. "How are you doing, Matt?"

"I'm fine."

Peter looked at Laura. "I'm going to go get us some punch."

He walked off toward the refreshment table.

"I see you brought Samantha with you," Laura said, nodding toward his date on the dance floor.

Matt nodded. "We've seen a bit of each other, and we get along well."

"She seems nice."

"Yes," Matt agreed. "She is very nice."

The conversation died off, and Matt watched Samantha laughing and smiling as she danced.

"Remember the last time we were here?" Laura asked.

Matt shook his head. He did, but he didn't want to be reminded of it, especially by Laura.

"It had to be before I left for the war," he said.

Laura nodded. "It was another dance. It was the end-of-the-year school dance."

Her end-of-the-year school dance. Matt hadn't finished school. He was working in the mines by then.

"Oh."

Laura arched her eyebrows. "Now you remember."

"I don't know what to tell you, Laura. I messed up. I know I did," he admitted. He wondered if this was the first time he had apologized for what happened at that dance.

"I guess that I didn't do much better trying to make you jealous," she told him.

"Oh, was that what you were doing?"

"You didn't think so?"

"No, I got jealous. You succeeded on that point. I just didn't think that you were trying to make me jealous. I thought that you were just enjoying yourself too much."

He remembered how they had come to the end-of-the-year dance together at the Literary and Sporting Club Hall. The dance had been for any young person, no matter what school they attended or even if they attended school.

At seventeen, Laura had been coming into full womanhood. She had looked radiant in her light yellow dress that showed off her legs quite well. Things had started out fine with the two of

221

them dancing and laughing.

By the end of the evening, she was dancing with any boy who asked her and kissing half of them right out there in the middle of the room.

Laura blushed. "I have to admit it was fun, but I think it would have been more fun if I hadn't been doing it to make you jealous. I kept watching you and trying to watch for your reaction every time I kissed one of those guys."

"Does Pete know you kiss and tell?"

She punched him lightly on the arm. "Yes. We've talked about each other's pasts in our conversations."

"So that's why he was brusque with me when I first came back to town."

"Probably, but I think it was more than that. He's usually not the jealous type, but he did get jealous of you."

That was true, and Matt had an inkling of why Pete had suddenly gotten jealous. Joseph may have had something to do with it. Pete had mentioned some of the things Joseph had said about Matt and Laura. Either Joseph was totally oblivious as to how what he was saying would sound to Pete, or Joseph had wanted Pete wary of Matt's intentions around Laura.

"I can see why he'd get jealous," Matt said. "You're his wife, and you are this beautiful woman. He has to know how lucky he is, and when people cherish something like that sometimes, they cling to it too hard out of fear of losing it."

Laura's mouth fell open a bit as she stared at him. "Wow, Matt, that is insightful."

"You sound surprised."

"Honestly, I am. You never said things like that before you left Eckhart."

"We both had to grow up sometime. I'm sure being a mother and a wife has changed your outlook on a whole lot of things from when you were an unmarried woman."

"It has. I'd like to think for the better."

"I think that's safe to think. You're more mature now. You seem to be a wonderful mother if Jacob's any indicator. He's happy, and Pete cherishes you. I guess you picked a good guy."

Laura nodded. She looked over at Pete who was speaking with another miner. "I guess I did."

Matt thought that she didn't sound too enthusiastic about what she was saying. Before he could ask her why Pete walked back over. He handed her a glass of punch and sat down beside her.

"Sorry, I took so long. John Montgomery was talking to me."

"That's fine. Matt and I were just talking," Laura told him.

"How are you doing this evening, Matt?" Pete asked. He must have forgotten that he had already asked Matt that question.

"I'm fine. My date is dancing right now with someone else, and I'm just relaxing until she's ready to pull me back onto the floor."

The song ended, and Samantha didn't return to him. He next caught sight of her dancing with a different miner. She must have been asked before she left the floor. Matt had a flashback to the dance that he and Laura had been talking about. It seemed once again that his date preferred someone else.

Of course, that hadn't been the case either time, he reminded himself. Matt was the one who had messed things up with Laura because Sallie Harcourt had just about thrown herself at him, and he had finally given in. Laura had only been trying to make him jealous.

As for Samantha, she just loved dancing and had the energy to do it. Dancing made her happy, and he liked seeing her so.

Matt looked over at Laura and said, "Would you like to dance? That is if Pete doesn't mind."

Pete nodded. "Go ahead. It's one less dance that I will make a fool of myself doing."

Matt led Laura onto the dance floor, and they started doing the foxtrot to "There's a Reason (and It's You)". Laura was almost as good a dancer as Samantha, and she seemed to enjoy it just as much. Matt just felt awkward.

He also kept remembering that last dance before everything went wrong. Matt and Laura had danced nearly every dance trying to get as close as they could without having the chaperone step between them. Those few seconds their bodies had been pressed together had been the most wonderful of his life to that point.

That had been another time, though, before the world had changed; before he had changed.

"What are you thinking about?" Laura asked.

"The last time we danced, I guess."

"Do you wish we could go back to that time?"

Matt considered the pros and cons of such a choice. "On balance, yes. Things were, for me at least, simpler. I didn't have to worry about work. I certainly didn't have this." He waved a hand at his scar. "I wouldn't have seen the things that I saw in Europe, but that's where there's another side to the choice. Because I got away from this town for a while, I saw wonderful things in Europe, too, not just war. Those things I love remembering. It's the other things that haunt me. So what kind of person would I be if I hadn't gone?"

"Do you know?" she asked.

"I think I'd be somewhere between Samuel and Enos. They both have good qualities I would like to think I inherited, but they seem short-sighted at times."

"I like them both. You could do worse."

"What about you? Do you wish we could go back in time?" Matt asked.

"Not really. I love Peter and Jacob, but I do wish I could have not hurt you before you left for the Marines."

"I got over it."

She smiled. "I'm glad. I really am."

The song ended, and Matt walked Laura back to sit with Pete. Samantha was still dancing, so Matt walked outside to get some fresh air.

He leaned against the wall. He could feel his damp shirt clinging to his chest and shoulders.

"Good night, Matt."

He saw Peter and Laura walk out of the hall. They were smiling and laughing. Peter had his arm around his wife's shoulders.

"Calling it an early night?" Matt asked.

"A neighbor is watching Jacob, and I don't want to impinge on her kindness too much," Laura said.

"Did you have fun this evening?" Matt asked.

"Yes, but certainly not as much fun as Samantha is having."

Matt smiled and nodded. "She does love to dance."

"She's very nice and smart, too."

"She's studying to be a teacher, but I would bet that she winds up running a business if not the state." He said it with pride in his voice as if it had been his accomplishment. He was proud of her, though. She would be a success at whatever profession she pursued.

Laura and Pete laughed.

"Good for her!" Laura said.

"I'm going to head home," Peter said. "Take your time. I'll get Jacob from Helen's house."

Pete shook Matt's hand. "I'll see you in the mine on Monday."

"Take care of yourself, Matt."

After Pete walked away, Matt said, "It's nice that he isn't angry with me anymore. It makes working together more pleasant."

"Yes, it makes things better for me, too. I think after seeing Samantha, he realized he's got nothing to worry about when you've got such a beautiful girlfriend."

"You make it sound like you're ugly."

Laura shrugged. "Not ugly, but I'm a coal miner's wife and a mother."

"What's that mean?"

"Well, I can't afford make-up or fancy clothes to make me look pretty, and having a baby has changed my shape."

"Laura, you're still beautiful," Matt said.

Laura smiled and looked at the ground. "Thank you, but I can look in the mirror."

Matt wished that he could say something to make her see herself the way that he and Pete and just about any other man saw her.

"Do you ever think about what life would have been like if we had stayed together?" Laura asked.

"Sometimes, but it's hard to guess. If we had stayed together, would I have even gone off to fight?"

Laura nodded. "Yes."

"You sound certain."

"I am. You always wanted to get away from here. I don't think that would have changed. What would have changed is that I would have gone with you."

"And what would you have done while I was in Europe?"

She smiled and turned around slowly. "I would have worked like other women did during the war."

"And when I came home?"

She laughed and grabbed his hand. "We would have started our family."

"You've thought about this."

"From time to time." Laura paused. "The thing I don't think you thought about was coming back here. It's obvious that you don't want to be here, Matt."

It was true that he really didn't want to be here, but obvious? He thought that he was hiding his feelings pretty well.

"I may not want to, but I need to be here," Matt said.

He still felt that he had done the right thing to try and help his family, and if he hadn't returned, he wouldn't have met Samantha.

"Laura, the reason that I cheated on you had nothing to do with you," Matt said.

"I know that now. I know I did nothing to cause you to cheat. I loved you."

Matt nodded. "And I loved you."

"So then why did you do it?"

That was a question that Matt had thought about more than once over the years. "Because I could. Sallie Harcourt was flirting with me, and I was flattered. I was a teenager who only really worried about himself. I didn't understand my feelings. I just acted on them. I wouldn't do that now."

Laura cocked her head. "Really?"

"You don't think so?"

"I don't know, but I heard about the woman in the hospital."

The town grapevine was working overtime. He wondered what other stories were whispered around town about him.

"She's a friend," he said.

"As I recall, that's what you told me about Sallie."

"I'm not lying."

"I'm not saying that, Matt. Samantha is a wonderful woman. Don't break her heart," Laura warned him.

"Like I broke yours?"

Laura paused and considered her response. "Yes. You did break my heart, and it took me a long time to get over it."

Matt saw a flash of pain in her eyes and looked away.

"I've had my own heart broken since then, Laura. I know what it feels like, and once again, I'm sorry for what I did to you."

"You don't have to keep apologizing, Matt."

"I think I do because it still bothers you," he said.

The door to the hall opened, and Samantha came out holding a cup of punch in one hand and waving her other hand in front of her face as a fan.

"Oh, there you are. I was wondering where you went," she said.

"It got too hot in there for me."

Samantha nodded. "I know, even with the windows open, I'm starting to perspire."

"Not surprising given the way you were dancing."

"I like to dance."

"And you're so good at it," Laura said.

"Thank you. You and your husband seemed to be having fun inside," Samantha said.

"We did, but we also have a young child. Pete already headed home, and I am on my way."

"Goodbye, Laura," Matt said.

"Goodbye, Matt, remember what I said."

"I could say the same thing to you."

Laura walked away into the night, and Samantha walked over next to Matt. He took her hand in his.

"Did I interrupt you two?" Samantha asked.

"We were talking. We've known each other since we were in school together."

Samantha leaned forward and kissed Matt.

"Thank you for bringing me this evening," she said.

"I'm glad that you had fun, but when we go back in, I want all your dances for a while," Matt said.

Samantha grinned. "I think that can be arranged, but I think I'd like being out here for a while longer."

He hugged her and leaned back to stare at the stars.

Chapter 29

March 22, 1922

Matt walked Samantha to her house after their dinner in Frostburg. As he was giving her a goodnight kiss at her front door, it opened. Her father stood there looking at them. His expression stayed neutral.

"Ah, Samantha, there you are. Look who stopped by." He opened the door wider, and Matt saw a man about his age, although he was well dressed, unlike Matt.

Samantha stepped back from Matt. "Vernon, I didn't expect you this evening," she said.

"I was in the neighborhood, and I thought that I would stop by to see you and your father," the young man said.

Samantha figured it would take a coin toss to decide whom Vernon wanted to see more, her or her father.

John Havencroft waved her inside. "Come, Samantha, don't keep your guest waiting. Matt, you'll have to excuse her."

Matt held his hands up in surrender. "That's quite all right, sir."

"I'm sorry, Matt, I'll talk to you later," she said as her father took her by the arm to lead her inside.

When the door shut, Samantha said, "Father that was very rude."

Ignoring her, John Havencroft said, "Why don't you and Vernon go into the sitting room and talk?"

Vernon Mitchell reached out for her hand to lead her into the sitting room, but Samantha pulled her hand away.

"Vernon, I've told you before that I'm not interested, and I told you not to touch me," she said through clenched teeth.

He pulled his hand back. "Just give me a chance."

"The young man is right, Samantha. Give him the opportunity," her father said.

Samantha glared at her father. She couldn't believe that he was putting her in this position. It wasn't even to make her happy. He wanted to advance his career.

"Vernon has been telling me that his father has a house at the ocean, and he's invited us to spend part of the summer with them," John said.

"His father the state senator," Samantha said.

Her father, at least, had the integrity to look ashamed. Samantha shook her head. Then she turned and went upstairs to her bedroom.

The door closed and Matt found himself standing alone on the front porch. Well, that hadn't gone the way he expected it.

He stared at the door for a few moments. He thought that he had gotten along well with Samantha's father when they first met.

Matt walked back into town and started to head towards Eckhart Mines. As he passed the Hitchins Brothers Store, he noticed a man talking loudly with a woman. He almost passed it off as a drunk, but then he noticed the man's bowler. Once he saw that, he noticed the man's height and size.

Matt slowed down so that he could get a closer look at the man. He had a break in his eyebrow above his right eye.

The stranger passed him by. Matt waited a moment and then turned to follow him and the woman. They went into the speakeasy in Failinger's basement. Tobacco smoke clouded the air making it harder to see. It was hard for Matt to stay inconspicuous in the basement room. It was small and a quarter of it was dominated by a cockfighting pit. The two roosters clawing at each other with the razors on their feet kept most of the people's attention. Men and some women cheered on their favorites.

Matt walked up to the bar and ordered a whiskey.

The stranger held one arm around the woman and watched the cockfight. The woman tried to turn away from the bloody fight, but the man laughed at her and held tight enough that she winced. The more that she struggled, the tighter he held on. Finally, she managed to grab a drink and throw it in his face.

He yelled and grabbed for his eyes to wipe the alcohol away. The woman took the opportunity to run away.

When the man had cleared his eyes, he looked around to see the woman had gone. The other men in the room laughed at him. He scowled and stormed out of the speakeasy.

Matt hoped that the woman had gotten far enough away so that this man wouldn't catch up with her because if he did, it wouldn't be pretty. This was definitely the man who had beaten Calista. There was no doubt in Matt's mind.

Matt followed the man out of the speakeasy and down the hallway. Rather than heading left for the stairs to the first floor, he turned right to walk down another hall and out the basement entrance at the back of the hotel.

That suited Matt fine. The National Road had too many street lights. As the back road passed behind the tall buildings on the National Road, it grew even darker. Matt quickened his pace and caught up to the stranger.

"Wait a minute," Matt said.

When the man turned, Matt punched him in the jaw. The stranger staggered back a step, but he kept on his feet.

"I hear that you like to hit women," Matt said.

The man laughed. "Who doesn't?"

"You hit the wrong one."

"I never hit the wrong one, because if I hit any of them, they deserve it."

The stranger was trying to anger him, and it worked. Matt swung again, but this time, the stranger blocked the punch with his left arm and landed his own punch in Matt's stomach. The breath went out of Matt, but he kept his senses long enough to block the stranger's follow-up punch.

The stranger had a couple inches and at least ten pounds on Matt, but Matt held his own as the two exchanged punches. Matt swung hard and knocked the man down, but the man grabbed a rock and slammed it into Matt's crotch.

Matt grunted and staggered back. Fireworks exploded in his vision. The stranger got to his feet and moved in on Matt, still holding the rock. Matt held his crotch and felt like he could barely breathe. He wanted to scream. He saw the stranger coming at him and wanted to get to his feet, but he couldn't manage it.

The tall man raised the rock to swing it at Matt's head. Matt grabbed his boot knife and stabbed the man in the leg. He let out a yelp and dropped the rock. He staggered out of Matt's reach.

Matt sheathed his knife. He pushed himself to his hands and knees and then to his feet. He started after the stranger in a shambling walk. The stranger wasn't moving fast with his leg injured.

Matt jumped on the man's back, taking him to the ground. Then he began pummeling the man with his fists until the stranger passed out.

Matt stood up and kicked the guy in the crotch for good measure. Let him see how that felt when he woke up.

He began searching the man's pockets looking for a wallet with some identification. He found a leather wallet. When Matt opened it up, something shiny caught his attention. It was a Pinkerton badge.

Matt found a piece of paper with the man's name on it. David Lakehurst. Matt dropped the wallet. This guy was an undercover detective like Matt. Matt had just beaten up someone who worked for the same company that he did.

He stumbled away from the unconscious man and headed home.

When Matt came into the house, Antonietta was sitting on the sofa knitting. She jumped to her feet when she saw him.

"Matt, what happened to you?"

"I was giving someone what he deserved and getting a bit of

what I deserved."

He started toward his room.

"It looks like you weren't even fighting back."

"I was."

"Get into your room. I'll bring you some towels and warm water. I want to make sure to wash those cuts."

"Do you really care, Aunt?" He said more sharply than he meant to.

"Of course I do. I may not like some of the things you've done, but you're still my nephew. Family is important, Matt, more important than an argument or the mine."

He nodded and staggered back to his room. He shut the door behind him and fell backward onto his bed. It even hurt when bounced a bit on the mattress.

Matt sighed and rubbed his face. What was he going to do now? When the agency found out that Lakehurst had been attacked, what would they think? What would they do? Would they blame the incident on the rowdiness of Frostburg or miners who discovered Lakehurst's identity? It was certain that the man wouldn't tell his manager that he had been beating up women.

The Pinkerton Agency would almost need to make some response to the incident. Would they send in more agents like Baldwin-Felts had during the trouble in Matewan? Matt shook his head. No, the outcome would be similar to what happened on Blair Mountain.

The Consolidation Coal Company was trying to avoid trouble. They didn't want to start more riots.

Matt heard a knock at the door. "Come in."

Antonietta walked in holding a wash basin. She set it on the nightstand next to the bed and dipped a washcloth into the water. She wiped at the dirt on Matt's face as he winced.

"Serves you right, getting into a fight like that," Antonietta said. "Was it worth it?"

"I hope so," Matt murmured.

Chapter 30

March 25, 1922

Matt stopped by Calista's house, knocked on the door, and waited. He looked around, wondering if any of her neighbors spied on her to see who visited. He heard movement behind the door.

"Who is it?"

"Matt."

He heard a door lock thrown back. Calista opened the door a few inches. Matt noticed the bruising on her face had nearly faded.

"Hello, Matt."

Her eyes darted around as if she expected to see someone else.

Calista opened the door wider. "Would you like to come in?"

"I need to show you something," he said without entering the house.

"What's that?"

"You need to come with me to the hospital."

"Matt, I don't want to. I just got out of there."

"It won't take long. Is there some reason that you can't come? Are you feeling bad?"

Calista shook her head. "No, it's just that …" She sighed. "I'm a little nervous about going out." Was she already back to work?

He wondered if she had gone out at all since he had brought her home. If not, that meant she wouldn't be working or buying food for herself.

"Why is that?"

Her eyes teared up. "Because I got beaten up."

"Jenny, that is something that happened in a dark alley at night. You were alone with the wrong guy. It's daylight now. We're going to the hospital, and we'll be in plain view of someone at all times."

"It's not that I don't trust you, Matt, I do," she said quickly.

Matt nodded. "I'm just trying to address your concerns, and you really need to see what I want to show you."

"Can't you just tell me what it is?" Calista asked.

"If I did, you might not believe me."

She sighed. "OK, let me get my coat."

She went back inside the house and came back a few moments later wearing a well-kept red flannel coat that reached her calves. She locked the door behind her, and they walked into town.

At Miner's Hospital, Matt led her to the men's ward. He stopped at the door and put his hands on her shoulders.

"I need you to wait here a second. I need to check on something," he told her.

Calista hesitated and then nodded. Matt patted her shoulder. "I won't be long. I promise."

Matt walked into the men's ward. When he came back out, he offered his arm to her and led Calista into the room where there were a dozen beds. Most of them were filled with miners who had suffered severe injuries. He led her about halfway into the room and pointed to a sleeping man. When Matt heard Calista's breath catch, he knew it was the right man.

"Is this the guy who beat you up?" he asked.

He looked over at her. Her lower lip trembled as if she might cry.

"Yes," she finally said. She looked at Matt. "What happened to him?"

"The same sort of thing that happened to you, except that he came out on the losing end this time."

Calista grabbed Matt's arm. "Did you do this to him?"

"It's not something you need to know. Don't worry about it,"

Matt said.

"Just like I didn't need to know who paid for my hospital stay?"

Matt nodded. "Right. Because it got taken care of, didn't it?"

"Matt."

"Jenny, he is a bad man, and he is going to get what he de-serves. So we need to make another stop now."

"Where?"

Her voice was stronger now. She didn't seem as timid as she had at the house. Her mouth held the hint of a smile.

"The police station," Matt said.

The smile vanished.

"What? No!" Calista said.

Matt laid a calming hand on her shoulder. "Hear me out. You need to swear out a complaint against that man, so charges are pressed against him," Matt said, pointing at the sleeping man. "He will be kept either here or in a jail cell."

"The police will want to know why I was going somewhere with a man that I didn't know. They can arrest me."

She looked panicked, and Matt thought that she might bolt. He grabbed her lightly by the arm and led Calista from the ward.

"Did he pay you any money?" Matt asked when they were in the hallway.

"No."

"Then tell the police the truth. Just don't mention you were expecting to be paid. You didn't do anything wrong." He patted her hand. "I will stay with you, so you don't get in trouble."

They left Miner's Hospital and walked up Water Street to Main Street where they could get to the police station. It was a small office with two rooms, and the rear room held two jail cells.

Calista hesitated at the door. "Matt, what if that man comes back and gets me for swearing out a complaint against him?"

Matt stopped and looked into her light-blue eyes. He said, "I can promise you that he won't."

"How can you do that? How can you make that promise? You don't know what will happen if this goes to trial or even if it will go to trial."

Matt sighed, leaned closer to her, and said in a low voice, "Because when I did that to him, I told him that if he ever came near you again, he would get even worse than what happened this time."

Calista stepped back and stared at him. "You did do that to him."

Then she just cried. After a few moments, she leaned against him, still crying, and hugged him tightly. She stood on her toes and gave him a kiss. It was a gentle kiss, a thank-you kiss, nothing like the faked passion when they had spent the night together.

Unfortunately, she did it on the street in full view of anyone passing by. Normally, Matt wouldn't have minded that, but this time, he heard a voice shout, "What is that all about?"

Matt stepped back, looked over his shoulder and saw Samantha walking down the street carrying a soapbox filled with her pamphlets about women's rights. She got in front of Matt.

"I thought I meant something to you," Samantha said.

"You do."

"You're here kissing another woman. How could you do this to me? I thought you were different from other men, Matt!"

Before Matt could say anything, she slapped him across the face. She spun on her heels and hurried off, crying.

Calista said, "Matt, I'm so sorry. I didn't mean to..."

Matt held up his hand. "I know. I know, Jenny, and it's not your fault. Samantha's scared that I was going to hurt her, and I did." He snorted. "I guess I'm doing a pretty good job of making women cry today."

"You need to go after her, Matt."

He shook his head. "She wouldn't listen to me now. She's angry and hurt. You saw how she was. That's a problem for another day. Besides, you and I need to go in here."

He glanced once more after Samantha and then opened the door. Calista stepped inside. A police officer sat at his desk.

Matt nudged Calista. "Officer, Miss Forrester here, would like to make a complaint against a man in the hospital."

The tall policeman fished a pad from a drawer and picked up his pencil. "What kind of complaint."

Calista took a deep breath, and said, "He ... he attacked me."

Chapter 31

March 26, 1922

Matt knocked on the door to his old house. Pete answered.

"Matt, I didn't expect to see you here."

"I'm sorry to disturb you all on a Sunday, but I have a problem I'm hoping Laura can help me with."

Pete looked confused, but he opened the door wider to allow Matt inside the small house. It looked very similar to the way it had when he had lived here with his parents. The furniture was different but just as well used. The walls had a permanent dinginess that came because scrubbing failed to remove all of the coal dust.

Laura was sitting on the floor playing with Jacob. Matt thought the boy would grow up looking more like his father than his mother.

"Hello, Matt, did you say you need my help?" Laura asked.

"Yes, I need advice from a woman's viewpoint."

Pete walked over and took Jacob's hand. "We'll go into the bedroom so you two can talk."

"It's all right, Pete. You can stay. I know this probably makes you a bit uneasy. If I knew someone else I could ask, I would. My aunt is too old to give me the right view, and she's mad at me right now, anyway."

Pete sat down on the sofa, and Matt sat in the rocking chair.

He explained what had happened with Calista and Samantha and who Calista was and why she had kissed him. When he finished, Pete looked embarrassed. Laura looked angry.

"I'm surprised at you sleeping with a prostitute," Laura said.

Matt decided not to tell her it wasn't the first time.

"And what you did for her," she added.

"I would have done it for any woman treated that way," Matt said.

"Are you in love with her?"

"She's half again my age, Laura."

"So?"

He made a conscious effort not to sigh. After all, he wanted her advice.

"I'm not in love with her, but I do like her," he said. "I don't think she deserved to be mistreated. I also don't agree with what's she's doing..."

"But you had sex with her."

"... or the fact that she does it. As for what I did, you better than most should know I'm not perfect."

"I never thought that you were," Laura said quickly.

That comment hurt Matt a bit. He had hoped that she might deny it. He had always thought he'd been at his best with Laura. Before their last dance, of course.

"So you think I shouldn't have helped Calista?"

Laura shook her head. "No, that was a kind thing you did–dangerous–but kind."

"Then how do I make Samantha understand?"

"You've got to talk to her, Matt, and tell her what you just told me."

"Don't you think I've tried? She won't see me. When I met her, she didn't trust men. I managed to get through that with her, but she saw Calista giving me a kiss, and she thinks the worst again."

Laura stopped playing with Jacob and looked up. "Is that why you came to me? That's kinda cruel, Matt."

He blushed and nodded. "I know, but I thought you would

keep me from making another mistake."

Pete leaned forward. "Did I miss something?"

"This is what happened with Matt and me at the dance years ago," Laura told her husband.

"The dance?"

"Before he left for the Marines." She looked at Matt. "I guess women can't help kissing you."

"Calista was different. Sallie was being forward, but Calista was thanking me. The result is the same. How do I keep Samantha from being you after the dance? If I don't fix things, she'll go back to not trusting men. Maybe worse than before."

"You don't know that, Matt. I got past our breakup." Laura patted Pete on the knee, and he smiled.

"I know she won't speak to me or listen to me. I'm not even sure how she will react to the truth that Calista is a prostitute. That will just make her think she's right about men," Matt said.

"You giving up, Matt?"

"I haven't yet, have I?"

"You asked for my opinion. You never tried to fix things between us after the dance," Laura said.

"You know why."

Laura nodded. "I was mad, yes, and I made you mad. You didn't even try then to fix things, but you're not stopping now."

She was right. He thought that he was trying to fix things, but he was ready now to give up. Like he had given up on Laura. Like he hadn't fought to stop Priscilla from ending things with him.

"I don't want to give up, but I don't want to hurt her anymore. I'm not sure how to be the person she wants me to be or needs me to be."

"But do you want to try?"

"I'm here, aren't I?" Matt snapped. "You don't know how hard it is for me to be here and tell you all of this."

She reached over and patted his arm. "I do know, and I know Samantha is a very nice girl. She is worth the effort." Laura paused and then asked, "Do you love her?"

Matt sighed and shrugged. "Sometimes I think I do, but that

scares me. I know what Priscilla did to me."

"Samantha's not Priscilla."

"When I first met her, I thought that she might be."

"And now?"

Matt shook his head. "They look similar, but once you get to know them, that disappears."

"So do you think Samantha will break your heart?"

Matt frowned. "She may already have."

Chapter 32

March 29, 1922

Peter heard the noise first. He stopped hammering at the coal seam and touched Matt's arm.

"Hold up," he said. Matt stopped. Silence fell in the shaft. The next pair of miners was too far away to hear. "Listen."

Then Matt felt more than heard the rumble of the earth. The ground trembled. Little bits of dirt fell from the roof, and small clods bounced around on the ground.

"We need to go. Now!" Peter shouted.

They tried to run out of the tunnel where they were working, but it was too low, and they kept hitting their heads and falling into the mud. Finally, they gave up and crawled as fast as they could. They were nearing the point where their tunnel intersected with the main heading when the roof in front of them gave way, and a wall of earth tumbled down. The gust of air it created blew dirt into Matt's face, and he scrambled backward with his eyes closed.

Matt heard Peter yelling above the sound of earth falling and timbers cracking, but he couldn't make out what he said.

Other miners had sensed or heard the cave in and hurried for the surface. Then all of the noise stopped, and they were surprised to find their way out still open, although the air was cloudy with dirt. They ran to the tool shed and hung their medallions on their hooks and began looking around for friends who might not have come out of the mine.

"Who's missing?" was the most common cry heard. No one asked what had happened. They all knew a cave-in had occurred somewhere in the mine.

The empty hooks slowly filled as medallions were hung on them, but it was the empty hook that drew attention.

Joseph McCord rushed down from the mine office, his face red from exertion.

"Where did it happen?" he shouted.

"I saw dust coming out of the northwest heading," one miner shouted.

"Anyone come out of there?"

"I did," another miner shouted. "It happened somewhere down there, but I couldn't tell where with all of the dust."

Joseph looked at the board. Still too many empty hooks. He hoped that they would fill up soon.

"Some of you go and see if you can help anyone still coming out. If there are any injured, come back out and let us know. The doctor's on his way."

Three men hurried forward and grabbed their medallions off the board and headed back into the mine.

"I heard something that sounded like a pop right before all hell broke loose," one miner said.

"A pop?" Joseph said.

"Yes, sir, like a firecracker."

"Where were you working?"

"In the northern tunnel."

So it wasn't the same tunnel. The sound might have been louder in the shaft where it happened. Joseph looked around for the miner who said he had come from the northwest heading.

"You there, did you hear a popping sound?"

The miner shook his head. "No, sir, I was working right up to the time the ground started moving under us."

Picking and talking. He might not have heard the sound. A

popping like a firecracker. If black powder had exploded, it would have made a louder sound. No one described that as a popping. It might have been a smaller explosion, but would that have been powerful enough to bring down a tunnel?

Joseph began pacing. He didn't need this now. It was going to hold up production when he needed to keep things as efficient as possible.

People from town started filtering down to the mine, drawn by the crowd or the news that would be spreading from house to house. He figured only a few people had actually felt the ground shaking, and they may have passed it off as a regular detonation. Joseph had thought so until one of the miners brought him the news.

He looked around at the anxious faces. They depended on him. He was a leader, the leader, in Eckhart Mines. He needed to take control of the situation.

"There's been a cave in, folks. It looks like it was a small one, but we're still trying to make sure everyone is all right," Joseph told them.

Wives started crying, and the younger children looked confused, not understanding what had happened. Joseph saw Laura standing with Jacob off to the side. She was standing on an overturned bucket looking for her husband.

Joseph walked over to her.

Laura saw him coming, and said, "I don't see Peter, Joey."

Joseph glanced at the board. A few more medallions were on the board, but there were still too many empty hooks. Everyone had to be all right. Too many dead miners would shut the mine down while inspectors checked everything out. They might realize that the timbers he was using weren't nearly as thick as they should be.

"Not everyone's out yet. He may be one of the stragglers," Joseph said.

"He was working with Matt. Have you seen him?"

Joseph thought for a moment. "No, but it's doubtful you'd see one and not the other. Since they were together."

Joseph saw the miners who had gone to check on the rest exit the mine.

"That's all we saw or heard from," one of them called to Joseph. They hung up their medallions.

"Anyone else holding onto a medallion?" Tom Gianconne called out. No one came forward. Tom looked at the board. "We've got six trapped miners."

Chapter 33

March 29, 1922

Matt opened his eyes and peered over the edge of the trench. He could see the yellowish cloud rolling over the field. Men ran toward the trench.

"Masks! Masks!"

The Marines scrambled for the gas masks hung on their belts or the underground rooms. They needed to get them on before the cloud hit them. It continued to roll across the field, and Matt heard a rumble like the ground collapsing around him.

"Masks! Masks! Matt!"

Matt shook his head and realized he was in the mine tunnel. His headlamp had gone out, and he was in complete darkness. A chunk of rock had hit his hart hat, leaving him dazed. Peter was calling out his name.

Matt coughed up some of the dirt he had inhaled when the roof collapsed.

"Pete! Where are you?" he called.

"Over here." It was a voice in the darkness.

Matt tried to crawl in the direction of Pete's voice, but he realized that his legs were buried. He sat up and felt large chunks of earth and rock covering his feet. He was lucky he hadn't been killed under all of that. He grabbed at the pile, but it came away in

246

his hand. He tried again and felt a small boulder.

"Pete! I'm trapped. I need your help."

"I…I don't know, Matt."

"Are you trapped?"

"We both are!" Pete yelled.

"No, I mean, can you move?"

"Yes." His voice trembled, and Matt wondered if his friend was about to cry.

He relit the carbide in his headlamp. Dust hung in the air, which cut down on how far the light from his headlamp could penetrate. Matt couldn't see Pete, which might be for the best.

The ground was still now. Everything that had wanted to fall must have fallen. Now it was just a matter of getting out. Part of their tunnel had collapsed, and it had been the wrong part, in front of them rather than behind.

"Pete, go back to the face and get our picks and shovels. We're going to need them," Matt told him.

"What if there's another cave in?"

"If that happens, then it doesn't matter where we are. We'll both be dead. Right now, I want to get my legs free and then start digging our way out of here."

"We'll never be able to do it. The whole mountain came down. It's trying to kill me."

"What are you talking about?"

"This is the second time."

"You can't call what happened to you before a cave in."

"I was nearly killed before," Pete said.

He was on the verge of panic.

"Pete, calm down. The ground has settled. They'll be checking who made it out on the surface. When they don't find us, they'll come looking and digging. I want to meet them halfway, but most of all I want out from under this rubble!" Matt used his officer's voice as he had done in Europe to get his men moving.

"Yes, yes, I'll go get the tools."

Matt couldn't help but smile. He wasn't sure what it was in his voice when he talked a certain way, but it certainly made men move their asses.

A couple of minutes later he saw the light from Pete's head-lamp shining in the darkness.

"I'm here," Matt said.

Matt saw Pete's headlamp dance over the wall of rubble. It had entirely filled in the four-foot-high tunnel.

"How far back do you think it goes?" Pete asked.

"I think our tunnel had another ten feet or so. It may have filled it all in." He didn't add that it may even extend further. Pete would figure that out soon enough for himself.

Pete passed him a shovel.

"Let's get my feet free, and then it will be easier to dig our way out."

Joseph knew the crowd, including Laura, was watching him. It was his time to shine; to show that he was a leader.

He sent a rescue crew made up of miners into the shaft. He had given Tom Gianconne the job of leading the rescue party. Joseph's place was here where he could be seen and bring the townspeople peace. The miners would start digging out the tunnels that had collapsed to find the six missing miners, hopefully alive.

Laura had collapsed when she heard that her husband was one of the missing. Joseph had helped her to her feet and gave her a hug as she cried into his chest.

People brought bolts of bed ticking and cloth to build temporary bratticing for the rescue crews to ensure air could flow into the mine. All of the actual brattices near the cave-in had been blown out by the explosion.

Joseph also sent men to make sure the fans were still working. The last thing he needed for was standing air to collect methane and kill the rescuers.

Some of the people began to filter away to return to their homes and businesses, knowing that it could be hours before anything was known about the trapped miners. Wives like Laura would be wondering if they would be widows before the day was out.

Word had slowly spread outside of town, and the townspeople who left were replaced by others. The first to arrive were people from Frostburg. Then came cars or people on the trolley. They didn't want to help. They just wanted to be on hand if something happened.

Samantha stood on her soapbox on the sidewalk next to the National Road proclaiming that women could run a business better than men. They ran families and what were companies other than large families? People passed by ignoring her, and some drivers honked their horns to drown out what she was saying.

Calista approached her from the side so Samantha wouldn't notice her.

"Have you heard what happened in Eckhart?" Calista asked.

Samantha turned, startled. "Why should I care?"

"Don't be catty, Samantha. It doesn't become you."

"Nor does being cheated upon by a man."

Calista shook her head. "You weren't, at least not by Matt. I can't speak for anyone else who knows you."

Samantha glared at her.

"There was a cave-in in one of the tunnels in the Eckhart coal mines," Calista said.

Samantha's eyes widened, but she didn't' say anything.

"I can't believe you," Calista said. "You won't even ask the question will you?"

Samantha pressed her lips together. Calista shrugged and turned away.

"Fine, I'll ask. Is Matt all right?"

"They don't know yet. He's one of six miners trapped in the mine. They think there's at least one dead miner."

Samantha put her hand to her mouth.

"What can I do?"

"For Matt? Nothing. They will find him, but it will take some time to dig through all of the rubble and not cause a cave in. His family will need support, though. I'm sure they are worried. I re-member those times. If the news is bad, they will need someone there to help them get through it all. If the news is good, they will want everyone around them happy."

"We have to go to him."

"We?" Calista asked.

"I thought you loved him."

Calista rolled her eyes. "I've been trying to tell you that it's not like that. Matt has been my friend, a better friend than I deserve."

"Then you should come with me."

"I want to, but I'm being his friend now and making sure you go. You'll be the one he wants to see when he comes out of the mine. I don't need to be there."

"But…"

"Believe me, it's better I not to be there. I might make some people uncomfortable."

Samantha hesitated and then nodded.

She dropped her pamphlets and stepped down off the soapbox. Then she started off down the street at a fast walk.

Calista smiled. She turned the soapbox over and dropped the pamphlets inside. She would drop them off at Samantha's house on her way home.

Samantha walked as fast as she could down the street. She wanted to run but held back not sure how long she could sustain a run in heels.

Was Matt still alive?

What if he wasn't? The last things she had said to him were so mean and hateful. She wanted to take it all back. She shouldn't have gotten so angry. It wasn't like her.

The trolley started past her, and she jumped on board. She dropped into a seat and paid the fare, not worrying whether it was too much or not. At least she wouldn't reach Eckhart out of breath.

She climbed off the trolley at Kelly's Pump. Should she go to the boarding house or to the mine?

The mine. Everyone would be waiting there for word of when each miner was found.

She wouldn't be able to do anything there but wait, but at least she would know about Matt as soon as possible.

Samantha saw the crowd forming as she drew closer to the mine. It appeared everyone in town was here and then some.

She moved through the crowd, occasionally pausing to ask if Matt Ansaro had come out of the mine. She was either told no or that the person she asked didn't know.

Samantha finally spotted Antonietta standing with her sister-in-law. She walked over and put a hand on Antonietta's arm. The older woman turned to face her. Her eyes had dark circles, and she looked forty years older.

"Is Matt all right?" Samantha asked.

"We don't know. Matt was with Pete Spiker. They're both missing."

"What can I do?"

Antonietta shook her head. "Oh, Samantha, Matt and I had such a fight a few days ago."

Samantha hugged her. "I got into an argument with him, too."

"Stubborn boy. If I didn't want to see him so badly, I'd want to slap him."

"Me, too."

Antonietta laughed. Then she smiled and said, "That felt good." She shook her head. "God! I love that boy!"

"So do I!"

Samantha stopped, surprised at what she had just said.

"It's all right, Samantha. Loving someone doesn't make you weak," Antonietta said.

"But it does. Look at us."

"Yes, look at us. We're able to endure because we have other loved ones with us." She squeezed Samantha's hand.

Enos staggered over and asked, "Any word?"

Samantha could smell alcohol on his breath.

"Not of Matt. Someone came out about half an hour ago, saying they had reached Harvey Eichorn and Joe Schellinghaus and talked to them. They're trying to dig them out now."

"Enos, couldn't you stay sober for this, at least?" Myrna asked.

"Can you think of a better time to be drunk? We just got Matt back, and now we may lose him," Enos told her.

"Don't say that! He'll be alive. He has to be."

"He had better be, or Joey McCord will follow him into the ground," Enos said, and he sounded stone cold sober.

"What time is it?" Antonietta asked.

"Four p.m.," Samuel said.

Samantha hadn't seen him approach. He was the quiet brother.

"I need to get dinner ready," Antonietta said without meaning it.

"How can you even think about eating right now?" Enos asked.

"I can't, but I need to do something to keep my mind off of all this. Samantha, why don't you come with me?"

"I don't know much about cooking," Samantha told her.

"But you can keep me company. I need that right now."

Samantha nodded, and they walked off toward the boarding house holding each other by the arm.

Chapter 34

March 29, 1922

When Pete and Matt cleared the rubble from around Matt's legs, they discovered that Matt's right leg was broken. The bone hadn't poked through the skin, but his lower leg was turned at an odd angle where there wasn't a joint.

In truth, Matt wasn't feeling any pain at the moment. He couldn't remember if that meant he was in shock or not.

"Let's keep going," Matt said when he was free.

"What are we going to do with the rubble?"

Peter looked skeptical. "You can keep working like that?"

"I have to. Just keep pushing it behind us. We don't need to save it for anything and moving it out of the way to the face will just make us tired all that much faster." *And use up our air.*

They started digging. It was easier going than working at the face because the rubble was loose. On the other hand, they had to be careful not to cause more debris to rain down on them.

They had been digging for a while when Pete said, "I used to hate you, you know."

Matt paused, surprised. Not knowing what Pete wanted to hear, he admitted, "I know."

"You're a good friend to her and to me, too, I want you to know that. I don't feel those bad things anymore."

"That's good to know, Pete, because I think of you as a friend, too."

Then, as if embarrassed, they shut up and just dug. They were making progress. Whether it was going to make a difference remained to be seen. They had no choice, though. If they continued to wait, either the lack of air or black damp would get them. Better to die trying than to just wait to die.

Matt's leg started to ache, and he wished he had whiskey to kill the pain. Heck, he wished he had water to quench his thirst.

"Hey, Pete, I just had a thought."

"What's that?"

"When we get ourselves out of here, I'm going to be telling people about how you rescued me from under all that rubble. Then you'll be a miner who rescued a war hero." Matt chuckled. "What do you think about that?"

"That sounds grand, Matt, but I'm not sure if I'll be around to enjoy it."

"What do you mean?"

"I got hit with falling rubble, too, when the roof gave way. It didn't trap me like you, but it did something to me. Maybe it broke some bones or something else, but I'm not right inside. I've been feeling it for a while."

Matt grabbed his arm and pulled Pete down. "Sit down, and let me look at you."

Pete shook his head. "It doesn't matter, Matt. You can't do anything about it. What's going to happen is going to happen. The mine doctor can take a look at me, but that's not going to happen until we get out of here, and that's not going to happen for me."

"What are you talking about? If you're standing, you can't be hurt too bad."

Pete shook his head. "I am hurting bad inside. Every time I take a breath, it feels like I'm being stabbed with a knife. And now, I can't even take a deep breath anymore."

"Then rest. Let me dig. They're coming for us, Pete, you just have to hold on until they find us. You don't want to die underground."

"That's what miners do, Matt."

"No, miners live above ground. Underground is where they go when they are dead. You aren't dead. You have a lot to live for. You have to hold on. When I was in the trenches in Europe, I had to fight to live. Sometimes living is not easy, but it shouldn't be. That's how we realize how precious it is."

Matt wasn't sure he even believed what he was saying. Oh, he thought that Pete had plenty to live for, but Matt wondered if his life mattered. Had fighting to survive the war made a difference to anyone? He didn't have siblings. His parents were dead. He didn't have a wife. Yes, he had fought for his country. When Priscilla dumped him, he had fought not for her but to move past her. Sometimes he thought that he had found his right direction. Not because he wandered into it but because he made the choice.

Pete wasn't convinced. "I'm just a miner. I'm nobody. This mine has been after me. If it doesn't get me now, then it will get me later. I'll die in the mines. That's nothing to live for."

"You've got a wife. You've got a son. You've got things that I can only wish for," Matt said. "Right now, and you've got them, but you've got to fight to keep them." Pete leaned his head back against the wall of the tunnel and shook it back and forth. "What are they going to do without you? You can't let them down. They depend on you." Matt snorted. "Not special? No one else in this world is Jacob's father. What would he do without you? No one else is Laura's husband. What would she do without you?"

"She'd have you," Pete said quietly.

"Pete, don't start that again. I thought we were past that. Laura loves you."

"I know, but you're special to her. If I die, she and Jacob would have you. You would watch over them. Right?"

Matt wasn't sure how to answer that. Certainly, he would watch out for Laura and Jacob, but he didn't want Pete to give up. "Yes, but I'd be a poor substitute."

Pete didn't say anything. He just nodded, and they continued digging. It was slow going because they weren't just moving loose dirt. Rocks and chunks of coal had to be cleared away; some of them large. Matt just hoped that people on the other side were working toward reaching them.

Joseph led Laura back to the mining office and had her sit at his desk. Then he walked next door and filled a cup of water for her.

"Drink this," he said, passing her the cup.

"I'm not thirsty."

"You're probably dehydrated. You've been standing out there for hours. You can rest here. Someone will let us know if … when they find Pete. We'll have time to get back to the mine before the rescuers bring them out."

Laura stared at the floor and shook her head. "He can't be dead. He just can't."

Joseph placed a hand on her back and gently rubbed her. "Everything will be all right, Laura."

She leaned against him and sobbed.

Joseph heard a knock at the door. It opened, and Adam Sivic walked in. "Excuse me, but you asked to be notified when they found someone."

Laura sat up straight. "Who?"

"Harvey Eichorn and Joe Schellinghaus," Adam said. "Rico Moretti died in the cave in."

"Is the doctor there?" Joseph asked.

Adam nodded. "Yes. He put them in an ambulance to take them to Miner's Hospital."

"What about the others?" Laura asked.

"We haven't reached them yet. Art Gallo and Rico were working the closest to the entrance. We're finding big pockets where the roof didn't collapse so hopefully, we'll find the rest of them in one of the pockets."

"Are the men using the oxygen helmets that the ambulance brought in from the hospital?" Joseph asked.

"Yes, but there's not enough to go around."

"Then be careful. We don't need men dropping from black damp. With passages blocked, the air won't be circulating well."

"Yes sir, Mr. McCord."

Adam left, and Joseph turned back to Laura.

"Those two were found okay. There's every reason to believe the rest will be."

Laura shook her head. "No, there isn't. Men die easy in the mines."

Matt wasn't sure how long they had been trapped in the mine. He was afraid to look at his watch. He worried that the air was no longer moving through the tunnel. That meant that gases could be gathering even now, and he and Pete would die from the black damp. He kept watching the flame in Pete's carbide lamp for any change in color to indicate disappearing oxygen.

He took breaks often to listen and see if he could hear anything. He usually only heard the sound of his own breathing or Pete digging.

"Any idea where we are?" Pete asked at one point.

"Judging by the distance between the walls, we're still in the branch tunnel."

"Then we're not making too much progress."

"As best we can without blasting, and we don't want to do that."

They passed the time in silence for a while. Then Pete came back from dumping a load of earth and said, "I love her, you know."

"I know," Matt assured him. He didn't need to ask who the her was.

"I wanted to do better by them and get a job somewhere else, maybe the shirt factory in Frostburg, but things never worked out."

"Keep trying. I'm sure you can find something. Business owners are always looking for hard workers."

They took a break to eat half of their lunches. They didn't want to eat everything because they didn't know how long they would be here. They also drank sparingly for the same reason.

Matt wondered what his family was thinking. He had come to Eckhart to protect them and had only wound up buried beneath the earth.

***

Supper at the boarding house was quiet. Antonietta prepared a meal, but the men stayed at the mine to help with the digging. She, Samantha, and Myrna passed the time quietly. That was a good thing. If Myrna had given one of her sermons, Antonietta might very well have strangled her.

"It could have been Samuel," Myrna said at one point.

"Or Enos or any of them," Antonietta added.

She remembered waiting when her husband had been trapped in the mine. Her mind had kept jumping to the worst case scenario, which was often the case with an accident in the mines. It had undoubtedly been for her.

It scared her just as badly now when it was her nephew. Why had he come back? He had been free of the mines. The war had given him that at least, but he had decided to return home.

How was Samantha dealing with this? What would the girl do? She didn't understand this life. It would be so much worse for her.

Samantha stood up and walked to the kitchen. Myrna hugged her and then handed her a large pail filled with tea. Antonietta and Myrna picked up the trays of sandwiches, and they all headed out the back door.

"Will he be all right?" Samantha asked.

Best not to lie to her. "You never know. So many things can happen, and what usually happens is not what you think will. All you can do is keep yourself busy until news comes."

This would be Samantha's first time having to deal with a mining accident where someone she knew was involved. Antonietta had grown up in Eckhart. She knew mine accidents happened at any time. She could remember miners coming to get her friends at school to tell them that their fathers had either survived or died in a mine accident. It wasn't something you ever got used to, but at least growing up with as she did, she had learned how to deal with it.

Samantha never had. Her imagination must be going in every direction at once.

It said something about Samantha that she was here, though.

She had cared enough to come check on Matt. And she wasn't afraid to help where it was needed.

Antonietta heard a knock at the front door and rushed to answer it, but Samantha beat her to it. A woman stood at the door.

"They've reached Matt," the woman said. "He's alive."

Samantha's knees went weak, and she sagged against the wall.

"What about Peter?" Antonietta asked.

The woman frowned and shook her head.

"We'll be down in a few minutes," Antonietta told the woman.

The woman left, and Antonietta walked over to Samantha.

"He's alive, Samantha."

Samantha lifted her face to look at Antonietta. She was crying.

"Why don't you wash your face and let him see a smiling woman greet him when he comes out of the mine?"

Chapter 35

March 29, 1922

Matt swallowed the last of his fresh water in his pail and went back to digging. He was about to stick his shovel into the loose earth in front of him when he heard a pick strike a stone. It couldn't be Peter. He was still taking away the rocks they had hauled out earlier.

He waited quietly and heard it again, definitely metal on stone.

"Hey, can anyone hear me!" Matt screamed.

The picking sound stopped.

"Can anyone hear me?" he yelled again.

"Who's that?" he heard a faint voice yell.

"Matt Ansaro and Pete Spiker."

"Thank God, you're alive. Hold on, we're coming for you."

"Pete, Pete, help me dig. They're nearby. They're coming for us," Matt called.

A few moments later, Pete scrambled up the low tunnel and lay next to Matt.

"Are you sure?" he asked.

"I talked to them. They heard me, and they're coming."

Matt and Pete dug furiously at the pile of earth in front of them, pressing and stretching to get a few more inches forward. Every once in a while either Pete or someone in the rescue party would call out just to make sure they were getting closer.

Matt could tell they were getting closer by the vibrations that he felt on the ground. Then something changed. He felt air moving.

"Hello?" he called.

He saw the light of a headlamp through a small hole.

"I see them," Pete called. He reached out for the hole. A hand came through the hole and grabbed his.

"We'll have you out in a couple minutes," the miner said.

Then a rock tumbled from the ceiling and smashed Pete in the head.

"No!" Matt screamed.

"What happened? What happened?" the miners called.

"Rock fall hit Pete."

Matt pushed the rock off his friend. He could see that the side of Pete's skull was bloody and dented, but he felt for a pulse at the man's neck.

The hole was widening, and Matt could see more than one headlamp now.

He leaned his head against Pete's shoulder. "No, no."

Matt felt a hand on his shoulder.

"Matt, Matt, it's me, Samuel."

"He was so close, Uncle. All he wanted to do was get back to his family, and he was so close."

"Give me your hands. We've got the hole wide enough that we can pull you through," Samuel told him.

Matt reached out his hands and felt the steel-like grip of his uncle. Then he was being dragged through the hole. Headlamps shone in his face.

"Are you all right?" someone asked.

"My leg is broken."

"We've got a stretcher. We can carry you to the coal car."

"We can't leave without Pete," Matt said.

A hand patted his shoulder. "Don't worry, we won't leave him behind."

"He almost made it. I told him he would make it, but I lied. He didn't make it."

"It wasn't your fault, Matt," Samuel told him.

The miners lifted Matt onto a stretcher and then laid it across the top of a coal car. As the mules started on their upward journey, Matt saw Pete's body pulled from the tunnel and gently laid on a stretcher. Someone laid his head on Pete's chest to see if there was a heartbeat. He lifted his head and shook it.

Why? Why was it always someone else who died? His officers and men in the war. His parents here at home. And now Pete. There had been close calls. The scar on his neck and his broken leg attested to that, but somehow he always came through things on the other side. Why should he be so special? He didn't have a family. No one depended on him. If he died, no one would be affected.

He coughed up some coal dust. The jarring sensation sent stabs of pain through his leg. They felt good like his body was punishing him for living when a good man had died.

He saw Enos hold a flask out to him. "Want something to kill the pain?"

"Not unless you've got an egg, too." A shot of whiskey and a raw egg was supposed to clear out the coal dust in a miner's throat.

"Enos, put that away," Samuel said. "If you get caught with that in the mine, you'll be fired, especially now."

"Seems like this is the right time to have it."

"Put it away. Now." Samuel patted Matt's shoulder. "Everything will be fine now. We'll be out of here soon."

"Not for Laura and Jacob," Matt replied.

"They aren't the first to experience such loss, and they won't be the last."

Matt had returned to Eckhart Mines to protect his family, and now the tables were turned.

"What happened?" Matt asked.

"We should ask you. You were there."

"We were just working. We hadn't even blasted today, and the ceiling gave way. Were we the only ones trapped?"

Samuel shook his head. "There six of you, and before you ask, two were killed, including Pete."

"So why did the roof fall in?"

"Who knows? We try our best to support it, but we keep taking out coal. We keep shaking the ground with explosions. It causes things to shift. I have my suspicions."

"Like what?"

"They've been having trouble keeping the fans running all the time, and we had just come back from a day and a half off. If the fans still weren't running right, gas and dust could have built up down here just waiting to be set off by a spark from a pick or shovel or the power line, which is down now."

As they approached the entrance, Matt shut his eyes against the bright sunlight. He heard the shouts of the crowd.

"Who is it?"

"Is he alive?"

Matt held up his arm and cheers rose from the crowd. When he managed to open his eyes, he saw the gathered miners, their families, and the townspeople.

Then he saw Samantha break from the crowd and run forward to hug him.

"Oh, Matt, you're all right," she said as she squeezed him.

He hugged her back, and then she lifted her head and kissed him.

"My leg is broken, but I should be fine. What are you doing here?" he asked.

"That woman ... your friend in Frostburg told me about it. Did you think I would stay home without knowing what happened to you?"

"Did I worry you?"

Samantha pulled back. "I may not need any man, Matt Ansaro, but you aren't any man." She blushed. "You are the one man I love."

He grinned. "Was that so hard?"

Samantha punched him in the shoulder. "Don't make me regret it."

He pulled her closer and kissed her again.

Then he saw his aunts moving forward. Myrna went to hug Samuel, but Antonietta grabbed Matt in a hug. After a moment, she pulled back and began running her hands over his body.

"Are you all right? What is broken? Are you bleeding?"

Her hands ran down his broken leg, and Matt sucked in a mouthful of air to keep from yelling. "There, Aunt, my leg is broken."

She pulled her hands back as if his leg had been a snake. "Yes, I can see that now. I'll get the doctor."

She stepped back and disappeared into the crowd. Matt slowly pushed himself into a sitting position. His leg throbbed, but the pain was replaced with a greater pain when he heard Laura call, "Matt! Matt!"

Laura pushed her way through the crowd carrying Jacob. He could tell from her red eyes that she had already been doing a lot of crying. How much more would he cause her to do?

She stopped in front of him. "I'm so happy you're all right. What about Peter? You were with him."

Matt wanted to say something, but he couldn't form the words. All he could do was shake his head.

"No!" she screamed. Jacob slid from her grip to stand next to her.

Finally, Matt managed to say, "I'm sorry, Laura. I tried to help him. He wanted to get back to you so badly. I tried to help him, but I failed."

She fell against his shoulder, crying. Matt just hugged her.

He looked over the crowd and saw similar scenes playing out as families who had lost a loved one in the mine this day wept. Others celebrated with muted happiness. Their loved ones had returned while someone else's had not.

Tears rolled down his cheeks as Samantha, and his uncles stood uncomfortably nearby. What can you do or say to someone who has had her life destroyed through no fault of her own?

The second coal car arrived carrying Peter's body covered with a blanket.

"He's here," Matt whispered in Laura's ear.

She pulled back and looked toward the mine entrance. Then she took Jacob's hand and slowly walked to the cart. One of the miners pulled back the top of the blanket so that she could see his face.

Laura started sobbing again. Matt turned away. He saw Samantha staring at him, but he didn't say anything.

Antonietta arrived with the doctor who began examining Matt's leg.

His leg was broken, which he already knew. The doctor set the fractured bone and then splinted and bandaged his leg. It throbbed, and he was finally starting to feel pain, so the doctor also gave Antonietta a prescription for a painkiller syrup.

She didn't even hesitate. She took the prescription in her fist. She kissed Matt on the cheek and headed into Frostburg to get it filled.

"I'll be back as soon as I can," she told Matt.

When the doctor finished with him, he limped back to the boarding house supported between Samantha and Enos.

"I'm so sorry, Matt," Samantha told him.

"I was one of the lucky ones."

She shook her head. "I don't mean that. I mean getting mad at you. Calista gave me a talking to. She set me straight. I guess I'm not as modern as I thought I was."

"No, you are, which is what I like about you."

She smiled and hugged him tighter. He winced but didn't say anything. His ribs weren't broken, but they were definitely bruised.

Enos and Samantha helped him to his room. He fell backward onto the bed and enjoyed its softness for a moment.

"Just get some rest, Matt," Enos said. "Toni will get back with the painkiller as soon as she can."

Matt was tired, but he doubted that he would be able to sleep. It wasn't that his leg had started to burn as well as throb. He kept thinking about what more he could have done to help Pete. What would Laura and Jacob do now that Pete was dead?

Enos left the room, and Samantha pulled the rocking chair over and sat down next to the bed.

"I'm going to stay for a while," she said.

"You don't have to. I'm home, and I'll be fine as soon as Aunt Toni gets back," Matt assured her.

"I'm going to wait anyway."

"Thank you."

Matt lay back on the bed and tried to close his eyes and get some rest. Every time he did, he felt like he was back in the coal mine and the walls were collapsing in on him. He and Pete shouldn't have been in that section. It hadn't been checked out properly.

He must have drifted off at some point because he looked over once and saw that Samantha had gone and that it was dark outside. He tried to remember when she had left, and if she had said anything. He could vaguely remember her kissing him on the forehead, but that was all.

His aunt opened to the door to his room and saw he was awake. She came in with his medicine.

"Are you in pain?" Antonietta asked.

"Some."

She poured the elixir onto the spoon. He winced as he swallowed it. It tasted like piss, but hopefully, it would stop his leg from hurting.

"That should last you until morning," Antonietta said.

"Thank you."

She walked back to the door switched off the overhead light.

"Please don't," Matt said.

Antonietta stared at him for a moment and then said, "Okay." She pushed the button and light came back on. "Will you be all right, Matt?"

"I don't know."

Antonietta frowned. Then she backed out of the room and closed the door behind her.

Chapter 36

March 31, 1922

The funeral for Pete Spiker and Rico Moretti was held two days later at the Eckhart Methodist Church. It was impossible to cram 2,000 people into a chapel that could hold a couple hundred, but the town tried. People stood in the aisles so that it was nearly impossible to move.

It was what happened when a miner died in an accident. The miners and their families showed up to pay their respects to the families who lost a father, brother, husband, or son because they knew that it could just as easily have been their loved one who had been killed.

Matt and his family had gotten to the chapel early enough to get a seat in the middle of the room in one of the pews.

Matt's leg had stopped hurting him, thanks to the painkiller the doctor had prescribed. He had hobbled to the church determined to say goodbye to Pete. He had to sit on the end of the pew with his leg sticking out because he couldn't bend it enough to fit under the bench. One woman had accidentally hit his leg while she was pushing past making her way through the crowd, and Matt had nearly passed out from the pain.

He could see the back of Laura's head from where he sat. She was in a front pew along with Rico's widow, Dora.

What could he say to her? He'd promised to bring Pete out of the mines alive and get him home to his family, and he hadn't. He'd failed, and Pete had paid the price.

The reverend kept his sermon short, knowing that an even larger crowd was waiting outside. The pallbearers carried the caskets out of the chapel to open graves in the cemetery next to the church.

The families sat in the chairs next to the graves. The reverend spoke loudly so that the hundreds of people gathered could hear.

Matt got a better view of Laura, and he saw her tear-stained face. She wiped at it with a tissue in one hand while she held Jacob's hand in her other hand.

Jacob was dressed in a white shirt and black pants. Matt wondered if Laura had had to buy the clothes for her son just for this service. Luckily, Jacob was still too young to understand what was happening around him. It probably also meant that he wouldn't remember his father too well. That was a shame. Boys should always remember their fathers.

Matt noticed that Joey was attending to Laura. At first, that seemed fine. As superintendent, he probably felt some responsibility for the cave-in. He had to feel some responsibility if he was human. Then Matt noticed that Joey wasn't paying too much attention to Dora Moretti. Matt mulled that over, remembering what Samuel had said about Joseph and the rumors.

The reverend concluded his sermon and the caskets were lowered into the ground. Laura sobbed and stood up. She wavered unsteadily, but Joey put an arm around her to steady her.

When the service concluded, the crowd moved to the Literary and Sporting Club Hall where the miners' wives had prepared a meal for everyone. The meeting hall allowed people to gather, express their condolences to the families, and share their memories of Pete and Rico.

More than a few of the miners cursed Consolidation Coal Company for running an unsafe mine. Samuel scowled a lot at Joey, but he didn't say anything. Enos muttered a lot about how if the mine had been union, Pete and Rico wouldn't have been killed.

Antonietta agreed with him.

Laura sat on a chair. She wasn't at a table because she wasn't eating, despite being offered food by friends. Joey sat in a chair next to her holding her hand and gently patting it.

That's when Matt realized the rumors had been true, and a terrible idea entered his mind he couldn't forget.

The next morning Joseph dressed in his wide-lapel, gray wool suit. It was his best suit and the one he typically wore when going to a meeting in Cumberland. He liked it because it tended to hide some of the coal dust that gave lighter fabrics a dingy look.

He drove his car down from the house because he didn't want to work up a sweat or get his oxfords dirty. He parked in front of her home on Store Hill and walked up to the front door. He took a deep breath. He needed to play this right if he wanted things to keep moving forward.

Laura answered his knock. She was still wearing her dress from the funeral. Judging by the wrinkles, she must have slept in it. That is if she slept at all. The dark circles under her eyes made that doubtful.

Joseph tried to keep a serious expression on his face. "I hate to bother you at a time like this, but we need to talk, Laura."

She stepped back and let him inside. The house was tiny compared to his. Even the ceiling was low. It had only two rooms. He stored the information away, knowing that he could use it as an enticement later.

He sat down in the worn green armchair. Laura sat across from him in a rocking chair.

"How are you doing?" he asked.

She shrugged. "It's so hard to believe it, although growing up in a coal town, I've known that it was a possibility."

Joseph leaned forward in the chair. "You have to know that I would let you stay here if I could, but this is a company house, and the company wants to reserve them for miners."

She nodded. It was no secret that if a miner in a company house lost his job or was killed, his family also lost their home.

Things weren't so bad in Eckhart Mines because there were plenty of non-company homes. Those had a more-expensive rent that a family without an income couldn't afford.

Laura looked as if she was on the verge of crying again. "Where can I go? I don't have any family here anymore. I can't work and care for Jacob."

Joseph nodded. "I know, I know. I'm sorry. I really am. I've tried talking to the company. I got them to agree to let you stay if you continue paying the rent. If you do that, they will look the other way."

He'd done no such thing. Arrangements for company housing were entirely up to him.

"But how will I do that? I don't have any money. We didn't really have any savings. I can't afford this."

Joseph rubbed his chin. Now things were falling into place for him.

"You need to figure out some way to earn money, Laura. You'll need more than rent. You have to think about food, too. You won't need much in the way of heat soon, but you will need coal or wood for a cooking fire. Sooner or later, the company will want this house for a miner."

She rested her head in her hands and sobbed. "I know. I know. I don't know what I'm going to do."

Joseph tried not to smile. This was the opening he had been trying to orchestrate. He had gently applied the pressure and allowed it to build up. He had wanted Laura to feel like her options were being narrowed.

"Laura, listen, let me help you," he said.

She looked up. "What do you mean?"

"I have money. I can pay your expenses until you get on your feet."

"What? Joseph, I couldn't let you do that. It wouldn't be right."

He reached out and took her hand in his. "Yes, it would be right. You're my friend. When you're hurting, so am I."

"But this is too much."

"It's the least I can do. I want to help you, Laura."

She stared at him without saying anything. Then her shoulders sagged, and he knew that he had won.

"I guess I don't have much of a choice right now, but I'll find a way to pay you back, Joseph," she said.

"I'm not asking you to. Your gratitude is all that I need." *For now*, he thought but didn't say.

She nodded. "Thank you, Joseph."

He stood up. "Now don't you worry about anything but taking care of yourself and Jacob."

When he left the house, Joseph had a smile on his face. Things couldn't have gone better. Once Laura depended on him, he could ask her to marry him, and she would say yes.

He drove the car up the mining office, even though it was only a couple houses away. He figured that he would work until lunch, and then change when he went home to eat.

He unlocked the door to the office and turned the lights on. The store's furnace also heated the office, so he didn't have to worry about getting dirty feeding coal into a stove. He took off his suit coat and hung it up. Then he walked into the store for a cup of coffee.

"What are you so dressed up for?" Portnoy asked when he saw Joseph.

"It was a special occasion today," Joseph said.

"And what was that? The town buried two miners yesterday. No one considers it a special occasion."

"For me, it is."

The phone in the office started ringing. Joseph carried his cup of coffee into the office and to his desk where the telephone was located. He lifted the handset from the cradle and put it to his ear.

"Hello," he said into the receiver.

"Joseph, this is your father."

What was his father doing calling this early in the morning? "Hello, Father."

"We just got word that the UMW has called a national strike. The miners will know about it by this evening. If the grapevine still is what it was, they will know about it by lunch."

Joseph frowned. The coal companies had been expecting something like this since Blair Mountain.

"Will it be bad?" he asked.

"They usually are."

"But we're not a union mine."

"It makes no difference. Your miners will either walk out in support of the union miners or be intimidated into it."

"What should I do?" Joseph asked.

"We're making arrangements to bring in strikebreakers and armed guards. You'll have to keep a lid on things until then. Remember the miners in the company houses may strike, but they won't want to roil the waters and risk being evicted, so don't push them right now. If you can find some men you can trust, you can hire them as armed guards. Do that tonight."

"Yes, sir."

"The strikebreakers and guards will be arriving within days, depending on where they are needed the most," Winston told him.

"I can probably find some men in Frostburg."

"That's fine." Joseph got ready to hang up, and then his father added. "And Joseph?"

"Yes, sir."

"Watch your back. Remember what happened in West Virginia."

"I will, sir."

Joseph set the handset back in the cradle and then dropped into his chair. He took a deep sigh and ran his hand over his face. Then he opened his top desk drawer to make sure his revolver was still there. Maybe he should start carrying it, but that would just increase the tension that was going to hit Eckhart.

He stood up and walked to the window to look outside. Everything was quiet right now. The miners were underground and working, but even now, word might be spreading from man to man that a strike had been called.

Things were about to get rough in Eckhart Mines.

Author's Note

I hope you enjoyed reading this story. It has been a long time in the making, and I haven't been this excited about a project in a long time.

The original idea languished on my to-do list for years. I would start it and then run into a problem. That would stop progress on the story as I tried to work out the problem, and I'd wind up getting caught up in another project.

Then in January 2018, I had a simple thought that changed the way I looked at the story and broke the logjam. That simple change was to make Matt Ansaro connected to Eckhart Mines. Once I made the decision to make Eckhart Mines Matt's hometown, I started getting all sorts of ideas about the characters, plot points, and the setting. I was carrying around a pad and pen to write down thoughts wherever I went. When I was in the car, I would record scenes, ideas, and snatches of dialogue that came to me. I would even be recording thoughts before I fell asleep at night.

I wrote more of the story in three days than I had in six years.

It quickly became apparent that the original story would take up more than one book and that the title. (It was called *In Coal Blood*, by the way.) I had planned on would no longer fit.

I researched like crazy. Because I was writing before I had a chance to research the setting, I had to make sure that the story fit the ways things were in Eckhart Mines in 1922 in later drafts.

That said, please forgive any inaccuracies that have made their way into the story. I tried my best to keep it as accurate as I could, but sometimes specific details just weren't available or couldn't be found. In these cases, I tried to find something similar that occurred nearby and failing that, I made an educated guess based on available information.

Also, don't try and draw comparisons between the characters and real people. For instance, James Widdowson, the president of the Frostburg Normal School in 1922 is not John Havencroft, the president in this novel. The characters are of my own invention. While I might have pulled an incident from a real person's life and incorporated it into the character's history, that will be as far as the similarity goes.

Finally, I'd like to think those people who helped me get the details right. They are all generous with their time and information. THANK YOU, Al Feldstein and Mary Jo Price. Any mistakes you find are my fault, not theirs.

THANKS to my beta readers who gave me a lot of good feedback and caught continuity errors and other mistakes. Elena Bittinger, Blair Thomas, Ila Reber, and Gale Rada help make me look like a better writer than I am.

This closes out *Smoldering Betrayal*, the first book in the Black Fire books. I am working diligently on book two, *Strike the Fuse*.

James Rada, Jr.
June 1, 2018

About the Author

James Rada, Jr. has written many works of historical fiction and non-fiction history. They include the popular books *Saving Shallmar: Christmas Spirit in a Coal Town, Canawlers,* and *Battlefield Angels: The Daughters of Charity Work as Civil War Nurses.*

He lives in Gettysburg, Pa., where he works as a freelance writer. James has received numerous awards from the Maryland-Delaware-DC Press Association, Associated Press, Maryland State Teachers Association, Society of Professional Journalists, and Community Newspapers Holdings, Inc. for his newspaper writing.

If you would like to be kept up to date on new books being published by James or ask him questions, he can be reached by e-mail at *jimrada@yahoo.com.*

To see James' other books or to order copies on-line, go to *www.jamesrada.com.*

PLEASE LEAVE A REVIEW
If you enjoyed this book, please help other readers find it. Reviews help the author get more exposure for his books. Please take a few minutes to review this book at *Amazon.com* or *Goodreads.com*. Thank you, and if you sign up for my mailing list at *jamesrada.com*, you can get FREE ebooks.

IF YOU ENJOYED

Smoldering Betrayal,

TRY THESE NOVELS BY JAMES RADA, JR.

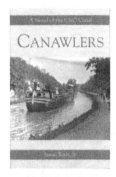

Canawlers: A Novel of the C&O Canal

At a time of war, the C&O Canal was caught in the crossfire between two nations. The Fitzgerald family makes their living on the canal, but now their lives are endangered by the Confederate Army's incursions into the Maryland and Confederate guerilla raids on the canal. When fate takes Hugh Fitzgerald away from his family, the Fitzgeralds, an orphan from Cumberland, and a disillusioned Confederate soldier, they will face the dangers presented by war, nature, and the railroad together.

October Mourning: A Novel of the 1918 Spanish Flu Pandemic

Dr. Alan Keener suspects the Spanish Flu had reached Cumberland, Md. He wants to take steps to prevent its spread, but a street preacher named Kolas aids the flu's spread, believing he is acting at the wrath of God. The fight becomes personal when Alan's family is struck with the flu. Can he find a way to keep them alive or will be they become part of the 100 million who died worldwide?

Available wherever books are sold.